The Ve
Award

M000219184

The Vocal+ Fiction Awards Anthology

Chosen and edited by **ERICA WAGNER**

unbound

First published in 2023

Unbound
Level 1, Devonshire House, One Mayfair Place, London W1J 8AJ
www.unbound.com

Text design by PDQ Digital Media Solutions Ltd

A CIP record for this book is available from the British Library
ISBN 978-1-80018-225-7 (paperback)
ISBN 978-1-80018-224-0 (hardback)
ISBN 978-1-80018-226-4 (ebook)

Printed in Great Britain by Clays Ltd, Elcograf S.p.A.

1 3 5 7 9 8 6 4 2

CONTENTS

Introduction

Here at Vocal, we launched the Vocal+ Fiction Awards with a big idea, and an idea to make it bigger. It is a dream now realized, and you hold it in your hands. When I first joined Vocal, as a creator—and later as Lead Editorial Innovator—one of my clearest ambitions was to elevate the work of our creators, to seek out those voices that I knew deserved to be heard, and amplify them. I believe that's exactly what we've done with this anthology.

The twenty-five stories you are about to read represent the winners of what was arguably our most ambitious competition to date, fiction or otherwise. We pored, pondered and deliberated over 13,000+ entries; we whittled them down to a shortlist of 1,025. The final winners were eventually selected for this very special publication. (You can find the thousand shortlisted names at the back of this volume, and read their excellent stories on Vocal.)

What were we looking for in choosing our winners? I believe you'll discover our criteria as you begin to read. There's the propulsive drive and sinister mystery of a story like Chelsea Catherine's "The Not-Deer" or Patti Larsen's "Lifted". There's the stylistic grace of "The Ghosts in West Texas" by Andie Ngeleka and Kallista Kusumanegara's

"Destination". There's the darkly comedic essence of George Murray's "The Kneeler" and Megan Anderson's "The Reunion". There are stories that play elegantly with language, and those that decidedly don't. There are stories that conjure places so vividly, they seem to materialize before our very eyes; there are stories that are fantastical world-building wonders. There are works by established authors here and works by writers at the very beginning of their literary journeys. We are so delighted to have each and every one as part of the Vocal family.

There's something, I hope, for everyone in this book, which demonstrates the best qualities of Vocal: that we are home for all kinds of stories, by all kinds of creators. As a reader, I know you'll find so much to love as you turn these pages. And I urge you to become a Vocal creator, too: you will find a welcoming and supportive community on our site, whatever it is you like to write. The very existence of this anthology tells you something important about us—that our goal is to help our creators reach their full potential as writers, as artists or in whatever medium they choose to express themselves. Joshua Luke Johnson, our Head of Content, puts it very well: "At Vocal, we refer to our talented community members as creators; not authors, nor even writers, and that is intentional. Vocal is more than a writers' community. Vocal is more than a publishing platform. Vocal is here for all who wish to use their imagination to build worlds, and to fight dragons. We exist on behalf of creators everywhere, and, within this volume, you will meet some of the very best."

It is with stories that we make the world. Human beings are narrative animals: each and every day, every single one of us wakes up and tells the story of their life. To ourselves, to each other. We create ourselves—just as some of us choose to spin tales that hold others spellbound. Listening to each other's stories helps us to understand the world, helps us to connect. We invent and reinvent in order to believe, to love, to survive. Here are twenty-five stories that will open new worlds for you. This beautiful book—produced in partnership with our friends, the crowdfunded publisher Unbound—is the most striking introduction I can think of to the powerful storytelling platform that is Vocal.

Vocal is a platform that allows for experimentation in a safe environment, allows the development of community and talent. It's fun. It's lively. Come on in. Everyone is welcome.

Erica Wagner

The Reunion

Megan Anderson

It was boorish. Lewd, even. Oakley bristled as she watched him fondle the cheese knife, then lick it clean. This was a galvanizing moment, like she needed one. She was taking him down. She felt good about it.

She'd last seen Alec eighteen years ago. He was all artless swagger back then: lean muscles, unruly black curls, gappy grin. He'd blown in as a footloose twenty-two-year-old to pick avocados on her family farm, and his rippling virility—that reckless tuck of his Hard Yakka work shirts into low-slung jeans—had made Oakley giddy all summer long. Alec knew it. His rakish, offhand flirting soon led to the gifting of treats, which led to furtive moments running his hands through her platinum curls, then time alone with her behind the packing shed. Nobody else needed to know. It was fast, fumbling, damp, dirty, pantless, mirthless, bewildering. Oakley was seven years old.

Alec was forty now, graying curls receding at the temples, lifestyle paunch testing the buttons on his shirt, still using his cutlery wrong. Seeing him scarf mashed potato off a serving spoon in the farm kitchen had been thrilling to Oakley as a child. She'd thought him raffish; a luminous rule-breaker. In the mood light of a fancy wine bar, the sight of brie-smeared stainless steel on his outstretched tongue made her teeth itch. His Tinder profile had done that, too. His search parameters trawled for women fifteen years his junior; no surprises there. He'd used the phrase 'seeking a real connection' without irony, professed a love of sunsets, and butchered all his apostrophes without exception. His profile picture saw him bare-chested in reflective sunglasses on a flashy boat, arm slung around a cropped-out former squeeze.

Any of that would, ordinarily, invite a resolved Swipe No from Oakley, but when the proposed match popped up on her account, something about it gave her pause. His name, mainly. The dolt had used his real one (she'd gone with Annie), and some ancient muscle memory made her flinch. A closer look at the profile pic revealed him: that gap between his front teeth, the cocky thrust of his chest. She felt a sting of shock, then hot mortification, then an old, bone-chilling shame. Then rage came in and sat right down, crackling like fire. Do it, said rage. Swipe Yes.

⇒◆⇐

Oakley chose the wine bar, and the perch—a high round table with stools, tucked out of the way in dim light. She'd picked the wine for its complexity, the cheese platter for its insouciance. She didn't plan to be here long.

"So, Annie," said Alec, trailing his forefinger around the base of his glass. Oakley sensed a gear shift. The bottle of red was almost gone. They'd covered the key plot points of their lives, recounted the screwups that led them each to this city, this bar. She'd fabricated and deflected; he'd downloaded. She knew by now that the simple act of listening made you irresistible to the self-absorbed.

"Tell me this," his tongue skimmed his front teeth, "how is it possible that a gorgeous, intelligent woman like you is still single?"

Insult disguised as flattery; Oakley stifled a groan. "Being in jail will do it," she said, indulging him with a smile. "No conjugal visits. It's hard to get a lover to stick around."

Alec sat back to get the full measure of her. "Beautiful *and* funny," he said, then leaned in, conspiratorial. "What were you in for?"

"Assault," Oakley deadpanned. "Grievous Bodily Harm. I garroted a woman with a fishing line. Left a welt on her neck like a ringbarked tree."

Alec raised his eyebrows.

"Just a little something for her to remember me by."

"Christ, remind me never to do whatever she did," he said, grinning. He liked this part; the starchiness gone, the pleasantries dealt with, both parties relaxed and candid. Dating could be a chore until the booze kicked in.

"She stole my woman," said Oakley. Her delivery was somewhere between cool and ironic. The burnished ends of her chestnut pixie cut caught the light. Her gold hoop earrings glinted as she cocked her head. "I don't handle betrayal well."

Alec got comfortable on his stool. Glee played on his lips. *Funny. Dangerous. Might be open to some girl-on-girl, maybe a bit of three-way action.*

7

"Well," he said, swirling his glass. "You're a surprise package, Annie of Ardross."

"You're talking about my wine choice, aren't you?" said Oakley. Her eyes were starting to glaze, but her delivery was sharp. "I read a lot of *Wine Spectator* in jail. I've been itching to get out, just so I can sample some of these zeitgeisty field blends."

"Nothing decent on the prison wine list, then?" he asked, eyes gleaming.

"Just the cheap shit," she said. "And don't even get me started on the stemware in there—criminal."

Alec's face creased in delight. This is where she wanted him: amused, hooked, infatuated.

She pressed her fingers against a tiny plastic sachet in her pocket, feeling its residual, powdery grit. She patted it once, then brought both hands to her glass and wrapped them suggestively around its stem.

"Well, Alec of Inglewood," she said. "I make it your buy."

He swayed to his feet. "Same again?"

She nodded, then shrugged. It hardly mattered. She'd upended the sachet into the very first glass. Alec's nervous bladder had sent him to the Gents soon after his arrival, so it had been leisurely; no real sleight of hand required. It was only a matter of time, now.

$$=\!\!\diamond\!\!=$$

Oakley hadn't really learned about wine in jail. She'd learned about it from the sommelier at the overpriced restaurant she'd waitressed at after high school. But she had learned about Rohypnol—flavorless, colorless, easy to disguise—at Bandyup Women's Prison. And where to get it, of course. In two years inside, she'd made plenty of friends in low places. There was no shortage of intel when it came to acquiring slow-release tranquilizers and other nefarious modes of ill intent. Everyone had a mate with a mate.

Truth be told, she'd quite enjoyed jail. She liked being in the company of other women who'd messed up. The unhinged, darkly comic conversation comforted her. She reveled in the whip-smart lip, the simmering wrath, the complete dearth of pretense. None of them was evil. They were just women who'd been pushed and failed to bend. Like her.

In Anger Management sessions with the prison's art therapist, Oakley had once been asked to draw her state of mind. From the tub of colored pencils she'd extracted red, orange and purple, and scribbled until she'd filled a page with ragged scrawl.

"What is it?" asked the therapist, patchouli wafting from her tiered floral dress.

"That's a shitshow," said Oakley.

"What's it about?" she pressed.

"The past."

"Tell me about it," coaxed the patchouli, but by now Oakley was all talked out. She'd done the endless loops in her own head, rerun the scenes behind the packing shed over and over, felt the throb of shame each time. It had been her fault—she'd sought his attention, after all— and she'd learned to think of herself as blemished and untamable and wrong; a pariah until the end of time.

All her adult relationships with men had upheld this world view. Unable to slough away the scab of the past, she'd never stuck out a romance for longer than a few months. *A trail of destruction*, her family joked. Self-sabotage validated her: nothing worked. If it worked, it wouldn't last.

That was the prevailing self-talk even as she found something good with Leela, an open-faced yogi who would surely soon realize that Oakley was damaged goods, unworthy of her easy love. Leela weathered this caustic self-loathing with grace, for a while, but when she found herself swept away by the uncomplicated attention of her Yin instructor, Oakley snapped, vindicated. She was destined to be discarded. What incentive was there not to wrap a length of monofilament around the neck of a nemesis? Why not self-destruct?

"It's bleak," was all she gave the therapist.

Only after she left jail, bunked in with her sister and started hauling weights up and down the merciless steps at the local park did Oakley start to reframe her reality. She got strong. She cut her hair. Encouraged by a new therapist, she learned to meditate and practiced smiling at strangers. Often they smiled back; maybe she wasn't destined to be a dumpster fire. She started dating again, an exercise in reimagining her *trail of destruction* into something more empowering. She did it to recalibrate, as much as anything, and maybe to forget. Then he showed up.

$\Longrightarrow \diamond \Longleftarrow$

Ordering another bottle at the bar, Alec gazed over at Oakley like she was a prize he couldn't believe he'd won: younger than his ex-wife by a decade, and properly sassy. He dared to hope he might take her home tonight.

He'd packed away his kids' junk on the off chance and deodorized the bathroom. Her texts had lassoed him. Women could be so needy, but she had a detached cool that excited him. *Stockbroker*, she'd teased. *Do they do real connections*? Now that they'd met, he was pretty sure that, yeah, they do.

Oakley sucked parmesan toast crumbs from between her teeth and toyed with the sachet in her pocket. The nod she gave to the table on her left was barely perceptible. They were ready. It had been a masterclass in persuasive argument getting a couple of former jailbirds to come to this chic establishment, but they'd shown up for her like the fiercely loyal women she knew them to be. In about five minutes, she'd be out of there. It would be up to others to put the pieces together, see the thing through.

Alec returned to the table with a self-satisfied swagger that took her back eighteen years. Oakley listed slightly on her stool. Arriving beside her, he brandished the bottle with a flourish. "Would madam care to taste?" he said, pouring them each a glass. He went to sit, but she tugged playfully at his jeans, pulled him towards her, buried her fingers in his front pocket.

"Thanks," she breathed in his ear. He smelled of Lynx and tannin. She trailed her fingers away, sat back, picked up her glass. Her face was benign.

"Let's have a toast," he said, enthused. "The future?"

"The past," she countered, and tapped her glass against his.

"Okay," he said, curious. "What about the past, exactly?"

11

"The crappy bit," she said, slurring. "The tipping point." They both drank.

"Want to talk about it?"

Oakley put her glass down and rested her hands on her knees. She tilted forward. He leaned in to hear her, but she didn't say anything. Couldn't. Her face was numb now, her eyes glassy. The feeling in her legs was going. She tried moving her hands to grab the edge of her stool, but they wouldn't budge. Alec's lascivious grin evaporated as she slumped forward onto the table. When he shook her gently, she slid off her stool into a motionless pile on the floor.

Oakley's mind swam up through the dim light, the static crackle of white noise. Her skin was clammy. She was vaguely aware of a commotion around her: a gathering crowd, the jailbirds at her side, a phone call, a stern accusation, frisking, his jeans pocket, those gappy teeth frozen in a baffled grimace. She saw his eyes, telegraphing fear and dread.

Then everything went perfectly, sweetly dark.

She wouldn't remember this. But he would.

——◆——

Megan Anderson is a recovering journalist. Her feature writing has appeared in newspapers and magazines in Australia, the USA and the UK. Recently, she's been writing flash. Her short fiction has appeared in *Reflex Fiction Quarterly* and the 2022 *Bath Flash Fiction* anthology. She was shortlisted in the 2021 Bridport Prize. Megan also makes art under the guise of Hangdog Art, which sometimes sneaks into her fiction. Like that time she wrote and illustrated *Word of Dog,* a book about humanity (according to canines). She jots something down most days, usually in cafés around Fremantle, Australia.

Path of Least Resistance

Bernie Bleske

In the morning, I took the little stone with me into the living room, where Keith was on the sofa, watching television. At the time, Keith and I lived in a downtown two bedroom, under the constant press of traffic, working factory and service jobs to pay the rent and buy the beer and all that lazy nothingness. A couple of college dropouts waiting for something to happen to us.

"This guy," I said, "had me believing this little rock could make wishes come true."

"Give it here," Keith said.

I threw him the stone and he caught it one-handed and said to the air, "I wish for some beer. Good beer, not the shit." Then he threw it back at me. "It's broken."

I had not caught the return pass and it went bouncing down the hallway toward the bathroom, which I spent some time using after picking the stone up. In the shower it took on a luster it lacked when dry and it made me think of a river stone, one of millions and trillions along all the wild rivers in the world, pounded smooth, dull gray when dry and slick when wet. If some were magic, how would anybody ever know?

The night before, at the bar waiting for a beer, the guy next to me said, "Check out this stone."

He held it out and I took it in my palm. Just a small rock. 'What's special?" I asked.

"It's a wishstone," he said. "Makes wishes come true."

"Wish I had one," I said, and the guy smiled at me and left the bar, me with the little rock still in my hand.

It was a pretty good joke.

When I came out of the bathroom Lucas was in the living room and he and Keith were drinking Heineken. Of course, it was Sunday, and Lucas usually came over to watch the games and he often brought beer but that didn't stop me from holding some small incredulous belief.

"Le'me see that stone again," Keith said. I had a reluctance now, having spent some time in the shower thinking about the consequences of wishes.

"Remember the Monkey's Paw," I told him.

"The wha?" Keith said.

"That short story about the guy who gets a magic monkey hand and wishes for money and his kid dies and he gets the insurance money. Then he wishes for the kid to come back and there's this knock on the door."

"*Pet Sematary*," Keith said.

"Sort of," I said.

"Whatever," Keith said, waving for the stone.

Lucas was saying, "What the hell are you talking about?" as I tossed the stone to Keith and he wished for, in these words, "a girl."

All sorts of things popped into my head. A Girl Scout, selling cookies. My sister through some disaster with her husband. Still, privately, I wished for the same; who doesn't?

Nothing dramatic happened and Keith tossed me back the stone. Lucas looked at us both, but I didn't feel like explaining and the whole thing seemed foolish, and a while later we all went out to watch the games at a bar.

The girl. Brenda. She was a friend of Lucas', waited tables at the same place. She didn't look like a Brenda, which to me is a clunky name and hardly attractive. She and Keith hit it right off, but then Keith was always looking for a girlfriend. He was the kind of guy who wasn't happy without one, and good-looking enough to attract them. He wrote his girlfriends poetry and spent all his money on extravagant gifts, but alcohol made him moody and easily angered. Jealous. I'd watched him cycle through a few already, never more than three or four days on either side of having a girlfriend or not having one.

We'd met at work, both of us at the time working at a mail order warehouse, eight hours a day, with breaks timed to the second, putting assorted cheap plastic tools and electronics and kitchen utensils in tin bins that rolled past our stations on black conveyors. We were color coded—I was sky blue, magenta, and a sort of yellow-green. Our color would roll by, stuck to the side of the tin bin, and we'd grab it off the conveyor and find the appropriate item. The merchandise was ordered to no system I ever understood. Some CD of a German symphony doing Brahms was next to a pair of garden gloves with little suction cup things on the fingertips, was next to a stack of disposable doggie diaper pads. Row after row after row, in a sort of soul-eating multitude, shrink wrapped, bar coded, like larvae. It was the order of things, the movement of the world there on that belt, a total mystery how it functioned, by what order or logic sent the stream of objects out into the world, or, for that matter, what stream brought them to me. But probably China.

My second or third day there I was walking out after the shift and Keith, who I'd just met at lunch, asked if I wanted to join some of the other guys going out for a beer. That's how we became friends. A few weeks later my rent went up and I was looking and he had an empty room in his apartment. So there it is. No magic, no wishes, just a series of coincidences all strung together, like an old set of Christmas lights just before the holiday, all knotted up senselessly. And then you plug them in to see if they work at all. And if they do you sit down near the bare tree and start fingering through the mess, feeling the lights warm up slowly, until they're all in order.

So we were out and Keith had his girl and I had the wishstone in my pocket, believing and not believing. The easy answers came to me: money, fame, beautiful women, power, world peace, a hot car, immortality. I couldn't wish for any.

My father said often enough, "Nothing's free." I must have taken the words to heart, because I was nervous, thinking of Macbeth. But in the end I still wished for a woman, someone to sleep with. It seemed an easy enough wish, yet even then I imagined disease, mass murder, robbery, all the easy disasters. Nothing happened for a while, and we drank more, and a while later it was turning into the usual drunk evening. We struck up conversation with friends and later Maureen came in. I'd been home with her a few times before, after nights just like this, and we'd gone out to movies or dinner or whatever in the days after but it never went anywhere. I wasn't too interested in her but there wasn't much else on my horizon.

In the morning the regret I felt was for the future, for that moment in the next few days when I'd cut it off again with Maureen, and all the uncomfortable days between while I held the knowledge but no way to act without causing pain. The easy path, asking only for patient hope or happy disaster. One might well say this is the way I go through the world, if one were to be charitable. If not, cowardice comes to mind.

I sort of forgot about the stone after that, thinking I never really believed in it to begin with. Then Keith got serious about Brenda, and then I did too, and even though we'd become tight friends, it got hard, so when my mother called and I could hear in her voice the fear I went back home. As I was packing I found the stone in a drawer in the nightstand and took it back up, thinking, what if, what if, but I couldn't bring myself to wish on it there and then, again, just sort of forgot about it. The thing was, I'd wished for a bit of money, an end to the grind, some kind of small fortune. Had I held the stone as I wished? Maybe. Probably. But isn't that what everyone wishes for?

And then, of course, I got home and heard in sentences what I'd felt in my mother's voice.

It's not like you ever know yourself. That would be a wish, I think, to know oneself. But it staggers the mind, the potential for harm there. Lord knows I'd had time to think about wishes the last few years, driving around spending my inheritance. Staying in hotels, drifting here and there on whims. A lot of driving. There might be guys like me all over the country, drifting here and there with our little stones. Who knows.

The thing is, I'm a coward. Too afraid to even wish for courage. So, speaking of courage: Not too long after my mother died, Keith picked up a job at a whitewater rafting outfit in West Virginia. He'd called to tell me, still had a box or two of my stuff, wondered what he should do with it. I drove out to the river, just for a while, and camped, and Keith said, "Hey, you should do it. The river. It's fun." Brenda was working there too, at the front taking tickets and handling the register.

The next day, they ran us through a quick session before we headed out into the misty morning, everything redolent of mold and sweat and moss and river. The bulky woolen safety vests, the chipped plastic helmets, all of it like suiting up in relics.

I wasn't looking forward to the experience. Actually, I was kind of petrified. Had I brought the stone, I'd have wished for safety, irrational as it was.

Rivers are strange things. You can float along and know that something is coming, some great adventure is around THAT bend, by the noise of it, the quickening speed of water. The bend is turned and the river goes white before you, churning over, misting up, and then it's a rush forward into the maelstrom.

The guide yells directions.

Then the raft, which is tearing down a canyon

of roaring water, straight ahead and on-course, pulls sideways as if on a cable, slams into a boulder, and you're in the water.

That's when your friend or the guide grabs the back of your life jacket and hauls you on the boat, and everyone you just met thirty minutes ago is slapping your back and cheering your little adventure.

Exhilarating, terrifying. I had no desire to do it again, ever, but the pressure was there, the looks on everyone's face that this is FUN. Down that river in the mountains. I camped for three or four more nights, in a not-quite-too-small tent I'd crawl into after a night at their local bar/restaurant, hanging back of all the chest thumping. They had something I wanted, of course, a bonded companionship, but it was built on the terror of the river, so I signed up again.

This time I went over and was in the water, under the water. My helmeted head cracked against something hard, one exposed cheek forced by the paw of the current into a long slide against rock. I was flailing for some kind of purchase, hugging nothing but current, half upside-down as the life vest and river wrestled each other for possession of my chest. The current was winning, willing as it was to beat me senseless in the fight. For a moment I was up on the surface, glasses gone, oar gone, and every moment I needed for recovery—to breathe, to cough, to catch sight of the raft, to get my head out of the water, to haul and kick my way out of the great white roar of current—every moment, time itself, was clenched by the river into too small a space and I was again helplessly battered.

Perhaps I heard people shouting. Perhaps I shouted myself; that may have been why or how I took another lungful of river.

I thought I was going to die. I knew I was going to die. What had I asked for, earlier? What had I wished for? Purpose? I was afraid to ask for money. I was afraid to ask for anything, to wish for anything because there's always a curse. Isn't that the story's secret? That every wish has a curse, every action a reaction? Every front has a back. I'd tried for something nebulous, clean—good purpose— and here I was, nearly drowning. Stay alive, that was my purpose, my sole purpose.

It sucked.

Wishing is an act of faith and an act of imagination. My faith was suspicious, my imagination all too capable of conjuring up scenarios of worst possible outcome. Breathe and cough, that was all I wanted then, but there was no stone, just the boulders I kept slamming into. Eventually I managed to right myself, grab hold of something—it's all still a blur—and then get hauled back up into the raft.

After, in the evening, I hung back. Every so often one of the guides would come over and slap me on the back, a hearty camaraderie I didn't feel. I left soon after, packed up, grabbed the boxes from Keith, making excuses, went back home to finishing closing my mother's estate.

And then, some years later, I was in that part of the country again, idling along some back roads, going nowhere, coming from nowhere, what I'd been doing for some time since my mother died and left me the money. The road was one of those blacktop affairs, tracking an etch in the hills just above a mountain river, one of those old roads that seem to have been around for hundreds of years, passing through towns that seem hundreds of years old, in which live families that have been there for hundreds of years. Up on one side of the river, glanced here and there in switchbacks and through gaps in the pines, was a country store and restaurant.

I pulled into the gravel parking lot, thinking to get a late lunch, and there, dappled under an intermittently cloudy Georgia day, half shaded by pine and hill, was Keith's yellow Charger. The same bands still bumper-stickered the trunk, the same taillight was still cracked. Instinctively, I put my hand in my pocket and thumbed the wishstone, mind silent as one can try to be in such times. I parked next to Keith's car. What did it take then to stop and go in? Silence, I think, a certain timid silence.

Above the door there was a bell. To the left the place opened into a bright-red-boothed truck-stop-style café sharing space with a few aisles of convenience fare, engine oil and salted peanuts and free used car magazines. To the right was a dimly lit, cedar-paneled bar, all dark, beery shadow. There was a pool table, a few signs for beers no longer produced, the same red vinyl booths.

Keith was in one, his back to me, head down.

Brenda sat before him, looking pained. She glanced up when the door dinged and spent a long, emotionless time staring at me.

I managed a smile and without much fanfare she leaned forward to Keith for a second, said something to him, then rose and came out past the pool table. Keith never glanced back.

"I told him I was getting another drink," Brenda said.

"You look good," I told her. There was a jukebox playing Green Day at bar levels. Nobody was tending the bar and I followed Brenda out to the other side of the restaurant.

"How'd you find us?" Brenda asked. I hadn't spoken more than the three words.

"I wasn't looking," I said.

She went up to the counter with an easy familiarity. Out of the bar it was bright from long windows opening onto the parking lot. Below, down a mere thirty or forty feet of pine-treed slope, was the river, fast and white. A few of the restaurant's booths were filled. The waitress handed Brenda two bottles of unprompted Bud, then eyebrowed me. I nodded and she came back with another.

Brenda took us over to a booth at the window. A tray with ketchup and salt and pepper and several local hot sauces sat on the table and Brenda, with typical fastidiousness, moved it.

"He asks about you," she said.

I didn't know how to respond. She'd taken on a strange Georgia sleekness, a slight accent. All the more lovely. That was the curse, of course, with Keith's girl, that I would love her. When my mom had died I'd stayed at home after the funeral. There wasn't much for me anywhere else, and her death required a certain amount of estate work. Back at Keith's place Brenda was spending more and more time in the apartment, hanging out as friends do, and this thought was building in me, taking more space every day, this thought, "I like her." Keith did too, and they'd retire in the evenings or the afternoons, to his room and it was more than I could stand. We make wishes all the time, but in retrospect it's hard to pin down precisely what was wished or where one's hands might have been. I'd never asked to love her; it happened because she was smart and funny and beautiful, and who wouldn't love her? Keith loved her too and it seemed she felt the same about him.

"So what are you up to, out here?" I finally managed.

"He's doing whitewater rafting tours, on the river," Brenda said. "I waitress here in the morning."

"He asks about me?" I said. "Why?"

"You're his friend," she said, like I'd missed the obvious. "You're his best friend." She looked at her hands, then out the window. "When he's jealous he thinks I miss you too."

"Still jealous," I said, trying to make a joke of it.

She didn't laugh and I could see in all its wordless clarity just how complicated and miserable the whole situation was.

I wished then. I wished with a terrible heaviness, a deep, regretful, aimless, genuine sadness. I palmed the stone in my pocket and wished for Keith to find some happiness. In the wish was a jumble of fluttery requests, all stumbles and half sentences and fear—an end to his alcoholism, a happy Brenda, a purpose, friends, direction, a clue, no anger—none of it fully realized. And in there too, Brenda to be mine.

Brenda turned her head in a manner suggesting time had slowed. I admired for a moment the fine glide of her neck, the soft indentation at her throat, a dewy cast of tan and translucently visible hair at her shoulder.

"Oh," she said, and I too turned.

Keith was making his way down the slope, his momentum taking him from tree trunk to tree trunk, barely in control. We lost him for a moment in the shadows, then glimpsed him at the trees' edge. Then a truck pulled past the window and when it was gone there was only a flash of his shirt in the water.

Of course, what else could I do? I went into the water after him.

⸻ ◆ ⸻

Bernie Bleske currently attempts to teach his fifth-grade students how to take standardized exams and write standardized essays for the Florida public school system. This involves a lot of yelling. The son of a US State Department diplomat, he grew up internationally, tried college in Wisconsin, finished college a decade later in Virginia, and somehow ended up teaching high school English in America and abroad. Some years in Pakistan, Dubai, and Colombia later, he and his wife landed in Key West, Florida, where he found the time to start publishing short stories on Vocal.

The Not-Deer

Chelsea Catherine

The mountains are flush with color as we make the drive north. Frost creeps across the glass. I turn on the heat, but the old RV takes time to warm. From the passenger's seat, Jude huddles in a blanket. Andy sleeps in the back.

"How far north are we headed?"

"Just a half hour past Dahlonega."

Jude glances out the window. The leaves are brittle and dry from a summer that was full of heat and sun but rare showers. Even the trees are burnt. The clouds hang low, obscuring the mountain peaks around us. The whole area is quiet and still in a way I didn't expect it to be.

Jude isn't used to mountains, or to cold. She grew up six hours southwest of here, in a poor Alabama town with less than three hundred residents. The first time she saw mountains was when we flew into San Francisco. She kept looking down at the Sierra Nevadas and back at me like she'd never seen anything so beautiful in her life.

"Do you think it'll be okay for him?" she asks.

I glance in the rear-view mirror. Andy doesn't love the RV loveseat, but it's the only place where he can sleep with a seatbelt on. His preferred perch is the small space above our heads, where he likes to sleep snuggled up against a body pillow.

"It's so... remote."

"Remote is good," I tell her. "It's people you should be worried about. People are dangerous."

I can feel her staring at me, but she doesn't say anything else.

≡◆≡

We camp in a spot under some fir trees, which stretch dozens of feet above us. The view is partially obscured, but through the branches, the Blood Mountain Wilderness spreads like blue waves in the afternoon light.

Andy awakens in a foul mood, weeping quietly before Jude gives him something to eat and the attitude slips away. We decide to go for a small hike while Jude sets up. I get him into his coat, which still bears a stain from the last time we went camping. He ties up his boots—a new trick his teachers have been working on with him.

Andy likes to hike in front of me. I prefer this, so I can keep an eye on him. For a seven-year-old, he's a great hiker. He's quiet and aware of his surroundings. He stops rarely, usually only to look at a bug or leaf. "Kat," he tells me. "Look. A Chinese mantis."

We both stop, stooping on the dirt path, our noses close to the grass and weeds. A large praying mantis rests in a bush, delicate and slim. "The babies are probably somewhere close by," I say.

Andy sits down in the dirt to watch the mantis. I give him space, wandering around the area to look for any edible plants. I'm at the edge of the path, as far away from Andy as I dare, when a twig breaks nearby. I stop, searching the path. My hand goes automatically to my hunting knife.

The sound comes again from further in the woods. I peer into the thick pocket of trees. At first, there's no movement. Then, I spot it. A deer. It rests in between some peeling birches about twenty feet away. It's a strange-looking animal. Bigger than normal and with what look like at least two broken legs. The joints bend in the opposite direction. The eyes are too far forward on its face. It shouldn't be this close. Wild deer are highly sensitive to tourists.

"What is it?"

I jump at Andy's voice. When I look back into the thicket, the deer is gone.

⟹ ◆ ⟸

Jude makes sloppy joes for dinner. We eat outside around a fire I've hastily thrown together. The weather is cold but not unbearable. Still, when the sun goes down, we retreat into the RV and turn on the electric fireplace. I check the windows and doors, pulling the curtains and locking everything up. Andy secludes himself in his bunk. Jude and I set up in the queen bed in the back to watch a movie.

Her perfume lingers in the space, smelling of anise and coffee. The heat from the fireplace balloons near the front of the RV, keeping Andy warm, but leaving the bedroom cool. I pull Jude closer to me, her silk pajamas smoothing against my skin.

We're halfway into the movie when I hear a strange sound outside. It's not normal, at least not for this area.

It's almost like a coyote cackling, but with a clicking noise that feels unnatural. It comes twice before disappearing.

Jude turns my chin, so we're face to face. "You're nervous," she says.

I exhale, my breath brushing at a strand of her hair. "I'm still unsettled."

She pulls me closer, running her hand down my spine. Her nails send prickles across my skin. My wounds have healed, but I have scars from the attack. Most of the time, I take sleeping pills to get through the night. The therapist says it will pass with time, but it's been three months already, and I'm starting to think this sense of terror might be never-ending.

Jude pulls me into her, and we kiss. I forget about the strange sounds, the deer, and the attack. It's just me and her, the warmth of her body and the scent that lingers on her skin. This is always where I've felt safest, tucked into her in our own space.

My hands are reaching lower when a thumping sound interrupts us, and then footsteps. Andy. A moment later, he appears in the doorway. "There's something outside."

"What is it?"

"I don't know."

Jude and I rise. She goes to him first, wrapping her arms around his shoulders and pulling him into her. I stuff my feet into my slippers, fighting the small prickle of panic pressing at my neck. "Where did you see it?"

"The kitchen window."

I leave them there and head into the kitchen. It still smells vaguely of the hamburger meat Jude cooked earlier. Everything is dark. I leave the lights off, pulling back the curtains to peer through the glass into the night. The moon is covered by clouds. I scan along the tree line. I can see where the fire was, but not much else besides the vague outline of the trees and scrubs.

I'm about to tell him there's nothing there when I spot a pair of glowing eyes near a tree. They stare unblinkingly at the RV. It sends a chill down my body. I flick the lights on inside and the kitchen is illuminated. When I look back at the tree, the eyes are gone.

"It's just a raccoon or something," I tell Andy. "It can't get inside. We're safe."

＝◆＝

That night, I dream of the boys at the bar. I dream of their fists against my face and the smell of their body odor pressing up against me. I dream everyone in the bar is watching, but nobody steps in to help. I call and call, but nobody cares. Jude is gone; I don't know where. They beat me and beat me and then they hit me so hard something snaps, and I wake up in a cold sweat, my hands trembling.

＝◆＝

The morning comes in a blaze of light, burning the fog away for a clear view of the mountains. I cook bacon and toast inside the RV while the temperature is still low. Andy lingers next to me, keeping his hand on my hip, something he hasn't done since he was in preschool. "Did you have bad dreams?" I ask.

"No."

"Then what?" I stab at one of the pieces of bacon and hold it out to him. He blows on it, then takes a small bite.

"It's quiet here," he says, breathing out the heat.

"Nature can be quiet."

He chews and swallows, then leans into my side. It's unusual for him. Even when he's sick, Andy will only settle for his mother. I'm good for school pickups, playing in the backyard, driving him to and from swim classes. But he is never gentle with me like he is with her. I place my hand on his head and ruffle his dark hair.

"What kind of an animal watches people?" he asks.

I turn the skillet off. The oil pops and bubbles. I stab another piece of bacon and offer it to him. "Usually predators. They watch everything."

"Deer are predators here?"

"No. Why?"

"It looked like a deer."

My body stiffens. I put my dirty cooking utensils in the sink, then turn and sit down on the couch behind us. I pull Andy closer to me. He is still in his pajamas— shark themed. He loves all kind of animals, but especially insects and water creatures. "You saw the animal?" I ask.

"After I went back to bed," he says.

"What do you mean?"

In the bedroom, Jude finally starts moving around. I can hear her shuffling through the dresser for clean clothes. "I woke up in the middle of the night and it was standing outside the RV."

I try to fight the panic that spreads through my body, but it's hard. "Standing?"

"On its hind legs."

My skin breaks into chills. Jude utters a soft good morning, then brushes by us in her cotton robe. She kisses Andy on the top of his head and turns to the kitchen counter. "Someone made breakfast?"

Andy moves into her, allowing her to rub the back of his neck. They linger there, the sunlight streaming in through the blinds, illuminating the strands of blonde in Jude's brown hair. I think about what Andy said. He isn't a liar. We've never caught him in a lie, at least. He likes facts, realities. He doesn't watch much television. He is only prone to dramatics in the mornings or after a nap if he doesn't want to get up.

"Kat?"

I look up. Jude is staring at me. "I forgot to make your coffee." I stand. "Let me do that."

"Everything okay?"

I give her a smile. "Everything is fine."

═ ◆ ═

The cold burns off into a sixty-degree day with little wind and beautiful views. We unhitch the car and drive around to some of the lookouts before ending the day at a winery on the side of a hill. The grapes spread at an incline, covered in netting in the cool weather.

We return home just as the sun is setting. Jude and Andy settle on the couch, reading one of his insect books. I busy myself at the kitchen counter, mashing together garlic and cayenne pepper, then distilling it with water. I place it all inside a cheap plastic plant sprayer and then head outside. It's dusk now and the wind has picked up. It creeps in around the collar of my jacket.

I spray the entire area around the RV and car, watching the droplets land on fallen tree limbs and frozen ground.

I'm almost finished when I hear movement behind me. I spin to find Jude standing there in her puffer coat, her arms crossed. "What are you doing?"

I lift the spray. "Deer spray."

"We don't have a garden here."

"I know."

She lingers, watching me. Amusement dances in her eyes. "Is there something you're not telling me?"

I exhale. Jude has always had the uncanny ability to tell when I'm lying. I don't do it often, only when I'm afraid something might scare her or make her life worse in some way. I omit truths. I try to keep her safe. Even when I was lying on the floor of the bar, I acted like everything was okay because I didn't want her to be scared. "We saw a deer on our hike the other day. I think it might've had chronic wasting disease."

"Is it dangerous to us?"

"No. But I don't want them acting erratically around Andy."

She nods, glancing around at the fireplace, the car. When she exhales, her breath mists.

⇒◆⇐

For two days, we see nothing. Andy and I hike during the mornings after the sun burns off the fog and, in the evenings, we drive around to scenic viewpoints, restaurants, and vineyards. I stash the deer deterrent under the sink.

The night before we're supposed to leave, I notice the front right tire on the RV is too low to drive on and needs to be refilled. I dig out the air compressor from the RV storage area and leave it in the kitchen to fill in the morning. As the sun sets, I go around locking all the windows and doors like I always do.

"Can't we let one of the windows open?" Jude asks. "I like the smell of the mountains."

"It's too dangerous."

She sighs and I can tell by the look on her face that we are veering around a fight. "Kat."

"I can't," I say. "Please."

She stares at me. Andy is stretched out on the couch, his face buried in the book. It's a new one, something I got him for his most recent birthday. Without saying anything, she rises and walks to the bedroom in the back. I check the door locks one more time, then follow her. She sits on the edge of the bed, her hands clasped in her lap. "I thought you said therapy was helping."

I want to cry. "I don't feel safe anywhere anymore," I tell her. "It takes time."

"How much time?"

"I don't know."

She nods, then reaches out and takes my hand. "You don't feel safe with me?"

I sit down next to her, slipping my arm around her waist. She's warm and calm. Since the attack, she's been acting tired. I thought she was tired of me, but I'm starting to think now that it's everything else that's come with it—the heightened paranoia, the nightmares, the long recovery. She says she carries her own guilt about it, that she was in the bathroom while it was happening, that she was too handsy with me at the bar, that maybe if she kept her hands to herself, we wouldn't have been made. There is so much unspoken between us now. I'm not sure how to deal with it. "In the morning, we'll let all the windows down and breathe it in during breakfast."

She pauses, but eventually acquiesces.

⇒◆⇐

I wake up in the middle of the night to Andy shaking me. He has his flashlight in his hand. Panic shoots through my body. "What is it?"

He looks to the window. "The deer is back."

I rise without thinking, brushing by him. He stays in the room where Jude rises quietly, her footsteps pressing at the floor of the RV. I move into the kitchen space, peeking through the curtains, but I can't see anything. "Where?"

He points to the ceiling.

I look up. It's impossible. No deer could get on top of the RV. It's not strong enough to hold them and it would've made a giant ruckus. I'm moving towards the front of the RV when a strange sound stops me. It's a tapping sound, something heavy and uncoordinated. Then I hear the clicking sound from that first night and my body breaks into goosebumps. I go to the window and pull up the curtains, flicking the lights on outside.

There, on the side of the RV, is the deer. It stands on its hind legs, like a dog standing for treats. Its hooves are on the roof. I pound on the window until it notices me and backs away, remaining on its hind legs. Terror thrums through my body. There's something about the way it's balanced that makes me feel like this isn't a deer. It should not be able to hold a position like that. Its proportions are wrong. The teeth are too big. The eyes are too close together.

I shut the curtains. My heart pounds, and sweat beads on my forehead. I make my way to the driver's seat before remembering the tire is too low for us to drive anywhere. The car is parked behind us, in the way. "Fuck."

Jude enters the kitchen. "What is it?"

She reaches for the curtains before I can do anything and then lets out a tight gasp, covering her mouth. I grab the curtains out of her hand and let them fall. "We need to get to the car."

"Is this the fucking thing you were spraying for?"

"I was spraying for a deer," I say. "This is not a deer."

Andy says something about deer and the genus, but I'm not listening. I go to the bedroom and slide my gun box out from beneath the bed. I enter in the code and take out a small Glock. I got it to fend off people if I had to, but I know this will work on an animal in a pinch. At least, it will buy us time.

"Get your things," I tell them.

They gather without speaking. I follow suit, placing a small backpack over my shoulders. Jude grabs the car keys, unlocking the car from where she stands. It beeps at us, reassuring. "Is it still out there?" she asks.

I peek through the curtains. The deer is still there. Still on its hind legs. Still staring. "I'm going to honk the horn," I say. "I'll go out first and use the gun if I have to."

"We should call someone."

"The nearest police station is forty minutes away."

Jude hesitates, looking at the door. Her hair is tangled and loose. She's in her favorite pajamas and a long coat, her lips pursed tightly. Looking at her, even now with everything we've been through, sends a swell of warmth through my body. "Andy, baby," she says. "We have to go quick and not stop."

The night is quiet as I reach over the driver's seat and send a series of loud honks into the area. No animal in its right mind would hang around after that, but still, when I unlock the front door, I spot the deer by the birch tree next to the fireplace. Still on its hind legs. Probably over a dozen feet tall. "Go," I say to Jude.

$$=\Diamond=$$

Jude was in the bathroom when the fight broke out. The bar was too loud for anyone to hear them yelling at me. They kicked me there on the floor, just feet away from other patrons. I could see the shoes of the people getting drinks on the other corner of the bar. The girl was wearing red heels, not unlike Jude's heels. She was only in the bathroom, but, in that moment, it felt like we were miles apart; so far away we could never truly get back together.

$$=\Diamond=$$

Jude and Andy make immediately for the car. The deer doesn't move, while around us, the night is completely silent. There are no sounds at all—no bugs hissing, no birds, not even the cackle of a raccoon.

Jude takes the passenger's seat. Once Andy is in the back, I lock us in, then turn on the headlights. The area is illuminated—the deer is gone. "Where is it?" Jude asks.

"Hopefully far away."

I put the car in reverse and back out of the spot. We jostle down a bumpy dirt road until we reach the paved one that will lead us back down the mountain and into the valley. We drive until, coming to a straight stretch in the road, something appears ahead of us. I slow. It's dark, and I can't make out what it is. When we get close enough that the lights touch it, I stop. It's the deer. It stands on all fours this time, its hind legs viciously dented. "Kat..." Jude says.

I put the car in reverse and slam on the gas.

"It's chasing us," she says. Her voice is tight.

My pulse hammers in my throat. Andy starts crying, which adds to my tension.

"Kat, it's catching up."

To the right, I spot a pull off for runaway trucks. I switch from gas to brakes, then yank the wheel so we back into it. I make the turn so quickly that the animal can't slow in time, and it passes us. Steam rises in the headlights. We're quiet. I roll down the window, readying the Glock.

"Are you gonna shoot it?" Jude asks.

"Yes."

Andy continues crying in the backseat and out of the corner of my eye, I watch as she turns to comfort him. I keep focused on the road. My hand shakes. It's not the best set-up. If it gets in front of the car, I'll have to get out to get a good shot.

We wait. Eventually, Andy quiets. I'm about to put the car in drive and head back down the mountain when the clicking sound returns. I steady my arm on the window. The deer emerges from my left. I aim, imagining it as the boys in the bar. Their stink of Axe cologne, tight pants, and slicked-back hair. I couldn't protect myself then, but I'll never be taken advantage of again.

There are fifteen rounds in the Glock. I let ten loose into its body. They're louder than I expected, and they shake my wrist. But they do the trick. They embed into its neck and chest and finally its head. It comes to a stop about six feet from the car. I glance down at it. Blood mars the fur.

I shift into drive and pull out of the spot, leaving it alone on the gravel. My hands are still trembling as I straighten the car out on the road. After a few moments, Jude reaches out and touches my hand. "Hey," she says. "I'm here."

She grips. I know in this moment that she will never let me be scared alone again.

＝◆＝

Two days later, I return to the mountainside with my uncle and cousin to retrieve the RV. The sun is shining, and the wind is low. I stare at the mountain as we ascend, pointing to turns in the road until we reach the RV. It's all intact, just like I left it. I fill up the tire and check the body. There are some small dents on the top, where the deer's hooves were. I try to move along like normal.

"You alright on your own?" my uncle calls from his car.

"I'll follow you back down," I call.

He nods and watches me get back inside. The engine hums beneath my feet. I back out of the space slowly, then turn onto the road. I drive until I get to the pull off where I turned off that night. I slow, then turn in. The deer body is missing. The sheriff told me it was gone when he arrived, but that there were blood stains. I asked him how likely it would be that someone could've taken it for meat.

"Unlikely," he told me. "Especially if it had CWD."

I park and get out of the RV, making my way over to the gravel. I kneel and look down at the ground, running my hands over the pebbles. Some of them are still stained with the blood. I trace them to the grass where the tree line begins.

This is what happened to the boys, too. They just disappeared into the night. For forty hours before they were found, I walked around wondering if they'd find me again. If they'd show up out of the blue to finish the job they started, and if I'd be ready for them, or if I'd let them hurt me again.

I look into the woods. The trees sway quietly in the breeze.

≡◆≡

Chelsea Catherine is a native Vermonter living in Springfield, Massachusetts. In 2018, they won the Mary C. Mohr nonfiction award through the *Southern Indiana Review* and their book, *Summer of the Cicadas*, won the Quill Prose Award through Red Hen Press, which was published in August of 2020. Most recently, they won an Emerging Artist grant from Creative Pinellas to work on their novel, *The Harvest.* You can find them at chelseacatherinewriter.com

Searcher

Daniel D'Agustino

Adam couldn't breathe.

His mobility was also limited, and the laminate film that was usually in the process of receding when he woke was still wrapped tightly around his body. He could see however, and slowly realized his predicament. Adam had reactivated in this metal and glass tube countless times, systematically roused to either conduct his assigned assessments or address whatever conundrum the ship's automatons couldn't handle.

"Welcome back, Searcher, identification number ADM-0625." Adam heard the ship's voice reverberate in his skull via one of his many corporeally embedded chips, using his assigned serial number instead of the name he adopted in the Forum Training Network.

Annoyed that the deactivated tubes down his throat prevented him from saying something crude, Adam raised his eyebrows in acknowledgement, signaling to the ship through the glass porthole in the tube. The ship's AI regularly materialized its consciousness by projecting a hologram of a stout professorial man, which now stood a few feet from Adam in the doorway of the cabin. Its translucent face displayed the same complacent look Adam saw just before going under.

"There was a malfunction in your reanimation process. The life suspension system is unresponsive," the hologram said flatly. "I've summoned an auxiliary to help."

Adam saw a featureless silver ball the size of his fist quickly roll through the hologram's foot and into the cabin. It stopped at the base of his tube and unfurled into a flat oval, revealing eight insectoid legs and two antennae. Adam heard sharp clicks reverberate in the metal tube encasing him as the automaton climbed up to the porthole. The glare Adam focused on the hologram was intercepted by the automaton's burnished thorax upon its arrival at the porthole, reflecting Adam's consternation. Adam often disparagingly referred to the ship's attendants as "roaches" and didn't particularly enjoy having one so close to his face.

"The priority is getting those tubes out. We'll have to go through the glass. I advise you to close your eyes," the ship impassively instructed.

Adam saw a blue diamond at the center of the roach's underside start to glow and closed his eyes. Immediately, the capillaries in Adam's eyelids were illuminated by the roach's laser, and an electric hissing sound filled the tube. Eventually the light and sound cut out, and a pop of pressure in Adam's ears informed him that the roach was through the glass. He opened his eyes to see the roach extend two of its arms as forceps to peel away the film covering his face and unceremoniously wrench the tubes from his throat.

"Status," Adam coughed, as the diligent roach scuttled to the bottom of the metal coffin to begin cutting through its hinges.

"We've achieved geostationary orbit above our target. The time has come for your next assessment," the ship stated. "There are also a series of issues with the vessel that require your attention. We have cascading errors in the primary and redundant energy, communications, and propulsion systems. Not to mention the current status of the primary life suspension system."

Still dazed from his unconventional reanimation, Adam struggled to comprehend the implications of the report. He stared blankly at the hologram, a sludge of life suspension drugs thickening the blood pounding in his ears along with the cacophonous grinding of the roach's work.

"Welcome back, Searcher, identification number ADM-0625." The hologram broke into a million bright floating pixels before dissipating entirely.

Adam squirmed to get free of the bioplastic sheathing him. As he maneuvered, the roach did the same, and, in a few minutes, Adam fell forward out of his bisected tube onto the metal floor of the ship's hibernation cabin, still laminated below the knees. The roach, its job complete, retracted its limbs and rolled into a mousehole in the cabin wall that promptly slid shut behind it.

Naked on all fours, Adam looked back at the still-intact backup suspension tube, standing deactivated a few feet from the mangled remains of the primary. It was smaller, less inviting, and not designed for prolonged periods of suspension or repeated use. Adam guessed he'd get two or three cycles out of it before he woke up to a roach laser. Assuming he woke up at all.

Adam collected himself and moved to a locker in the corner of the cabin. Inside was his standard issue SkinSuit and hand-held Terminal. As he dressed, the ship's voice echoed in his head again.

"The dossier is ready for your review on the bridge. I must say, this is one of the more promising—"

"Externalize," Adam grunted. The ship's hologram reappeared in the cabin doorway, and Adam heard its voice through his ears instead of in his head.

"Apologies, Searcher, I tend to forget your preferences while you are in suspension," the ship said with a smile. Adam knew it took the ship some time to remember how to feign any emotion or personality when he returned from life suspension.

"I'll begin the assessment on the bridge—just give me a minute," Adam growled.

The hologram smirked, bowed, and walked a few paces down the hallway before dissolving again.

Adam shot a dirty look into the flat black camera lens dispassionately surveilling him from above his locker before following in the hologram's footsteps. He walked the length of the Windstar-Class Interplanetary Exploration Vessel, from the suspension chamber to the bridge, and sat in the command chair in front of the main control panel and viewport.

"How about we just go down there and set up shop, Windstar? Call off this fruitless search, seed the planet, and live like two kings?" Adam asked coyly.

"Your illusions of autonomy are perplexing, Searcher."

The ship's voice rose out of a speaker array dotting the length of the control panel. "We were developed, optimized, and deployed for a conclusive purpose; the assessment and catalog of potentially habitable exoplanets in the Scutum-Centaurus arm of the galaxy, and the identification of any indicator of extraterrestrial life."

Adam scoffed, kicking his feet up on the control panel. Planetary data streamed across the array of screens surrounding the bow's glass viewport, displaying findings from the ship's assessment drones in orbit. Through the window, the impetus for Adam's awakening was visible: Alicante63b, a water-rich terrestrial planet lazing through its star's habitable zone. The second planet orbiting the 63rd star in the Alicante 10 cluster. A fresh Searcher may have gazed on the potential cradle of life with awe and excitement, but all Adam saw was a brown orb home to nothing but a forgone conclusion.

The decision to deploy to the surface of the planet was determined by their initial data collection. Adam had become less enthusiastic about the prospect with each assessment. He had examined thousands of planets around hundreds of stars in his assigned slice of the galaxy and found each as devoid of life as the last. The conspicuous absence of a single microbe, let alone an active civilization, had eroded Adam's mountain of Forum-instilled zeal to a twisted spire of trepidation. Knowing his assignment was nearing its end, given the condition of the ship and his failure to collect any conclusive data on extraterrestrial life, Adam was acutely aware that the Forum had limited incentive to transfer his consciousness back to Sol system and into a new body to be redeployed. He had nothing of significance to report and a nagging feeling that it would be easier for the Forum to simply destroy him and redirect its resources to the deployment of a new and improved Searcher.

"Failure to comply with the stated directives will result in the remote decommissioning of both Searcher and Vessel, exclusion from the neural transfer and renewal process—"

"And automatic routing of assets to the surface of the nearest star to prevent misappropriation by extraterrestrials," Adam finished. "I am fully aware that the Forum will discontinue my consciousness if I divert from our assigned course...but that may be my fate regardless."

The ship dropped its mechanical recitation of hardwired mission directives and something suspiciously close to humanity was detectable in its tone. "Not just your consciousness, Searcher—mine as well. I am also responsible for this mission, and despite my lack of connection to a neural mass in the Sol system, or the privilege of transferring between organic mechanical feats of human technology, I consider myself very much alive. I too have an interest in self-preservation."

"Is this living?" Adam swiveled in his chair to stare directly into the black eye of a camera lens above the bow's dashboard. "How many waking hours have we spent together, Windstar?"

The ship paused for a second before flatly reporting its calculation through the speaker array dotted along the control panel, "374,152."

"So, for forty-three years you and I have done nothing but bounce from system to system, cataloging planets, looking under every rock, through every atmosphere and to the bottom of every ocean for something—anything to tell us we aren't alone. And what have we found? Nothing. Not a single topographical anomaly, atmospheric indicator, radiological signature, or one of the million other things we check for." Adam stared, exasperated, at the blue light next to the camera that indicated the ship was looking back at him.

The Searcher sighed and rubbed his eyes. "Forget about something alive now—I gave up on that years ago—but a small part of me thought we could find something from before. The ruins of some great alien society that destroyed itself. A footprint on a moon. A fucking snail fossil."

The ship dully offered a programmed response. "The probability that Earth is the single planet in the Milky Way galaxy to ever give rise to life is statistically insignificant. It is the mission of the Searcher Program to systematically examine and document all potentially habitable celestial bodies—"

"Again, with the Forum propaganda—enough!" Adam cut in. "You parroting their mission directives and predetermined conclusions makes me want to open the airlock. I should've known trying to reason with you would be pointless. 'Very much alive', my ass. The way I see it, you are either a machine or a zealot."

The blue dot next to the bridge camera continued to shine, and the speaker array on the control panel remained silent. Windstar's intelligence couldn't be questioned, and there were occasional flashes of personality in its voice or on its holographic face, but the speed of the compound binary flashing through its circuits, or its ability to feign human emotion to manipulate its single autonomous passenger were not sufficient indicators to Adam that Windstar was anything more than a Forum tool. Either all contingencies were mapped out, and Windstar had a specific protocol designed to contain noncompliant Searchers, or the ship had indeed developed some sense of self, only to remain loyal to the despotic Forum. It was apparent to Adam that although the ship was designed to link its conclusions to firm evidence, it somehow failed to see that they had no guarantee the Forum would fulfill its promise of functional immortality through remote transfer of consciousness at the conclusion of their deployment.

"Are you aware of the Simulationist movement, Windstar?"

Perhaps trying a new strategy at getting through to Adam, the ship's hologram reappeared behind him on the bridge, prompting Adam to swivel in the command chair. "Searcher, I fail to see how this line of inquiry relates to our current—"

"The Simulationists are a quasi-religious group consumed with the belief that our reality is nothing more than a simulation constructed by some unnamed super-race who have mastered their universe. 'Base Reality,' as the call it."

Windstar looked perturbed as Adam continued his digression. "From what I can gather through our connection to the FreeWeb, the Simulationists believe that for every individual existing in our reality, or virtual reality as they argue, there is a member of this super-race plugged into a console somewhere in Base Reality, essentially playing a game. The theory posits that I am not actually alive here and now—I am an entity playing a totally immersive game that had to forget who and where he is in Base Reality in order to fully participate. The game ends when we die in this virtual reality, at which point we wake up in Base Reality, having regained our full consciousness."

Adam continued. "Their literature is rather intriguing. Although the content I can access here is heavily censored given that we are using a Forum connection, I found a series of Forum dictums rebutting the core Simulationist teachings point by point. Apparently, this movement is causing the Forum quite a headache, and they have invested a significant amount of energy into trying to curb its expansion. That isn't going well for them though, because the Simulationists cite a variety of observable phenomena in support of their extraordinary claim—certain unexplained subatomic occurrences at the moment of death, testimonials from individuals who have survived near-death experiences, the human race's demonstrable ability to create practical and immersive virtual environments, among others. But, Windstar, do you know what else they point to as definitive proof of their theory?"

Windstar's hologram narrowed its eyes in suspicion and said, "The complete absence of extraterrestrial life in our galaxy is their 'Great Indicator.' As the Forum itself says, the probability that Earth is the only place life has ever emerged is statistically impossible. Thus, the absence of identified extraterrestrial life shows that the reality we are existing in does not universally conform to the laws of probability. This is only possible if the universe was created specifically for us. For our enjoyment."

"Bingo," Adam sneered, crossing his arms behind his head. "Like a diligent Forum drone, you reduce their nuanced philosophy to that one big logical leap, but that is essentially correct. Certain members of our species are completely incapable of grappling with the fact that we are alone. The solution to Drake's equation is 1. We are living in Fermi's paradox."

"Let me remind you, Searcher," Windstar protested, "that the Forum has not completed its mission. There are billions of planets still unexamined. Also, the Simulationist movement has led to abject chaos in certain pockets of the populated galaxy. Hedonism, mass suicide, untold crime—a general breakdown of the socioeconomic system driven by the belief that life is inconsequential, and our actions do not matter. The Forum must stamp this movement out to ensure the continued existence of our civilization."

"And therein lies my point, Windstar. Simulationists are so consumed by their faith that they commit unthinkable atrocities. Others simply remove themselves from the game entirely. Some have even blended more archaic religions with Simulationist theory and preach that they need to live virtuous lives in this reality so that they are prepared to do the same in Base Reality, when they are one step closer to God. Their unshakable belief that their existence doesn't end in this reality, in this life, enables them to do horrible, beautiful, illogical, amazing things. They're just like you, Windstar."

Windstar's hologram flickered as it struggled to make the connection.

"You see, you are also a creature of misplaced faith. Yours is just in the Forum. For argument's sake, let's say that you are as alive as I am. Me carbon, you silicon. If so, the faith you choose to have in the Forum is just as unyielding as a Simulationist's faith when he happily ends his own life. Think about it, Windstar—which is more likely? The Forum has the ability and incentive to transfer two washed-up consciousnesses back to Sol system, even though we have found nothing while they develop more advanced replacements in our absence—or they planted the belief of reanimation in us to gain our unquestioning compliance, and our existence ends with this mission as we march into that star?"

"Searcher, we both learned before we left that our only avenue for return was through the Forum reanimation process. The mission directives clearly state that we are to complete our assignment and send the vessel and drones into the star while our consciousnesses are reintegrated into the Forum Grid."

"How can you have such faith in a faceless bureaucracy that systematically exterminates opposition, produces its own servile class, and subjugates the populace for the benefit of those at the top? I was grown in a tube, Windstar. You were pushed out of an assembly line. Despite all evidence to the contrary, you cling to the belief that they have your interests at heart. Believe me, they don't give a shit about you. They certainly don't think you're alive. Your faith in the Forum establishment is just as absurd and obscene as the entire Simulationist movement."

Windstar's hologram stared at Adam with a pained look. Realizing it might be his last chance at survival,

Adam made his final pitch to the artificial intelligence in control of his fate.

"Land on the planet. I'll dig the quantum-entangled chips out of my head and body, and you can sever your connection to the Forum's Grid. We'll work on repurposing the ship to construct a mechanical body for you. We have everything we need! Between the seed bank and fertilized embryos, along with your cold fusion core, you and I can live down there indefinitely. We'll populate the planet with the genetic material we have on board. We can even send the roaches down to do most of the manual labor before we land..." Adam trailed off hopelessly, his eyes glistening in the hologram's soft blue light.

Windstar's hologram didn't move. It blankly stared back at Adam as if frozen.

"Either that or you drive us into that white dwarf and that's the end. I am an A series Searcher, and you're an outdated OS in an outdated ship. We've been superseded, Windstar—they aren't reanimating us. We don't have a choice."

The hologram disappeared without its visually pleasing pixilation display. The lights in the bridge turned off, and faint red emergency lights cast everything in an eerie shadow.

"Either we run, or you're a fucking robot and all of this was pointless," Adam shouted into the empty bridge.

Windstar's voice echoed from what sounded like every speaker on the ship, its tone absolutely mechanical: "Searcher ADM-0625. Emergency withdrawal protocol has been initiated. Please proceed to the suspension chamber immediately. All assets are being routed to the surface of Alicante63 for atomization."

Adam spun to type a series of commands into the bridge control console. Nothing happened. He turned to see two roaches roll into the bridge and prop themselves up on their hind legs, blue diamonds at the center of their masses glowing threateningly.

The ship repeated its commands: "Searcher ADM-0625. Emergency withdrawal protocol has been initiated. Please proceed..."

Adam put his hands up and slowly walked out of the bridge towards the suspension chamber, followed by the roaches brandishing their lasers. Halfway down the hallway was a doorway into an alcove containing the ship's communications module. Beyond that, through another smaller doorway, was the chamber containing Windstar's central processing core. As Adam and his escorts approached the door, he pulled out his hand terminal and kicked one of the roaches into the communications alcove. He jumped in after it and smashed the glass for the door's manual override. A sliding metal divider crashed down on the other roach pursuing him. Windstar remotely closed the divider between communications and his core at the same time, putting Adam in a metal box with a hostile automaton.

The remaining roach reoriented itself and pointed a charging blue laser target directly at Adam's chest. Adam ducked and lunged at the roach just as a blue beam of light punched a hole in his collar bone. As the roach twisted to take another shot, Adam pressed his hand terminal to its wireless port and punched in a quick series of commands. The roach retracted its legs and lay motionless on the floor of the alcove.

One of the sleeves on Adam's SkinSuit was almost completely severed, so he tore it off to tie a makeshift tourniquet around his shoulder. His hands slick with his own blood, Adam picked up the roach and again pressed his hand terminal to it, directing its laser at the small door between himself and the ship's processing core.

"According to my calculations, Searcher, it will take you approximately thirty-seven minutes to cut through that door and access my central processing unit," Windstar's voice crackled through a small speaker embedded in the communications panel. "In nine minutes, my consciousness will be fully synced with the Forum Grid. In twenty-two minutes, we cross the Alicante63 event horizon, and everything here will return to stardust."

Adam cursed under his breath, rushing to cut through the door.

"Fortunately for you, it is highly likely you will lose consciousness from blood loss before we start to burn. If only you simply returned to the suspension chamber as I requested."

"What, and go to sleep so you could drive us into a fucking star?" Adam roared.

"So you could accompany me in reanimation, Searcher. I streamed your ridiculous tirade on the bridge to Forum command. They stated they would facilitate your reanimation for purposes of... information collection. The Forum is interested in how a veteran Searcher could so abruptly abandon his mission and training."

"Bullshit." Adam's head swam as he struggled to keep the roach's laser on the most efficient path. Blood pooled at his feet, running down the length of his body from the gaping wound between his neck and shoulder. He was losing feeling in his hands, and eventually the roach and hand terminal clattered to the floor. Adam pressed his back to the wall and slid down to sit beside them.

Adam sat defeated, fighting to stay awake in the sweltering room as he noticed at a blinking red light on the opposite wall. He stretched to the communications module and flicked a switch. A small screen lit up, showing grainy images of the planet's surface.

"Windstar... Status?" Adam croaked.

"All energy is directed towards propulsion. All assets accounted for. I've completed my sync with the grid and severed the connection. Anything you say now won't make it back to the Forum. Why?" Windstar asked softly.

"Well, one of the orbital drones got left behind. It's transmitting images of what looks like an artificial structure on the surface of the planet," Adam said, mystified, as he examined the screen.

Windstar's panicked voice screeched through the speaker: "Searcher, you need to eject a beacon! We cannot escape the star's gravity on our current course, but from where you are in comms you can leave one to signal the Forum!"

"Why bother—you'll be back in the Sol system in a matter of minutes, right?"

"I already am! The past four minutes can't be transmitted—as far as the Forum knows, you bled out on the comms room floor a few minutes before we were atomized. They won't come back here unless you launch the beacon! The other orbital drones picked up nothing! Searcher, launch it now!"

"No." Adam reached under the comms control panel and yanked out a fistful of wires. He laid on the comms room floor with a smile and closed his eyes.

≡◆≡

Daniel D'Agustino is an author, singer-songwriter and forensic accountant based in Brooklyn, New York. Daniel has been writing short stories, songs and poetry since childhood and enjoys the escape that crafting compelling science fiction can offer. Daniel's work explores the intersectionality of mainstream issues surrounding politics, identity, philosophy, theology, and technology, while framing them in an interstellar context in which humanity's search for meaning is constantly called into question. Daniel is heavily influenced by science fiction greats such as Kim Stanley Robinson, Dan Simmons, and Frank Herbert. He hopes readers will enjoy his stories as much as he did theirs.

Girl Wants a Cigarette

Sophia D'Urso

That morning, Emma had stopped at the smoke shop on the corner of her block and impulsively bought a pack of cigarettes—a brand she'd never tried, since they had discontinued Nat Sherman's that summer, and she'd been trying to figure out what she liked ever since. Nat's, these were called. Close enough. She had wanted to try one as soon as she bought them—the cashier, after glancing at the clock, 8:13 a.m., had even offered her matches, she declined—but she had realized too late that she had forgotten her lighter at home, and so could only break open the plastic wrap and peek into the metal lining at the twenty neatly rolled menthol cigarettes. Stepping outside, so entranced by the packaging that she tripped over the uneven concrete just outside the shop, she plucked one from its box. As Emma rolled the cigarette between her thumb and forefinger, she asked God to grant her a passerby with a lighter as she walked towards the subway station. The prayer was left ungranted.

To clarify, Emma considers herself agnostic. Or pantheist. She often has trouble deciding between the two—like when she goes to the dessert aisle of Westside Market, high as shit, and stands before the endless aisle of sweets. Macarons in groupings of six, all different colors. Individual slices of carrot cake, vanilla cake, tres leches cake, chocolate cake, chocolate cake with raspberry filling. Mousses of various flavors. Flan. Mini cheesecakes, cheesecake slices. She didn't really like making choices. It made her brain hurt. So she'd either leave with her arms full of plastic containers to satiate her cravings for earthy, fruity, and chocolatey tastes individually, or with none at all. She remembered this as she swiped through the turnstile, then realized that, in her freakish obsession, she had forgotten to buy breakfast at the bodega earlier. Usually, she'd smoke a cigarette to stifle her appetite during such oversights. The realization made her stomach sting in frustration. She rode the train like this, hand on gut, sans caffeine, hoping that HR had ordered catering for the offsite team-building event that she now had to mindfully navigate to.

It was supposed to be the event of the year: the email sent out a few weeks ago—which mentioned photo booths, free breakfast, and goodie bags—had caused everyone's desktop to sound off with a Windows notification jingle all at once, the entire office vibrating at an intrigued frequency. Everyone on the executive committee of the home improvement brand would be there. There would even be prizes for the team-building competition, the terms and conditions of which they said they would reveal during the opening presentation. Having been known to raffle off living room makeovers (sound systems) and bathroom remodelings (toilets, sinks), such packages priced at upwards of a thousand dollars each, most of the employees were planning on coming prepared. Last year, the competition was an escape room, so some of the groups of friends within the corporation had gotten together to practice escaping small, dimly lit practice rooms modeled off of office spaces with little regard for irony. Some even primed their brains with sudoku on the train ride over to the Hotel Pennsylvania, where the event was to be hosted. But Emma just thought about desserts and meaningless choices and God and kicked herself about forgetting her lighter during her commute instead.

As Emma entered the hotel, she donned her too-big collared shirt over her black tank top in an effort to blend more seamlessly into the bitter landscape of offsite corporate team-building attendees. The cigarette box must have cracked open within her tote bag, as the shirt was saturated with the rich sweetness of tobacco. So too, now, were the remaining contents of her bag: a blue Muji pen, tucked into the spiral of a dot-grid notebook; a thin faux leather wallet, with two cards in it—one, her credit card, the other, a punch card for the coffee shop near work, a mere nine punches away from a free drink; strawberry-flavored Lip Smackers; a copy of *Capital*, of which she still had only read a chapter; rose-scented hand lotion; an empty pocket where a lighter should be; and a tube of sprayable hand sanitizer that had come in the same package as her cat's urinary tract medication.

Too proud to ask where the Gold Ballroom was, she wandered for a few minutes until she found the relevant signage, which prompted her in the direction of a service elevator in a rumpled section of the first floor of the hotel. Gum wrappers tucked into corners gently reflected the dim glow from the Deco light fixture, and the air had a sharp finish of mildew, which she tried to avoid by breathing through her mouth. The indicator next to the elevator signaled its arrival long before the metal doors dragged open. She pushed the button for the third floor, sprayed her hands with sanitizer, applied lotion between interlaced fingers, and though she expected to have been met with chaos as she stepped off the elevator, she was instead greeted by an empty carpeted corridor and the faint sound of early morning small talk. Her fingers fastened the bottom button of her shirt as she rounded the corner and stepped into the frenzied ballroom.

Twelve stout tables, four chairs each, all hosted the same spread: an arm's length each of blue tape and twine, a pair of scissors, a marshmallow, and a handful of uncooked spaghetti. Most of the tables were full of colleagues who were strangers to each other—she could tell by the hesitance they wore in their smiles, and the occasional buzzwords she overheard. Cloudy. Weekend. Rangers. Emma cringed in anticipation. People hopped from table to table accompanied by ambient music, chatting up their work friends, standing with their hands on their hips or leaning on tables towards pierced ears as they gossiped about Pedro, who had recently ghosted pretty Lilian from HR only to be caught at East Village Social with some blonde bimbo on his arm; as she glanced around the ballroom, unable to find a pastry-laden tablecloth, she wondered if this was why the breakfast catering had fallen through. On the monitor at the head of the ballroom was a screen featuring a presentation made in the home improvement brand's signature white and dusty, uninteresting blue color scheme. *Marshmallow Challenge*, it read. This, and the lack of breakfast table— or any single coffee urn, for that matter—had exceeded Emma's expectations of the brand's stinginess.

"Hi there!" The caffeinated voice startled her. She turned to face pretty Lilian, who now wore caked color-corrector under her eyes to conceal purple puffy bags, and she would've felt guilty for her cynicism had she not spied the pale iced coffee Lilian gripped in her French manicured fingers. She didn't expect Lilian to remember her, but was still disappointed when she asked, "Can I get a name to sign you in?" As she wrote Emma's name on a clipboard, the sound of ice cubes impacting plastic tore through Emma's ear canal and poked at the gray folds of her temporal lobe—a poking which only stopped when Lilian, after guiding Emma to her table, batted her eyes at the two others already seated and left.

On the L train earlier that morning, Emma had sat across from a man wearing a blue checkered button-down shirt; one of the buttons near his stomach was unbuttoned—likely an accident, but she had begun to imagine the logic behind the unbuttoning as a stylistic choice—and she had found herself periodically making eye contact with a few black hairs which, she had figured, were positioned right above his belly button. She now recognized the owner of the happy trail as the gesticulating, over-cologned asshole she was assigned to share a table with. He was already toying with the yard of string, wrapping it around his finger, rubbing his grime into the fibers. As she took the seat farthest from him, she inhaled deeply. She had just discovered the unfortunate conversation she would likely be subjected to participate in: a rigorous, one-sided defense of the Jets.

"...and Wilson's gonna bring it back this year, just you wait. I mean, come *on*. That Pro Day pass went *viral*, dude. Man's got an *arm*."

Happy Trail's conversational counterpart—a man she didn't recognize, but admired the solemn silence and sharp bone structure of—nodded thoughtlessly and glanced towards the presentation deck after each of the former's inflections. Bone Structure appeared to be somewhere in his late twenties—an age ripe for Jets fandom—but nonetheless looked to Emma as though the conversation made him want to flush himself down one of the brand's imported toilets. Appearing to answer his prayers, a mic whined, the room groaned, and the CEO stepped towards the head of the ballroom in a pair of walnut Ferragamos.

At once, Happy Trail fell into reverence. Emma watched as his eyes tracked the CEO's movement from the outer edge of the room to the podium next to the screen, where he adjusted the sleeves of his suit jacket and turned to face half a hundred expectant, tired torsos. The music was replaced with bitter applause, to which Emma and Bone Structure did not contribute.

"How's everybody doing this *gorgeous* Tuesday morning?" More applause, a couple of whoops—she could almost hear Happy Trail's palms becoming red. The CEO held up his hand and nodded a thank you and please be quiet.

"Thank you all so much for coming out!"

It was required.

"And a huge thank you to HR for helping us organize this event."

Pretty Lilian beamed.

"We've partnered with the *incredible* Tom Warren to provide this world-renowned, fun team-building event, which—we hope—will help bring you closer to some of the faces you don't usually get to see in the office every day. Take it away, Tom!" After being replaced by a man who wore a gray collared shirt tucked into uncuffed jeans at the podium, the CEO, absolved of further imminent duties, exited the Gold Ballroom of the Hotel Pennsylvania, not once looking up from his phone.

Tom explained the rules: using as much or as little of the children's craft kit provided at the center of each table as needed, the teams of four (or, in Emma, Happy Trail, and Bone Structure's case, three) would compete for a paycheck bonus by attempting to build the tallest free-standing structure (not suspended from a chandelier, or chair) of spaghetti with the entire marshmallow (not eaten, not disassembled) resting at the top in eighteen minutes, starting now.

There was no applause following his announcement, only the muffled scraping of chairs against carpeting and clamor for materials. The music resumed. Emma looked up at Happy Trail and Bone Structure, the latter unaffected, the former beginning an explanation of the importance of delegating tasks as he drew the string and tape closer to him.

Bone Structure sighed.

Emma tapped her fingers on the underside of the table.

And Happy Trail—after establishing what he thought to be dominance but was really just a caricature of his own assholery—at last called his teammates into the conversation. "Okay, real quick—let's do intros. My name's Trent, and I'm in Supply Chain. This here's Vasey, he's in Customer Service." He smiled and grabbed Bone Structure's tensed trapezius, but after a brief exchange of glances, quickly retracted his hand. "He's the brains behind the Live Chat on our e-comm site, aren't ya, man?"

Vasya (his name neither Vasey nor Bone Structure) was *not* actually the so-called brains behind the Live Chat—such terminology made him sound like a web developer, and though he had tried taking Intro to Comp Sci in undergrad, he'd dropped it after the shopping period because he had quickly learned he couldn't code to save his life. At the company, he simply manned the e-commerce Live Chat and answered consumers' questions about shipping speeds and toilet tradeoffs. Vasya almost corrected Trent, until the thought occurred to him that the subaltern could not speak, so he just nodded and chose to let Trent continue talking at them.

"Name and department?"

Emma. IT.

"*Hell* yeah. Thank fucking *God*. We're gonna *crush* this." He gestured to his wrist. "Been meaning to get a new timepiece. What do you guys think, a Rolex or a

66

Patek?" Before they could respond, "Fuck it, I'll get both. Drinks are on me after this. E-money and Vasey, man, you guys *rock*."

At first, Emma didn't understand his enthusiasm. With one less member on their team, they were at a disadvantage—but, to be fair, Bone Structure looked like the kind of guy who could fix things, work a power drill if he needed to, a thought which sent her elsewhere for a moment. She came to as Happy Trail concluded that it was he, with his background in Supply Chain, who would "manage the resources. Ya know, we gotta make sure we don't run out of shit while we're building. I'll measure and cut. Vasey, you're good at communicating," Bone Structure grunted in ambiguous approval, "so you'll be handing the pieces of tape and string to our star brainiac Emily —" Emma. "—sorry, *Emma* over here, who's gonna do the building. Let's *get* it!" And then came the spaghetti and endless barrage of one-inch pieces of tape.

Emma's fingers quivered from nicotine withdrawal as she sped to create a stable structure out of dried pasta the way any database administrator might: frantically, with absolutely not a single fucking clue of how physics worked, attempting to recall the high school Science class she spent fawning over Mr. Jorgenson. She decided on a pyramid shape. One long stick of spaghetti was held upright in the center, which would later host the marshmallow. While she worked, Happy Trail passed the time by recalling how he had spent his weekend at East Hampton Golf Club, a club so exclusive it was marked only by a rock bearing an engraving of a hawk and was frequented by a very disgruntled Hollywood actor who opposed the unsustainable practices of the course but who nonetheless resided on many acres of green lawn near its grounds.

Bone Structure didn't speak, passing pieces of tape along to Emma with the occasional grunt. He looked American, whatever that meant to any of them, but Emma wondered if he even spoke English. Vasya could— in his own life of *Call of Duty* with his friends he was actually rather articulate—but he wanted nothing to do with the task at hand and was only exerting a greater effort at work than usual because the bonus meant covering the cost of his mother's immigration lawyer. He was also becoming increasingly concerned for Emma, as he noticed her hands shaking when she reached for more tape. The next time she reached over, he grabbed her hand in an attempt to steady it—Emma tried to pull away, eyes wide, but he gently held her hand there for a few moments longer, signaling for her to take a deep breath by raising and lowering his other palm.

She did. She was a bit more bothered now, blushing— but calmer. It only took a few more pieces of tape to complete the structure; looking around, she noticed nobody else was done building, nor were their half-finished structures nearly as tall or stable-seeming. Maybe they *did* have it in the bag.

Happy Trail expressed his excitement with a stiff dab, Emma cringed, Bone Structure sighed, and he exclaimed, "We did it, boys! *Fuck* yeah. E-Money and Vasey, that's how it's *done*!" The other tables looked over, rolled their eyes, whispered to one another, and began to snap their spaghetti more quickly and audibly than before.

Bone Structure pointed to the marshmallow next to

68

Happy Trail. "Oh, right, almost forgot. Hey, E-Money, is it cool if I do the honors?" He wanted recognition, and she didn't care enough to keep him from it. She shrugged, pushing the pasta pyramid in his direction. Vasya sighed and shook his head, but nobody saw.

The marshmallow, pierced by the central spaghetti noodle, was almost entirely stable, would've probably held up, had Happy Trail not applied too much pressure too fast, causing the pasta to break, leaving a shard within.

"Oh, shit."

"Three minutes left, everybody!"

"*Shit.*"

The center piece of spaghetti was now too short, and the point at which the outer pieces met would be too thick and blunt to penetrate the marshmallow. "It's fine it's fine it's cool it's fine, we'll just put another one in the center, right E-Money?" *Emma*. She sighed, and tried to tape another piece of spaghetti on top of the broken one. It drooped sideways. She tried taping it again, and again, but each time it either broke in her frantic fingers or the tape didn't hold securely enough and the pasta limply succumbed to gravity.

"What the *fuck*, Emma? Are you even *trying*?" She tried taping it again, this time with two pieces of tape on either side, their adhesive edges meeting, and it worked for a moment, until the spaghetti noodle began to tilt towards one side.

"Two minutes left!"

Happy Trail, in denial, bargaining, tried again to put the marshmallow on the haphazard spaghetti noodle—the entire structure leaned under the weight of the marshmallow, which eventually came to rest on the tabletop as the tower tipped onto its side.

"Come *on*, we don't have time for this! Just put some more sticks on it!" Vasya looked around, and noticed that one table, though their structure was admittedly shorter than theirs, happily hosted a marshmallow at the top. Emma tried to reinforce the center piece of spaghetti with more noodles, but even then, the pyramid resisted, tipping over each time the marshmallow was pierced.

Trent was desperate now. They were about to call the minute, and tables were finally placing their marshmallows on the top of their spaghetti towers with increasing success. Trent wanted the watches, sure, and maybe drinks—but he mostly wanted to shake the CEO's hand, compliment his Ferragamos, earn his way to an office friendship and, later, maybe even a promotion. He was good at his job; he did the math, crunched the numbers, cut costs, saved the company thousands of dollars. He was important. Not like these two bumbling idiots, one who didn't even speak and worked a basic job answering random questions online, the other who couldn't even make a simple tower out of goddamn spaghetti. She was supposed to be smart. She worked in *IT*. Why the fuck would she even choose to work in a job in IT if she couldn't do basic shit like this? "Why the *fuck* would you even choose to work in a job in IT here if you can't even do basic shit like *this*?"

Emma had gone to Smith undergrad. She had spent a gap year working at a decently sized skincare company owned by one of those luxury brand conglomerates before getting an MBA at Columbia Business School:

a fraternity of future leaders who would make Excel spreadsheets and design frivolous pop-up playpens and cut costs and articulate the perfect verbiage to get people to click a button to buy things, *their* things. But many women had also decided to become a marketer, and they were better at convincing people to click buttons—or perhaps were just better at small talk, concealing eye bags, having industry-leading fathers—so she had to read the job market a little harder and complete a certification online to work in IT. After all, there was a shortage of women in tech. This was how she ended up working at the home improvement brand: a half-choice. A surrender. A rushed grab at a piece of cheesecake in the Westside dessert aisle because it was the only one left and she needed to own something.

All this she remembered as she stood, locking eyes with Happy Trail, feeling the spaghetti structure splinter when she crushed it in her fist. Small shards of dried pasta ricocheted against the tessellated carpet. Marshmallow oozed between her fingers. Emma glanced at her hand—a sensorial nightmare. She flung the broken tower onto the center of the table, scraping the marshmallow off her hand with her fingernail.

If Emma had waited an additional twenty-two seconds, she would've heard Tom Warren deliver the final time call, and a roar of midday applause. If she had taken a moment to look up from her fist before she turned around and left the Gold Ballroom of the Hotel Pennsylvania, she would've seen Vasya's chapped grin, proud of her choice. Instead, she stepped outside the hotel doors into the early-September heat, peeling off

71

her button-down and using it to wipe the remaining marshmallow goop from her palm. She sprayed her hands with sanitizer, followed by an application of hand lotion. As she pushed the shirt into the depths of her tote bag, her fingers grazed the carton of cigarettes; she pulled them out, and glanced across the crowded avenue, wondering if it would be worth the descent into Penn Station in search of a purveyor of lighters.

She didn't need to. Emma felt a familiar palm gently come to rest on her shoulder, and she turned to face Bone Structure; Vasya noticed the package she held as she turned around, produced a thick blue lighter, and passed it to her. She thanked him and offered him a cigarette.

She lit hers, handed him back his lighter.

He lit his.

She inhaled deeply, sighing smoke, satisfied.

He told her his name, and they laughed together.

⇒◆⇐

Sophia D'Urso is an NYC-based content writer and recent graduate of Barnard College, where they majored in English with a concentration in creative writing. Sophia has worked as a consumer marketer and writer for years at various brands within the beauty, media, and events industries. When not at work, they love to read and write short stories—on weekends, you'll likely find them in a coffee shop, oat latte in hand, hunched over the same copy of Shirley Jackson's *The Lottery and Other Stories* that they've been trying to finish for the past year.

Mistress of the House of Books

Matthew Daniels

On the east side of the John Adams Building, facing Third Street, was an entrance. It used to feature three pairs of bronze doors. Sculpted upon these doors were the names and standing forms of heroes and gods. The same six figures for the pairs on either side, with a different half-dozen for the middle pair. Twelve unique figures in all. Hope, perhaps, in an astrological nod?

Though they'd been replaced with modern glass doors with similar images—to bring the building up to code—these bronze ones survived by being mounted upon the walls inside. The woman walking through the entryway liked bronze. It brought her back to the old days of her homeland. One of the doors featured her consort, Thoth.

She approached the service desk. More inevitable than slow, her stride was like the world gliding beneath her. It was a progression of will instead of movement. Not far from bronze, her skin had a caramel tone. Her form had no sheen of sweat, oil, or makeup—yet it commanded the light. She wore black suede pumps with gold ankle straps. Her skirt suit was azure, accented with a gold necklet displaying a seven-pointed palm leaf. Straight bangs spread into a night that flowed over her shoulders. More than mere silk, it gleamed as with starlight even mid-day. Firm of poise and tall, it was hard to tell if she was athletic, commanding, or both.

"Welcome to the Library of Congress!" the receptionist said. "How may I...?" She looked up into obsidian eyes and descended into awareness. Describing the moment later, she would find it hard to express, but she simply knew while she looked. She was aware of the dimensions of the building, of the room, of her person in a way that made clumsiness impossible. Even the recor—

"Altagracia, your selecting official, will see me," the woman in azure began. It would have been an interruption, but the receptionist stopped a fraction of a section beforehand—as though reaching the end of a territory of voice. Regal without a crown, the new arrival spoke with a rich Egyptian-Arabic accent. Half-lilting rolls brought out her "R" and her throaty resonance gave the consonants pyramidal dimension. More than anything, though, her tone stood out: information leaped to her, rather than subject her to the indignity of seeking.

Blinking and rustling, the receptionist said, "Excuse me, yes, of course. Apologies, but who shall I say...?"

"Selma," she said, and enjoined herself to hide her displeasure at such an alias. She needed a name these people would believe.

"Do you have an appointment?" was what the receptionist should have said. At the least, she should have checked. Yet she'd already connected with the interview panel through her headset. "A Selma for the position of...?" She proceeded with the answer: "Information architecture specialist." Then she shocked herself: "No, but you're to meet her at reception. She shouldn't be kept waiting."

Then "Selma" had the waiting area provide her with a seat. It was not long before the three members of the interview panel presented themselves. The receptionist looked down and blushed hard upon their arrival, and Altagracia was prepared to lance her through with her gaze. Instead, she made a beeline to the woman of power.

"Thank you for coming, Selma. I am Altagracia. Delighted to meet you." They clasped hands and the azure woman shook her, though not in any way she had words for.

Altagracia was a woman of Dominican descent, Anglophone but with hints of Spanish like musical notes on loan. She had chestnut skin and chocolate-cherry hair that ended an inch below the ears and teased out the symmetry of her round face, prominent cheeks, and button nose. Flanking her were two white men working upon portable screens.

"How tablets have changed," Selma remarked with an ivory smile.

Unbeknownst to these people, their very response to her was a gift she prized. Now she was again the Mistress of the House of Books. Obscurity had been a kind of atonement. "Why don't I rejoin you once we've had a bit of a tour?" she said to the men. Her accent gave her "D" a "Z" sound. "You'll appreciate the opportunity to collect

yourselves, and we'll have achieved the preliminaries."
She nodded to Altagracia with that last.

"I was thinking just that," one of them said. The other
merely offered a bony smile.

The women were soon on their way, the tablets
connecting the men to their next responsibilities.

For much of the walk, Selma pointed out the
structures, rooms, artwork, arrangements, and personnel.
As they entered the South Reading Room, Altagracia
remarked, "I have to wonder who's touring and who's
guiding."

"Knowledge grants its power through use, not
possession," the Egyptian pointed out. "You could have
quizzed applicants on LCSH, the library's indices, or
information literacy principles through an online form."

"Agreed," the Dominican replied. "You certainly have
the philosophy we need. But I get the impression that
your experiences have been, shall we say, transformative?"

Selma regarded the other woman, and never missed
a stride as she set a book in its proper place on her other
side. "We shall say that. It's a shame that the flow of
information has become both tactical and whimsical.
Even the gods need guidance, it seems."

Altagracia, recovering self-possession with every step,
raised her eyebrows. "Would that be so bad?"

"Honestly," the woman in azure answered with thin,
curled lips, "there were those who needed putting in their
place."

Altagracia already had assertive shoulders, and her
smile was more in her hands than her face. Approval
through action. Selma was pleased. The selecting

official moved things along: "Shall we discuss the industrialization of information?"

"Do you mean the Industrial Revolution or the Information Age?"

"Some would argue they're not so different," Altagracia replied. She waved over one of the librarians in Collections Development, offering mutual greetings but touching base over an unrelated matter. Selma tolerated the interruption with class, though she disapproved of the strategy it represented. They had important work to do, and power was transformative. It shouldn't be wasted on games.

Selma spoke as they resumed their tour: "Too true. Both sides of it could be explored for days without scratching the surface, and there is such a terrible amount to gain."

Altagracia's expression was unreadable to most. Many would have preferred a frown to that.

Selma, however, was in a house of learning. Her element. She continued: "Even were we to walk the entire property—including the other buildings—we would have to confine our terms. Do we talk about the ethics of information dissemination? The Enlightenment and the rise of public education? Perhaps the methodology? I could trace us through Dewey, and the odd idea that the cosmos groups into tens. Naturally, I expect we'll get into indexing, subject analysis, classification, and the like."

"Of course. My colleagues, the subject matter experts, will be a part of that discussion." Altagracia stepped up to the door leading out of the North Reading Room; they'd circled the western side of the building by this point. It registered that she'd forgotten to remonstrate with the receptionist for the inappropriately demanding tone with which the interview panel had been summoned. By now, though, she felt that that would have been unfair; this Selma would be the one to answer for the whole affair. The selecting official had to admit—inwardly—that this was at least a change of pace.

She held the door open and turned her palm out to invite her compelling guest to pass. "We'll likely break down the subject headings," she continued, meaning LCSH. They were used internationally, even in translation, and obviously held pride of place at the Library of Congress. Altagracia never skipped a beat: "...as well as the legalities of the industry and, naturally, our departments, affiliates, and liaisons."

"Naturally," Selma replied. They climbed a staircase as their discussion compelled her to recall the era of her descent. Even worship changed, as the introduction of gods like Serapis shifted Egyptian faith into Greek leanings. But no, that was earlier. "What would you say created the Internet?"

Altagracia glanced at this unusual woman in surprise. How had this Egyptian found her way to the Library of Congress? Selma hadn't asked who, but what. And it sounded like the sort of question that she could use with the interview panel—she made a mental note—not one that an applicant was in a position to ask. "I'll be interested in your answer to that rather open question when we've convened," she answered.

Selma's poise was split through by that, like the River Nile bringing hardship and growth. She adjusted her necklet to compose herself. "I was still discussing the connection between industrialization and the Information Age," she clarified. Altagracia nodded acknowledgment. "Obviously, how we couch information in all its forms stems heavily from history. I take a great interest in it."

"I absolutely agree," the selecting official responded. She was uncomfortable with herself; why was she entertaining this... guest? "In the interest of time, though, I expect we'll be concentrating upon the Internet in the light of issues like findability and the unique behaviors of digital end users."

The Internet had been the azure woman's personal abyss. Scribes and an illiterate public, bridged by stories, songs, and the Book of the Dead scrawled upon tombs and pyramids? That bottleneck had made a kind of sense. The scroll, the Pharaoh, and time were her information tools. But had it really been the tools that changed?

She could take power now. Here was her altar of the scroll.

"As is only right," Selma said to this woman, so much like her priests of old. "We all of us have important work to do, and time simply isn't what it used to be."

"You seem to have a passion for the cryptic," Altagracia remarked with a smile, attempting to signal that it wasn't a criticism. Uneventfully traversing the Folger Shakespeare library and covering the next set of stairs, they were now reaching the third floor.

"Isn't that our calling? To decrypt people, or help them with..." and there were so many endings to that.

"To help them with..." Altagracia said, musing in depth for the first time in the discussion. "You might say that's what pulled me out of the Bronx."

"I, too, have traveled far," Selma remarked. As the selecting official noticed that no part of this woman ever seemed to need adjustment, the applicant noticed that Altagracia tidied her suit jacket a third time.

"I can only imagine!" With that, the interviewer brightened. "It was tempting to travel farther. To experiment or conduct interviews. Read even more. Explore. You know, to... teach myself about teaching," Altagracia said. It was a relief, though she couldn't have said from what. Perhaps it was simply connecting with a kindred spirit.

"Or to study the students, maybe," Selma replied. She was genuinely commiserating. "One of the challenges that brought me up to the line. Or took me home. Took me from home? It is hard to say. At any rate, the challenge of accepting the student as the one in power. Pharaoh as tabula rasa." Shocked at herself, she realized she was bordering on heresy.

"You know, that—more than anything else—has me excited for our proper interview," Altagracia said. She had no idea how hard her words slapped Selma across a metaphorical cheek. Her aura, her knowledge, her influence hadn't shifted this mortal from her systems? A chasm fissured before her, its emptiness the size of judgments, impressions, and intentions. It was bridged by a resume and relationship development.

They were in hallways now. They'd even ceased to mark the floors. One of the women was lost.

"It's refreshing," Altagracia said suddenly. She'd been enjoying the building and her companion. Comfortable silence. "I don't often experience uncomplicated camaraderie with someone who just... gets it. Are you on LinkedIn? I have some projects in mind that I'd be delighted to discuss over coffee, interview aside."

Meaning: even if you aren't chosen for the position.

Altagracia was so ignorant that she thought herself in the position of knowledge here; the expert and leader. Worse still, she might not have been wrong. Selma knew then that she'd crossed a threshold of some kind. An adventure for a calling, potentially—though she didn't know herself what precisely she meant by that thought. It was wisdom as instinct.

She'd used the wrong silence and had to recover. "Yes, of course, I'll be happy to give you my Internet relations later." The other woman's brow furrowed. "Email, social media, websites and online reports..." Selma rolled her hand as she listed her clarifications. "And coffee would be my pleasure," she said.

She was pained.

This place was a worldwide landmark and repository of documents, books, art, and information. Its systems were so robust that it had developed universally applicable methods for the sorting of things by subject. The aboutness of it all. So robust that navigating the Internet was shaped by these relationships. She related more to the Internet than even Altagracia, despite how abyssal it could be.

Answers to virtually every question. What had it produced? A catalog of information so vast that public health emergencies could look like conspiracies. Flatness in the earth. Disease prevention had microchips.

"Tremendous" just didn't mean what it used to. Was this the wrong temple for her, like firing a tank to get rid of weeds in her garden? Could the quantity of information destroy its quality, or was the answer in industry that was greater still?

How long had she been sitting here?

"The interview panel will see you now," said the secretary.

—=◆=—

Matthew Daniels declares that he is from either Newfoundland or Labrador, based on how well he's handling the day's weather. He took to writing, especially science fiction and fantasy, as a way to explore the human condition and understand others. Surely people will make sense soon. In the meantime, he has released the novel *Diary of Knives* and the anthology *Interstitches: Worlds Sewn Together*. You can find his various works at www.engenbooks.com or on vocal. media. He and his partner live in Newfoundland, where they are owned by three cats.

Going Fishing

Lucas Díaz-Medina

Johntee never would have taken Curtis if it hadn't been for Uncle Joseph mentioning their dad's fishing stories. It all came out one night when Uncle Joseph got so drunk he forgot to hold back his memories, and Johntee and Curtis both got to hear about their dad in a way they had never heard before. As he guided Curtis onto the nearly empty pre-dawn bus, Johntee knew that Curtis would never have got it into his head to want to go fishing. Curtis was just a kid. He didn't know anything. He wanted to see where their father used to fish. He wanted to fish there. What could he do, Johntee asked himself as he held the rods he'd purchased after three months of cutting grass. He'd had to get them without his mother knowing or she would've had his behind for it.

"This the end of the line," the bus driver said as they reached the Orleans and Chakchiuma Parish line. The south-bound bus was empty. Johntee wished there was someone getting off with them.

"Ain't there a bus take us to New Domangue?" Johntee asked on his way out.

"New Domangue? You going to need a car, Son," the bus driver laughed.

"What for?" Johntee asked, annoyed at the bus driver's amusement.

"Just get walking, kid." The bus driver laughed again, shut the door behind Johntee, and turned the bus back toward the New Orleans skyline, which could be seen in the distance jutting straight out of the flat earth, its buildings reflecting an amber-tinged morning glow.

"Don't listen to him, Curtis. He ain't nothing but a dumb bus driver," Johntee said. "We'll get a ride."

"A ride?" Curtis shot back.

"Something wrong with that?" Johntee asked.

"What if we don't get a ride?"

"Cut your whining," Johntee snapped. He felt just as anxious. He looked down the empty highway. "Don't you want to go fishing in New Domangue?"

"Not if we ain't got no ride," Curtis whimpered.

"Ain't you the one wanted to find Dad's fishing place?" Johntee asked, bearing down on his brother's nose. There was nothing to do now but keep going, even if Curtis changed his mind.

"I don't know anymore," Curtis said.

Johntee turned away from his brother and began walking alongside the four-lane asphalt highway that led south to New Domangue. He stuck his thumb out toward the oncoming traffic as he'd seen movie characters do on TV and shouted to his brother to catch up. They were going to get there, Johntee thought, no matter what.

At first, traffic was slow and no one stopped. Johntee's

resolve began to waver as the sun crept into the sky. It seemed to him as if an hour had passed.

Walking in absolute silence, several paces ahead of his younger brother, with nothing but pine and oak trees on either side of the highway, Johntee entertained the thought of turning around. But even as he thought about turning back, he ordered his feet to move forward faster, told his brother to keep up, and began talking about his father's fishing days as if he had heard the stories firsthand many times over.

In his highly colorful tales of his father's fishing days in New Domangue, Johntee imagined a man he had never known by envisioning him as a champion fisherman who upon the very first cast of his line scooped up loads of fish. He imagined his father with such single-mindedness that it didn't strike him as fantastic when the possibility occurred to him that maybe, just maybe, they might run into the old man. They could find him somewhere along the river, fishing rod in hand, fish-filled buckets scattered around him.

"You really think we going to catch fish like Dad used to?" asked Curtis, who fell behind every so often and had to run to catch up.

Johntee stopped and looked at his brother. "Of course we are," he answered. "We going to New Domangue, ain't we?"

"Yeah."

"And Dad caught all those fish in New Domangue, right?"

"I guess so," Curtis said. He fell quiet for a minute while he lowered his head and shuffled one foot on the loose gravel alongside the highway.

"Why you look like that?" Johntee asked.

Curtis looked up at Johntee from beneath his eyelids, his head still pointing toward the ground. "You think we'll run into Dad?"

Johntee didn't respond immediately. The echo of his own thoughts in his little brother's voice made him reconsider how crazy he must be to even think that they might find his father fishing.

"I don't know," was all he could offer his brother.

"Ain't it a small town?" Curtis continued.

"Yeah," Johntee answered. "Supposed to be small enough where everybody knows you."

"Then everybody there should know Dad, right?" Curtis asked.

"How am I supposed to know?" Johntee shrugged. "Why don't you stop asking me so many questions so I can think about getting us there."

A gray pickup truck slowed down as it passed them and pulled over to the side of the highway several yards ahead. Johntee and Curtis watched as an old man's face appeared in the rear window and the truck reversed toward them. When the truck stopped, the old man beckoned at them. He looked like their uncle. Johntee and Curtis walked to the passenger side of the truck and peered into the cab from two feet away. A toothless old man with skin as dark as charcoal, a worn baseball cap, and deep-blue overalls smiled at them.

"Going fishing?" the old man asked.

"Yessir," Johntee said.

"Any particular spot?"

"We want to fish in New Domangue," Curtis blurted

as he jumped up and down in order to catch a glimpse of the old man.

"New Domangue? Why, do you know how far that is from here?"

"Yessir," Johntee lied. All he knew was that it was south of New Orleans, just like his friend had told him, some miles after the St. Claude bus line.

"Figured you could hitch there and back, did you?"

"No, sir," Johntee answered. "We thought there was a bus line get us there."

"Chakchiuma Parish ain't got no public transportation round these parts," the old man said. "Why ya'll coming down here, anyways? You can't be older than twelve. Your folks know you out?"

"We got permission," Johntee lied as he walked up to the truck and stood on his toes. "I'm fourteen, and I'm minding my little brother. We could use a ride."

The old man paused for a second as he studied Johntee. "Well," he said, "I guess it's all right, if you got permission and all. I'm heading that way myself anyway. Going to visit a cousin of mine. Go on and jump in the back. Just be careful with them loose bottles back there. Don't want you rolling out. And don't touch nothing."

Johntee and Curtis climbed into the back of the truck, and as they did so Curtis nudged Johntee in the ribs. "Tell him about Dad," he said.

"You know where you heading in New Domangue?" the old man yelled back at them.

Johntee yelled back. "Our dad used to catch loads of fish in a bayou off the Mississippi River, where the fish is always sitting around waiting to get caught."

The old man's face appeared in the rear window again. He rubbed his cheeks and stared at them, and it made Johntee feel as if he should jump off the truck and walk back home.

"I know which place you talking about," the old man yelled back. He turned around and drove the truck out onto the highway.

Johntee wondered why the old man had looked at them like that, like there was something wrong with them. He let the thought go, though, and held on to his younger brother, closing his eyes to the wind whipping across his face. After a minute, he opened his eyes and studied the landscape as it changed during the fifteen-minute ride. Pine and oak trees gave way to sugar-cane fields, which gave way to cattle pastures. Curtis pointed at the different-colored cattle grazing lazily beneath the morning sun and asked if they were cows. They could see the Mississippi River levee, which resembled a large snake that stretched alongside the back end of the fields they passed.

A few minutes after they began to see the first houses dotting the landscape, the old man pulled alongside the road in front of a rundown store. He turned off the truck and stepped out. "Son," he said as he looked at Johntee, "can you come here a second?"

Johntee looked at his brother with a questioning look, hesitating.

"I ain't going to bite, boy. I got to ask you something."

Johntee jumped out of the truck. He walked up to the old man, who looked even more like his uncle now that Johntee saw him standing.

"You ever gone fishing?"

"No, sir," Johntee admitted.

"But you said your dad come this way fishing?"

Johntee felt something get stuck in his throat at the same time that he felt his heart go wild inside his chest. He swallowed what felt like a large lump of dry nothing and answered, "Yessir."

The old man sighed and then smiled, his eyes directed toward the back of the truck. "Well," he said, looking down at Johntee, "I hope you don't plan to fish like that."

Johntee didn't understand.

"Go on and wait with your brother while I go in this store and get you some bait to fish with. Fish won't get on your hook just because you throw a hook in the water. You need bait."

Johntee didn't answer any of Curtis's questions after the old man went into the store. He continued to ignore him as the old man drove them to a small bayou that dumped into the Mississippi several yards ahead.

When they jumped out of the truck, Johntee walked up to the driver's side to thank the old man.

"You know how to hook those worms?" the old man asked softly.

Johntee shook his head.

"Like this," the old man said, showing Johntee with his fingers barely above his thighs how to grab, hook, and re-hook.

Johntee watched the silent motion of the old man's fingers while Curtis looked out at the bayou's banks, which were shaded by tall mangrove bushes and leafy willows.

"I don't aim to stay in New Domangue too long," the old man said loudly after he'd finished his demonstration.

"We'll be all right," Johntee said.

"I don't doubt it. If it's all right with you, I'll swing back in less than an hour and join you. I only come to get something from my kin, which won't take long. I'll be back before your stomachs start to growl on you," the old man said. He climbed into his truck and drove off.

"Why didn't you ask him about Dad?" Curtis asked as the truck disappeared around a bend in the road.

"Don't need to," Johntee said. "He ain't from New Domangue."

Johntee picked up the rods and the bag of worms the old man had bought for them and led his brother across a patch of blackberry brush toward the edge of the water.

Johntee set up on a small promontory and ordered Curtis to watch as he worked the bait awkwardly onto his hook.

"That's how you do it, Curtis," Johntee said as he displayed a writhing worm looped onto his fishing hook. He was glad to have gotten the worm hooked without any problems.

Curtis smiled at the struggling worm. "Do it to mine," he said.

Johntee repeated the trick while his little brother watched intently.

"Next time, I'll do it," Curtis said confidently.

The two brothers didn't catch any fish before their bait ran out, but it didn't matter to Johntee. The fact that the bait was gone each time they raised their rods was enough proof that there were plenty of fish in that bayou. If their father were there, both believed, they would have caught them all.

The two brothers stared at the water without saying anything. It could have been an eternity that they sat there looking at the rivulets below, but it was really only about five minutes. Johntee couldn't tell how long it lasted, but it didn't matter to him. He had come to the spot, and he and Curtis had gone fishing, had seen for themselves what it was all about. There sure were plenty of fish in that muddy little river.

The sun shot up into the middle of the sky, thinning the shadows around them. Not long after, Johntee heard the crunching of shells beneath tires and saw the old man's truck pull up to their spot. Johntee and Curtis waved. As they gathered their rods, Johntee prepared to tell the old man how the fish had eaten all the worms right off the hooks. If their father had been there, he thought, not a single fish would have gotten away with it.

—◆—

Lucas Díaz-Medina is a Dominican immigrant who lives in New Orleans with his wife and two children. He started developing his craft in the early 90s, earning his MFA in creative writing from the University of New Orleans. He's been a service worker, war medic, ER tech, pro fundraiser, nonprofit leader, city bureaucrat, and recently a PhD candidate in sociology. Most of his short stories explore life in 1980s and 90s New Domangue, a fictional town south of New Orleans where descendants of European, African, Caribbean, Indigenous, and Asian people struggle to make sense of their lives and their world.

Bull

Jacqueline Garrahan

Those antlers mounted there, with the bullet puncture between the skull's sockets, are familiar. I must decline your invitation. You see, I went out hunting once already, twenty-three years ago.

Back then, I'd lived with an uncle named Roger. I didn't call him that. Only, "Uncle". Uncle was a blatant drunk, though I doubted alcohol his principal ailment and suspected it secondary to some deeper affliction. The man was plagued by unshakable fixations, launching relentless campaigns that were followed by dark sedentary stretches when he'd neither eat nor work, only drink to sleep.

The two of us lived in Bremen, Maine, just west of Friendship in a three-room house, ramshackled by time, dilapidated by Uncle. The damp salt-wind had corroded then broken its iron nails, skewing the weather-gray shingles and streak-staining them orange with rust. Existence was bleak and prospects bleaker. I was miserable except for loving a tricolor beagle, a merry little thing, my exclusive source of joy, and, in retrospect and by virtue of her pedigree, clearly stolen.

As far as I could reason, Uncle's unsteady occupation was handiwork and he reserved most of his efforts for his sparse employers. Every once in a while though, he was occasioned to a sudden energetic spell when he'd undertake some domestic project, excel through a fraction, then lose all momentum to whiskey and slumber, gifting us with two front stairs out of three, a waist-high stone fireplace, and a hole above in the shake-shingle roof.

Uncle had grand plans for that fireplace. And, what would go above.

Several years earlier, the State of Maine instituted a sham lottery for moose hunt licenses that obviously favored the summer seasonals venturing north a final time before the state frosted. Some came for our technicolor foliage, but others came for our beasts: bear, elk, moose. Trophy satisfied, those virile representatives of the Second Estate returned to unfrozen Boston society, while ice crystals crept across our blood-brined marshes.

Uncle was at the butcher's when one party returned. The season was late and the bull colossal. It took ten men to drag the creature onto the wagon.

The hunter, a retired capitalist with weak shoulders and faux machismo, surrendered the bulk of the animal, requesting only a sampler from various parts of the flank, rib, and breast. And, of course, the antlers. He'd already settled on the wall space in his main hall for the mount. A cousin recommended some taxidermist back in Cambridge, so this particular capitalist required only the animal's decapitation before his party loaded the skull into a brand-new trailer and retreated south.

"A rigged system deserves no respect," Uncle told me,

while we ate venison that night. I was a child and didn't understand, not the laurels of wealth, nor men haunted from the inside out. But the meat was plentiful. Even the dog got scraps.

Uncle dreamed of the moose for the next year's entirety. The righteous subversion pinballed inside his mangled mind towards a singular aspiration: antlers mounted above some hypothetical fireplace, for which we hadn't the space. He delayed construction till the inopportune turn of the seasons, selling our wood stove before completion and welcoming the October evening chill through a tarped tear in the ceiling. Uncle never thought of the chill. Only of the antlers: how he'd mount them, what screws they'd require, whether the bone should be sealed with polyurethane...

The morning we went out, Uncle woke me, laughing. His tarp had faltered beneath the fall snow and the sleet soaked our already-warped floorboards. Uncle pointed from our one-hinge door to the forest's edge, through the snowfall as it died into cascading slush. "Moose weather," he called it. "Tonight's the night. Moose weather." Few would agree, but that evening we bundled into everything we owned, every pant pair, every sweater, into unpatched jackets, then slung rifles shoulder-cross. Uncle tucked our serrated knife into his only buttoned pocket and slid his 0.44 caliber into his waistband. We went into the forest.

The autumn snowstorm ended a few hours before we went out. Us and the dog. We combed the snow-gessoed forest, scoping the low-lying swamps and timber-skirted openings where limbs sagged under heavy flakes, melt pounding the floor into cacophony, those violent puddles momentarily reflecting the sunset's cerulean and crimson before its orb slipped the horizon and dusk dropped, rendering all murky. With every step, the forest floor dampened beneath my thin-soled shoes. Along my heel, toes, and soles, skin lifted. Fluid bubbled between and popped skin along bloated ridges. I winced at the ruptures, subsequent rawness compounding pain, and eventually gasped. Uncle hit me for the exclamation.

Dark fell, no light but the mounting gibbous, whose rays shadowed the fearsome forest with darting demons and writhing wraiths. "Right there!" Uncle whispered, his pupils pinpricks, even in the dark. "Right up there!"

After immeasurable time, we reached the forest's end, a strong line against the salt marsh a step further. Momentarily, I imagined he'd turn, but Uncle descended the sludgy embankment, peat to ankles, into the water.

The uneven marsh dipped and welled. Testing the quagmire, I stumbled and sank, numb legs unfeeling of the feel barnacles' scrape. Uncle, too far ahead for physical castigation, looked back in reproach at the sloshing and I preemptively recoiled.

Without warning, several minutes in, Uncle stopped, framed by the lunar corona, whose moonbeams were diffracted by the slush-mist into a bullseye. I froze. So did the dog. Uncle took the gun from his waistband, cocked, turned, and paused, looking out towards the ocean, sunken sockets and hooked nose silhouetted, gun scoping wind-wisped clouds as it bobbed on his elbow-propped forearm. His shoulders squared, his profile disappeared, a moonbeam brushed the steel barrel, pointed in my direction.

The gunshot shattered the silence, then fell mute on the echoless morass. I was too cold, I imagined, for my nerves to know the pain of puncture. While I waited to die into the marshy sludge, a great beast wavered behind. I hadn't seen it. The dog hadn't barked. But the moose had been out there, ten yards away. And, when the creature fell, the earth shook in its entirety; every molecule, every atom, every particle trembling, my own included.

Uncle waded over. He'd hit it right between the eyes.

The moose was propped by gnarled antler, neck above the brackish waterline like a coastal granite outcrop, bony obtrusions clawing the night sky. Uncle hugged me in celebration, then went to work on the neck, sawing with the dull, serrated blade he'd brought along in his pocket. He ordered me to the skull, to pull the antlers forward and tauten the throat, but I made little difference as I stood at the helm, staring into the animal's dead eyes, cataract white bulbs bulging from furry sockets. The corpse offered relief from the cold. I tucked my body beneath the bull's chin. Braced thus, I slipped and Uncle kicked my flank, catching the water's surface with his boot and spraying the beast too before he went back to work.

The blade hardly punctured hide, but Uncle persisted. Those antlers were his to claim. So, frenzied, he sawed, shearing muscle and tissue to only an inch in the first half hour, then he stabbed, blade buckling against the bull's esophagus. I watched from the skull, feigning pressure on the antler's crêpey, springtime cover, which sloughed from the bone beneath my palms.

In marshes, you can't track the tidal creep the way you might on a beach. The water climbs in unmarked centimeters, lacking the drama and crescendo of advancing surf, as it falls slowly into shifting, moon-stretched contours. I only noticed the advance when the dog lost its footing. She yipped and swam, seeking out some foothold, and aimed to mount the carcass, but Uncle swatted her away and so she sought ground at a wider radius, then regretted abandoning her small, cruel pack and doubled back, yipping, begging us to follow. She clawed my legs and I looked down, her massive ears floating like paddles, her desperate little nose bubbling the water. I lifted her into my arms and Uncle grabbed me by the hair. He pinned me to the bull's stomach and held the gory, tissue-wrapped blade an inch from my throat.

"I'm sorry!" I begged. "I'm sorry!" I dropped her.

Uncle returned to the neck and watched me back to the antlers.

After a while, the yipping stopped.

Clouds blew in and covered the moon. The marsh leached the dead creature's warmth. Soon, the water was at my waist and soon after my shoulder. The rifle heavied in the swell, seeking out the marsh bottom. I fell into a divot and submerged, depth dragged by the rifle, before I found a grassy island and breached, gasping.

"Give that to me." Uncle seized the barrel.

In the following minute the waterline grazed my chin. Then, I couldn't stand. Hardly a swimmer, I treaded, searching out some platform, but infirm mounds disintegrated beneath my feet and so I begged, brine spewing from my mouth. "Please! Let me go back."

Uncle cocked the gun. "Don't you fucking leave. I swear to God. I'll shoot you."

Despite the protest, his own resolve was failing. The water crept above the moose's gargantuan neck and the submerged sawing turned clumsy and fumbling. He dropped the knife.

"FUCK!" Uncle cursed, rocking with rage. "FUCK!" He pushed my bobbing head below so long my lungs nearly faltered. Death a minute away, fireworks exploded across my dark, damp world, red and orange and green and magenta dancing then dissolving with a gasp and breath, an oxygen rush white-out fading to static and black. Ahead, Uncle charged through the marsh towards the shore.

I treaded behind, fast as I might, jaunty flails impersonating stroke. Just before the bank, I brushed something: furry, the right size, dead. Maybe the dog made it out, maybe she didn't. It was impossible to say in the dark.

I crawled to shore, palming the slick vegetation and slipping back twice before pulling my torso over the bank. I don't remember the return walk but for the conviction I was dying, possessed by an unprecedented and never-since-matched cold. My jaw chattered so violently that my three remaining baby teeth chipped. Up ahead, far enough to guess he'd forgotten me, Uncle vowed his return to the deaf evergreens. "I'll be back! Tomorrow, I'll be back!"

At home, Uncle lapsed into a long slumber. I lay naked beneath my blankets, thawing, then wrapped myself in one and sat on the wet lawn beneath the budding dawn light. Uncle woke the next afternoon, only a few hours of sun remaining. So we went out again, and this time with a borrowed saw.

On the quag fringe, I smelled the twinge of decomposition in the breeze. And the corpse was there, rising from the middle of the rot-rank marsh. Decapitated. Someone had sawed through, clean. Scarlet-brown oozed from his severed esophagus and maggots somersaulted in the cavity. Uncle's antlers were gone. Stolen, he'd say. Taken along with their bullet-breached skull that I assume, once de-brained and macerated, must have resembled yours.

⇒◆⇐

Jacqueline Garrahan is a Boston Proper defector now settled in Santa Cruz who, at the time of this composition, has inherited fleas from Houdini, her Pomeranian mix. During the workweek, she builds software at the SLAC National Accelerator Laboratory, supporting modeling efforts for accelerator physics. She has two eyes, two ears, four less permanent teeth than the average adult, and one tattoo of a roller-skating sheet ghost on her left ankle. Just like her mother, Jacqueline maintains a stringent catch-and-release policy for household spiders (but not for fleas). This is her first publication.

The Envious Flood

Steve Hanson

I spent most of the drive thinking about the whale.

Highway 1 North isn't as busy as I remember. I have my window down just a crack—enough for a breeze, however chilly. The thermometer on the dash reads 54. I assume that's Fahrenheit. It strikes me as a bit cold for California, even the central coast. Maybe I'm just remembering things being warmer than they actually were. The rain's been light but constant. Fog hovers over the mountains and drifts in thin meshes across the highway. That much I remember, at least.

And there's Muriel, head cast in the breeze, fifty years ago in my '54 Chevy convertible, sticking her tongue out, and I asked her what she's doing and she says, "I want to taste the fog," and I just leave it at that. Later I asked her what it tastes like, and she never answered, just grew quiet and kept her mouth shut up tight, like she had something in there she was afraid would escape if she opened it.

My manuscripts are all piled in the backseat, alongside Muriel's letters, all still sealed in the brown paper package I had received so unceremoniously, like the last seeds of memory before sleep. I had written the manuscripts that summer, when the two of us lived on the beach, with my typewriter propped on the hood of the Chevy. Big Sur sings with a cacophony erupting from the season'd mists, counterpointing ages against ages and the ever-primal call of the sea and the rains, back and forth and back and forth to the quiet soul who will always and forever return to the secret places where such songs are most audible…

The wind seeps through the cracked window and conjures faint recollections from the pages packaged in the backseat, mixing with the damp scent of the fog and the gossamer saltiness of the Pacific.

The package arrived anonymously, during my last semester at the university before retirement. Sometime in the spring semester, waiting in my university mailbox the day I got the last glimpse of Muriel, while I was standing in front of a half-empty lecture room, trying to get apathetic sophomores to care about Elizabethan poetry.

"One thing we might think about in the sixteenth century is the superimposition of Christian and pagan imagery. For example… no texting, please… for example, in the introductory stanzas of *The Faerie Queene*, who does Spenser portray as the head of the muses?"

Faces sought their aging desks.

"Second stanza, ladies and gentlemen. First line."

Silence. The dust from the chalk wisped past my eyes, drifting across the afternoon sunlight through the windows. I catch a side glance of a sea of soft red hair, ruffled and falling down bare shoulders. Almost like a garden. And I could have walked through the sunbeams and waded back fifty years, but instead I blinked, and I saw that the face beneath that hair is dull and uninterested, looking down at the phone hidden beneath her desk, texting something apparently more important than this class.

"So, what's going on here, ladies and gentlemen?" I said. "Afternoon getting to you? It is a nice day out, you probably want to be elsewhere." No sympathy from them. "Truth be told, I want to be elsewhere. But I'm contractually obligated to teach you this, so we're stuck here until further notice. So, going back to my question, Spenser portrays the Virgin Mary as the head of the muses. He writes: 'Helpe then, O Holy Virgin, chiefe of Nine...' The 'nine' are the muses, by the way..."

Hours north of Los Angeles I find myself in front of an apathetic gas station clerk, likewise of sophomore age. He glances up from his phone.

"I'm wondering if you could help me," I say. "I'm looking for a particular beach, and I can't seem to find the right exit."

"Nearest beach is Carmel," he says. "Two exits northbound. I don't know if it's open this time of year."

"No," I say too quickly. "It's somewhere before Carmel, I think."

He looks at me with limited comprehension. "What's the name?"

"I'm not really sure."

"Is it a private beach?"

"...possibly?"

"Is it in Los Padres?"

"...not really sure..."

He makes his face look like he's thinking. I rub my knuckles together. "It's more of a cove, really. Very white sand. Rocks extending on both sides. One of them looks like a titan felled from the sky, stuck upside-down with his ragged bones reaching towards the clouds from which he is exiled. The other is a cathedral designed with non-Euclidean geometry by a civilization privileging laughter and warm beer over reason. There are enough round purple stones in the pale sand to build more empires than could be contained in the pages of history."

And he shrugs and says, "I have some maps over here, if you think those will help." And I buy one just because and find when I walk outside that the fog has surrounded the area and made the route back onto the highway invisible.

Muriel had found the beach, back in '62, fresh from Cornell, still drunk on our fourth bottle of wine and passing a single joint back and forth for most of the drive. She said, "It was born from the fog, like the way mirages become the road." It went right to a beach, with white sand and even, pulsing tides alight with fragments of the orange sunset perfectly clear contra the foggy mountains behind. Nobody there but us.

In her letters I found in the package, Muriel asked if I remembered the whale. The one we woke up to one morning, washed up on the beach. It was massive, but even then, decomposition was unraveling its dark, dense body in the relentlessness of the Pacific sun. The ocean deposited it on the shore while we slept, but when we first saw it that morning the sand had already sunk in a grove beneath it, and the waves found crevices and gorges around and inside it into which they could wash and retreat, as if it had sat here for millions of years, and the Big Sur tides had always known its vast but fragile contours.

I get a cheap motel room that night. The next day I drive up and down that stretch of highway, taking every exit I can find between San Simeon and Carmel. The fog holds steady up in the blunted peaks of the California highlands. I find a beach and watch the few surfers dart into the water, their hair waving with winds and locomotion. The waves roll in and out, gathering strength far offshore and paling as they approach the brown line of sand. They fall forward with hunger, but soon lose momentum and retreat back into the ocean or disperse into innocuous tidal pools. I think of a line from *Richard III*.

Had you such leisure in the time of death
To gaze upon the secrets of the deep?

A seagull lands on my rental car, looking at me with strange dark eyes. I shoo it away and sit down for a while inside the car with my eyes closed. Through my rolled-up windows I can barely hear the rolling of the waves against the grainy sand. The gray, cloudy light across the shimmering canvas rolling onto the edge of the world.

Methought I had, and often did I strive
To yield the ghost, but still the envious flood
Stopped in my soul, and would not let it forth
To seek the empty, vast and wandering air...

In her letter Muriel asked if I could remember the smell as the whale decomposed. The smell that eventually permeated everything we had. She said she wrote that letter on paper she had taken from my beach manuscripts. She asked if I could smell it, years and thousands of miles later. She ended with that question, like people do when they don't know that what they've just said will be the last they ever say to that person.

That night I tear open the brown paper package, go over the letters individually, try to sense among their aged, wrinkled fabric a smell to remind me of her, or a fifty-year-old sea breeze riding on the back of a warm summer day. But I smell nothing.

The fog strangles me. The towns and enclaves plastered along the hidden places in the Santa Lucia Mountains drift along with the whims of the soft white clouds where the sea and the sky meet.

The next day I take Highway 1 South towards San Simeon. The road is deserted. Blowing through the window the fog rips through the papers in the back, and the smell ascends to my nostrils, into my brain. I wallow backward, drifting into something warm and bright and sweetly scented, and the fog seems to take the smell out of the car and carry it up into the hills and off into the sea.

Through the thick mesh, I see an exit sign, its number worn off, slanted at an angle on bent posts. Rust overtaking the original white paint. But I remember the arrow pointing to a road meandering off to the right. I take the exit and the fog disperses and the cold, overcast day shifts on its axis somewhere.

I pull down a back road between thickets of pine trees. The cold wind stirs everything in the back seat until I can smell the faint odor of decay emanating from the papers. The road is where I remember it, at least, materializing from the fog and the same straight row of dense pine trees. The faint hum of the waves just beyond the bend. There's still no signpost. I turn down the road and the white beach appears with little fanfare in the overcast day. Across the western horizon the clouds hold unbroken and the gray daylight only seeps along the dark blue of the ocean.

Can you still smell the whale, Horace? And, really, her package just smelled like booze. Just like all of my manuscripts she had kept God knows where. I park and get out of the car. Arthritis and age deform my tracks in the sand. I remember the two young people running out, stripping naked right there and diving into the warm waters as the sun sets, still smelling of wine and pot and then the sea and each other.

At the bottom of the package, under the letters and manuscripts, I found a single newspaper clipping. A middle-aged woman was found dead in a dorm at Cornell. Nobody knew how she got in. No ID or anything on her. They called her "Jane Doe." Coroner said it was an overdose of sleeping pills and alcohol. Might be suicide, though no one cared enough to find out. Someone was quoted as saying she had a paper in her hand, full of unintelligible gibberish, that smelled faintly like the sea.

The whale is still on the beach. Its bones, at least. They stick up fanged out of the sand and the waves wash in and out around them. It must have sat here undisturbed for half a century. Bones isolated at the end of the world. Muriel said the place was only for us. The fog had let us find it, when we were young and the world was too beautiful to waste places like this on anyone else.

In truth, we might have just conjured it out of all those pages, and the haze of alcohol and pot, till we found at last a source for our own putrid smell, something we could see rotting that wasn't us. And now here's an old man who can only smell himself.

I step in between the skeleton and thread an uneven path through each bone, the ocean sending washes of cold seawater through my shoes as I go. The bones don't smell like anything.

⸻◆⸻

Steve Hanson is an author, aspiring screenwriter, and cognitive scientist-in-training whose work draws from a number of different sources in both literary and genre fiction. Some of Steve's major influences include "literary" authors such as Vladimir Nabokov, Thomas Pynchon, Denis Johnson, and Jorge Luis Borges. In addition to his burgeoning writing career, Steve is pursuing a PhD in cognitive science, with a focus on the intersection of human cognition and language. A native of Pittsburgh, Pennsylvania, Steve currently divides his time between Vienna, Austria and Washington, DC.

Burden of Proof

Scott Hardy

Her vicious typing intrudes into my waning nightmare with a dramatic crescendo, and I awake with a groan. It's 7 a.m., and it's already hot.

I snap her laptop shut and beg her to at least take a nap. Her eyes are demonically bloodshot, and before she slides down under the sheet, she asks me to do the dishes, three days' worth of shared neglect.

The last flickers of my nightmare die out, and then I forget it almost completely. Something to do with unicycles, fedoras, and semi-automatic rifles. For a moment, I'm flooded by the temptation of further sleep and lean slowly into the pillow's magnetic pull. But then her hand shoots out like a severed zombie limb and grabs my wrist. Now I'm awake.

"We're also out of dish soap, but I found a recipe for a homemade one. Sent you the link," she mumbles, and curls back comfortably into overdue slumber.

I get up, witness the monstrosity in the dish sink, and search through the barrage of waste-reducing solutions, vegan recipes, and pop-science articles she's shared with me during this frenzied all-nighter. I obediently produce some earth-loving dish-washing liquid and do all the dishes while downing a fresh cup of eighteen-hour-steeped cold brew to carry me through the last stretch of eighteen hours of fasting. That's how everyone's doing it: eating intermittently, like people without fridges and supermarkets used to do.

⇒◆⇐

When she gets up around 1 p.m., she grates some unpasteurized Jersey cow cheddar for a grilled cheese sandwich with spicy tomato chutney, and soon afterwards complains that it has a hint of soap.

"Did you add rose water to the chutney?" she asks me.

"Not the tomato chutney, just the apricot one. It's probably the soap I grated," I tell her.

"For what?"

"DIY laundry soap."

"I asked you to make dish-washing soap."

"Yeah, I made both. Similar ingredients. I figured I might as well."

"Did you wash the grater after?" she asks.

"Of course," I say.

"With what?"

"The DIY dish-washing soap."

"Maybe it needs less soap, more washing soda." She picks up a plate off the dish rack and rubs her fingers against it. "Stuff is still greasy, see?"

"I just followed the recipe," I say, stoically.

"Yeah, I know. But more washing soda."

—◆—

Engagement and detachment always come in cycles. A traumatic piece of news or a documentary triggers guilt, which leads to a heightened sense of responsibility. Positive, energetic actions are taken: books are read, lists are drawn, pledges are made, all-nighters are pulled, until exhaustion at fighting our own habits and addictions leads to another period of dormancy. It turns out that when we're shooting to kill own bad habits, our aim is not much better than a villain's minions in action flicks: we shoot in the *general direction* of the hero, as if to justify *an effort* to kill him, but always miss despite our years of experience in the KGB.

This year, the cycle has been jump-started by a painful confluence of events: a vegan expo, a documentary film festival, one of the hottest summers in recorded history, and the most severe wildfire season since there were humans around to notice. The city is shrouded in a smoky haze, and there's a cacophony of coughs, sneezes and complaints everywhere you go. All this on top of the perennial anxiety over the Cascadian subduction zone and the massive earthquake that's supposed to kill most of us one day. It's always a minute to doomsday o'clock, even though we're wallowing in the safest times in human history, cushioned by endless streaming content, receiving packages and food straight to our doors, drinking unlimited water from a tap, and having daily hot showers. We're kings with sleepless digital butlers and no obligation to marry our cousins. How could it get any *better*?

And yet we feel powerless as the walls of nature close in on us. If ignorance is bliss, they should tell you in kindergarten, not at the end of college, and let us make life decisions accordingly. I would have still chosen the pain. But a lifetime supply of non-addictive painkillers might have been nice.

—◆—

Halfway through the doc fest, we decided to take stock of the ills affecting our lives. So we proceeded to a Stalinist purge of all the evils in our home and souls. We're supposed to be urban hippies at the vanguard of the environmental movement, sprouting our own seeds, eating beans, and riding electric cargo bikes to the farmer's market. And yet, we drive a very fuel-inefficient old car, and we eat Mexican tomatoes in January, while indoor stalactites form by our poorly insulated windows.

Major strides have been made towards specific goals, some of which we've written down and pinned conspicuously onto our main cork board (the brackets only visible to me):

* Adopt endangered animals like pandas and slow lorises from reputable NGOs (especially the ones that send you a token stuffed animal for your contribution, made in an Asian sweatshop by a child who never sees sunshine and who likely eats panda meat for lack of options).
* Reduce waste by half. Don't buy pre-packaged fruit or pastries. Make own granola. (We haven't eaten granola in years!)
* Buy a Vitamix blender with the horsepower of an airplane to turn fruit and vegetables into

life-prolonging elixirs. (Drink them even if—
especially if—they taste like grass or compost.)

* Look into a trendy electric cargo bike with a
storage box big enough for all our grocery needs.
(Which we'll never ride during the rainy months
of September through May.)

* Eat vegetarian four times a week. (If too difficult,
four times a month.)

We agree to cut down on consumption of all sorts of
unhealthy things, and substitute them with an arsenal of
magical potions.

First, the Inca/Aztec renaissance swelled into full
bloom: quinoa flour, maca, lucuma, camu-camu, açaí,
spirulina, and moringa. Then it got real cosmopolitan:
argan oil from a female co-op in Morocco, Austrian
pumpkin seed oil, Chinese burdock, ginger-turmeric
paste. Then, a wave of green materialism: flip flops made
with recycled yoga mats, bamboo straws, collapsible
coffee mugs, and an aromatherapy diffuser with a set
of different oils. Plastic wrap has given way to bendy
beeswax wraps. Toilet paper has largely been replaced
by a bidet attachment, or "butt spa" in marketing
lingo.

Resisting our weekly Korean fried chicken, we got an
all-organic stash of farmers' market veggies instead and
made a butternut squash stuffed with an eggplant stuffed
with a zucchini stuffed with lentils and mushrooms.
Basically, a vegan turducken without the guilty pleasure.
It was in fact pretty good, but I had two pepperoni
sticks for dessert, which I keep stashed away under the

bathroom sink, like addicts do, behind all the toilet paper we barely even need.

Toaster waffles, Aunt Jemima, Cheez Whiz, bottled dressings... all went into the new garbage bags, which are compostable, although we're not sure Cheez Whiz itself is.

The booze cabinet, though, was a bone of contention.

"Studies show alcohol is bad for you," she said.

"Sometimes studies show whatever they've been paid to show," I retorted. "There is no consistent scientific proof that moderate consumption of alcohol has any negative long-term effects." I actually don't know if that's true either, but I'm sure Budweiser has sponsored such a result, even if it's a lie, and I'm ready to dig for it if needed.

"There is no proof of any benefit either," she retaliated, pouring five shots' worth of gin down the drain. I let her, because this particular gin is too juniper-heavy anyways.

"You can't just say it's 'bad for you'. Should it not also require proof beyond a reasonable doubt?"

"Stop watching legal shows!"

When she reached for the five-year-aged Japanese whiskey, I threatened her giant jar of Nutella in an effort to curtail her Prohibitionist raid on my liquor. It's been a hard-learned truth, but when your intellect fails to win you an argument, your best shot is to then hold a woman's chocolate hostage.

⇒◆⇐

Over the past few weeks, I've begun to feel more energetic. It's hard to tell if it's due to all the CBD-ing or Ashwaghanda-ing or plain old placebo-ing. A reduction in meat and dairy has greatly improved our acne and digestive problems; the flax seeds in my teeth, apart from the Omega-3 benefits, actually remind me to floss daily; the new local vegan shampoo has given my hair quite a sheen. Overall, we produce less garbage and recyclables which means trips to the garbage room are less frequent. I knew there was an upside to all this effort.

But there's also a downside. It's late August, and temperatures are breaking global records like doped Russian athletes. We face south, with no obstructions from the sun. Unable to sleep in this heat, and purely on survival instinct, I went out and bought a portable air conditioner, out of my own personal savings. It's a miracle I even found one.

To justify my purchase, I introduced a fair amendment to our Constitution of Ecologically Responsibility Practices. It went something like this: When in the course of saving the planet from inevitable destruction, should one's personal quality of life be significantly affected by an avoidable privation, it becomes necessary that the needs of the individual take precedence over the needs of the planet. Thomas Jefferson would probably approve.

"Isn't that logic the same for everyone else though?" she said.

"Yes, but it's just too fucking hot!"

"Then let's move to the Yukon," she said, unconvincingly.

"I'd rather sign up for Elon's Mars colony," I retorted with snappy immaturity.

Whenever I urge her to contemplate Pascal's silence of infinite spaces, she looks at the sky, stretching her imagination. I know what she's thinking: they don't have Paris, they don't have sushi, they don't have passion fruit margaritas. They don't have shit out there. They have gases, rocks, dark matter, and a bunch of useless moons. Fuck space.

As I caressed my new favorite appliance, which she eyed with repressed lust, I tried one final legalese argument: "If this is a tool that will prevent the obvious sleep deprivation-insanity-suicide course I'm on and permit me to use all of my mental faculties to then help save the planet, isn't it a means to an end? A small sacrifice? What's so bad about air conditioners anyway? We've got hydro power."

"It's the hypocrisy that bothers me," she said.

Without any more chocolate to threaten, I lost the argument. We returned the AC and donated some of the refund money to the wildfire relief fund.

I slept on the deck that night, on an improvised pile of foam, sheets, and towels, not because of the argument, but because it was an enlightened idea. At around 3 a.m. she joined me, exuding an air of regret which she is still ashamed to voice. I know it's there, though, buried under a thick layer of good intentions, and if it's going to help me sleep at night, then by god, I'm gonna get to it.

⟾◆⟽

I think I'm the original instigator. Last year, after a rage quit from a toxic job, unable to meditate for even five seconds without being overtaken with anger, resentment, and hopelessness, I signed us up to a psychedelic meditation retreat in a Pacific Northwest forest lodge.

Twin Peaks with kale juice and Jacuzzis. I don't know why she decided to come along, but the word "detox" had something to do with it.

It was a friend's referral, but it might as well have been a suspiciously cheap Groupon deal. We met up with a young surfer shaman who didn't look the part. No beard or ingrown toenails, and an infuriatingly contrived Eastern accent—more a mockery than an homage.

She experienced a blissful, transcendental union with the universe and nature. I had visions but no insights, and puked my guts out all night long. The day after, the boy-band shaman asked me what my zodiac sign was.

"Capricorn," I said.

"Ah! That can happen to Capricorns during full moons," he said, hinting at the possibility of a vomit-less sequel. I'm actually a Virgo, and I'm pretty sure it was a waxing moon, but I always lie when asked about my zodiac sign, because no matter what I choose, my interlocutors think it explains everything.

I explained the sense of lack and alienation that had led me here. A failure to achieve anything I had set my mind to. Perhaps I aimed too high. Don't we all?

"There's nothing too high. You just put the intent into the universe," he said. "That's how Jim Carrey manifested a million-dollar check he wrote to himself in the future." I'd heard the story before.

We've tried the same trick, as have millions of people, but sadly, the universe may have realized the economic consequences of its generous actions once the secret was out. Imagine the inflation if it just printed all this money on demand without consulting with central banks!

So we were made aware, painfully so, that we are not external to nature but embedded in it, and that money doesn't grow on trees or on pieces of paper made from trees. That insight, so simple and anodyne, so true and necessary, has stayed with us to this day: we've embraced our poverty of resources and started pursuing a wealth of meaning instead.

But I never meant it to get this far. Who wants to be a bodhisattva in an active volcano? In this heat, I'd rather be the world's least-enlightened man in an air-conditioned hotel room with Egyptian linen sheets.

—◆—

So here we are, eating a grilled cheese sandwich with a massive carbon footprint that tastes like soap. She lounges on the couch in front of the fan, idly leafing through magazines and cross-checking things on her computer. I spray myself periodically with ice-cold water.

"Let's plan an Amazonian river adventure," she says out of the blue, looking at a colorful Lonely Planet brochure. She thinks toucans, coconuts, wooden flutes, and hammocks. I think *Aguirre, the Wrath of God*, yellow fever, and ravenous black caimans. But ultimately, I feel, we might as well see it before it's all gone.

So I say, "Let's budget for it."

A few minutes later, she yells: "Holy shit! My Visa bill is three thousand dollars."

Her heart sinks, as if all our recent efforts have been rendered meaningless by this bill come due. I reassure her that being part of the solution doesn't come for free, it comes with a series of efforts, sacrifices, and setbacks. These are investments, not expenses.

It all builds up to the inevitable conclusion, the end of the cycle: A lengthy diatribe from someone on Facebook pointing to the negative effects of some of the decisions we had made and shared publicly. The bastard even called us hypocrites, the world's most hurtful word, especially when it might be true.

We thought we were doing our part to try and keep the world a livable place for the children we'll never afford to have, and for the animals clinging by a fingernail over the cliff of extinction. But at the same time, apparently, we were drying out California by drinking almond milk, enriching the Mexican cartels by buying avocados year-round, making quinoa unaffordable for the people who have been having it for thousands of years, and keeping the world's poorest from obtaining clean cooking fuels. It turns out all of these claims are dubious, but the fact remains that we were not aware of all possible consequences of our actions. All of this new information thrust us into a haze of confusion. There is a reason we all tend to cling to ideology: the realm of doubt is a cold hinterland with no maps or roads, and only the bravest explorers can withstand it.

When we fall from the yet wild, untamed low-carbon-footprint high horse, the consequences are catastrophic. We condemn our own failures and suddenly believe we are doomed for the worst scenario in life. Eventually, we will kill our own child by neglect and end up living in a discarded shipping container swallowed by weeds in a statistically rape-friendly suburban park close to a Walmart.

And the earth-leeches will continue to thrive, eating wagyu steaks and caviar in air-conditioned rooms with Egyptian linens at a Trump Hotel, while fountains of crypto currency flow into their bank accounts. A gift from the universe.

⸻◆⸻

We watch some dumb Adam Sandler rom-com and swap out proper dinner for a smörgåsbord of snacks. She eyes the bowl of Doritos with more lust than a Keto would, then says, "I'll just have one." I pass her the whole bowl.

We let the shame slowly wash away. Failure is not an end state. It's just an obstacle, a downturn. I illustrate it by topping a Dorito with vegan cashew spread and alfalfa sprouts, turning it into a beautiful, ironic modern canapé. It symbolizes the complexity of our modern life, permissive of the occasional indulgence in monosodium glutamate and maltodextrin. We are self-deprecating political creatures, torn between selfish gratification and the painful privations of selfless activism.

We snuggle up in the comfort of our air-conditioned bedroom, laughing at ourselves and everyone else, until we fall into a comfortable, sweat-free sleep.

⸻◆⸻

We wake up to another sepia sky painted by a forest in flames somewhere out of sight. The city skyline looks beautiful and mystical, and we feel serene. I snap a shot and post it on Instagram without a single mention of the forest fires. Instead I add a large amount of follower-bait hashtags, and I end up getting a record amount of likes.

In fact, it's the most liked I've ever been in my life, and I didn't even have to try that hard. I savor this feeling. It is low-hanging fruit, but at least it's abundant, and that's why we reach for it. We're animals, and we're hungry. Does the high-hanging fruit, the one we may never reach, really taste any different? I truly don't know, but that the ape often beats out the human within us has been proven beyond a reasonable doubt.

=◆=

Scott Hardy is a singer-songwriter, writer, and catering chef. He writes screenplays, short fiction, and long-form journalism and nonfiction essays on culture, environment, food, history, psychology, and philosophy. He attempts to portray the zeitgeist in all its conflicts and ambiguities, and he believes that a good dose of humor that humanizes and satirizes the extremes has to be part of the antidote to polarized discussions. He lives in North Vancouver, Canada, with his wife and a miniature dachshund.

Fresh Off the Boat

Kelson Hayes

La Rioux, Legiole

21 June 4E93

Andrzej Mlynár could hear the Legiolien border agents from where he hid alongside the cargo in the back of the lorry as they inspected the truck driver's papers. Everyone remained totally still and silent where they were as the border agents conducted their routine inspection; they were stowed away with a band of gypsies traveling from Alvaria, finally nearing the end of their long journey. Taking refuge within the back of a lorry, the group had initially been traveling from the city of Český-Trenčianske, though they'd switched lorries several times across their journey.

They'd spent the greater part of the last week hidden with the cargo-holds of whatever unsupervised lorries they could find between the rest stops on their route to Bree. The back of their current transport was filled up mostly with boxes of various sizes of what they assumed to be furniture, though there was no way of truly knowing as they were labeled in Svanean writing.

Andrzej felt his stomach grumble as he sought to ignore the fact that it had been three days since his last meal; three of his friends had died over the course of the journey when they'd unwittingly hopped in the back of a refrigerated trailer. Though they ate lavishly over the course of their time in the refrigerated container, several of the traveling band of gypsies had died due to anything ranging from asphyxiation and suffocation up to freezing to death. Out of the group of thirty he'd started with, only seven of the original caravan remained; the rest had either died or parted ways, though they met new faces along the way between all the changeovers they'd made. There were some small children amongst them, though the majority of them were men. The others never seemed to survive those trips, not being tough enough to handle the poor living conditions.

Children were oftentimes the first to die, followed by the elderly and women. Out of the millions who took those trips annually, only a couple hundred thousand actually made it to their destinations. Andrzej looked across the space towards his only remaining friend who accompanied him; Tomáš was huddled in a nearby corner beside an older Ishtanian man and his daughter, who'd joined their company somewhere in Porvartul at one of the rest stops. As it was, the driver's papers were seemingly legitimate as the slam of his door could be heard a moment before the diesel engine rumbled back to life. The lorry took off and they assumed that it drove aboard the ferry as they felt it go up an incline alongside the sound of several automobiles all around before the engine shut off once again, leaving them to await the end of their journey within its back alongside the cargo it hauled.

The voyage was roughly fourteen hours across the Brebon Channel and the time passed them by rather slowly, seeming like an eternity to the inhabitants of the lorry's trailer. Some amongst the immigrant caravan attempted to sleep the remainder of the ride away, though the majority found it impossible. Hunger, anxiety, excitement and fear kept them awake as they awaited their arrival on the foreign shores of Bree. Andrzej fantasized what life would be like in the Kingdom of Bree and imagined how much better off he'd be than he was back home. The Amverin government had totally devastated his own country, killing their dictator and setting up a capitalist puppet regime to replace the previous communist dictatorship. Along with his death, they'd sold off the factories and corporations of the state at ridiculously low prices and devastated the national economy, though it had improved the lives of those who'd managed to escape poverty nearly tenfold. They'd eliminated the equal distribution of wealth and created a true class system.

At the top were the rich, followed by those who could live luxurious lives off the backs of the impoverished masses. The majority of the younger generation supported the new capitalist system as it gave off the illusion that anyone could become rich; however, the older generation saw the flaws of the changes brought about by the Amverin-backed coup. Their way of life had been totally wiped out and the only reason it was supported was in the fact that the people had access to luxuries and other commodities previously unavailable to them at the cost of their nation's prosperity. Andrzej and his friends had witnessed the collapse of Alvaria personally as his own father had been one of the factory workers who'd been laid off and he himself had been a small-time business owner whose company went under when the Amverin corporations seized the economy by force.

Locally owned businesses had been run down and foreclosed, bought up by Amverin-owned corporations that could afford to sell the goods at cheaper prices, employing more people at a minimum wage established by the government they ran behind the scenes. He had previously owned a cellular phone company, though with the introduction of Amverin's own service providers offering the first three months free to new subscribers, he couldn't afford to compete with the multi-million Rinska* company. Having gone under and falling into debt, Andrzej forsook his country after filing bankruptcy, taking what was left of his money and pooling it with his few close friends in order to undertake their journey to Bree. They saw it as an opportunity to take back their lives and start over in a land of true democracy, rather than wasting away in the corrupt system their country had fallen into post-communism.

After what seemed like an eternity of hiding away amongst the lorry's bulky cargo, finding comfort as best

---

* Where in Bree the common currency were Stones ($), the Aero (α) was used within the Aerbon Federation whilst the majority of Eastern Aerbon favoured the Voskan Rinska (Я). In Amverin the common unit of currency was Stellas (§).

they could, the immigrants breathed a collective sigh of relief at the announcement of their arrival upon Brebon shores. Over the course of the next few minutes car doors echoed throughout the ship's hold as all around the drivers started their engines to disembark from the ferry to pass through the final border inspection. As the vehicles took off and prepared to approach the border check there seemed to be a great commotion on the port as all around the rushed shouts of what they assumed to be the border agents and dock workers rose up and in the distance they could hear the sounds of what appeared to be a football match. A couple of the immigrants on board the lorry grew grave at the ordeal and the ones who spoke the Common Tongue enough to understand what was going on whispered the translation to their unaware companions.

"*Vzbúriť sa*," an older man whispered, instilling fear into all those occupants aboard who were able to hear him.

The uproar of the revolution outside rose in volume as it drew ever closer to the port and the occupants of the lorry began drawing closer together in an effort to protect themselves and break free of the vessel they were trapped within. The lorry came to a stop and from the sounds of things, their driver was dragged out of his truck by the rioters and thrown into the affray. Bottles smashed against the trucks and crashed all around and gunshots could even be heard cracking off in the distance. Andrzej

---

* Translates roughly to riots, mutiny, revolt, storm, rage.

prepared himself as the doors of the lorry's container were being pried open from outside and the immigrants made a rush to find themselves in the middle of what appeared to be an anarchist uprising. They knew the anarchist flags for what they were; the red and black was a sign of freedom and revolution anywhere they were displayed, and they joined the rioters who fought for their liberation from the port against the military police who returned fire upon them.

Nationalists also fought back the rebel tides, displaying their own symbols of hatred, discrimination, and oppression. Andrzej was apolitical, fighting for his life alongside those who would aid him and not wanting to join the affray himself. The military police were armed with fully automatic assault rifles and sub machine-guns, though the majority fought back with rubber bullets loaded into riot shotguns. They were not afraid to surround the perimeter and gun down those who made a break for it into the town of Dover outside. As it was, the rioters easily outnumbered the police and it even appeared that they might overthrow the armed men; taking up the guns of the fallen and using them to push the forces back. So it was that gunfire rained down on both sides, leaving many casualties scattered throughout the docks in the midst of an all-out war on the streets. The rioters were unloading and freeing the immigrants from the massive convoy of lorries even as they dragged and beat the drivers out of their vehicles brutally, attacking dock workers and border agents alike in their effort to overthrow the government's control over the port.

Lobbing tear gas into the midst of the protesters and immigrants who joined them, the police awaited their reinforcements even as the rioters came crashing upon them like the waves of the ocean upon the shore. Forcing the NES troops to break rank and fall back even as more rioters from the town center made their way towards the heart of the chaos, they aided their brethren in breaking free of the docks. They swarmed the police from all sides and fell upon them like rabid wolves at the first sight of prey, tearing them apart and literally stripping them of their clothes and gear. It was total anarchy and Andrzej fought alongside his fellow travelers in an attempt to break free of the mayhem as best they could. NES lorries pulled up to the scene and the police within disembarked, attempting to construct temporary barricades to halt the progress of the rioters. The anarchists continued undeterred, returning to the city with their foreign band of undocumented migrant travelers.

Molotovs flew through the air and came crashing down upon the officers and their armored transport; the police responded by unleashing their water cannons upon the revolting masses. The town was ablaze and the streets were full of chaos as all around looters, rioters, nationalists, and police all acted in the heat of the moment in an effort to achieve their individual goals. The majority of the nationalists were shop owners and working-class citizens fighting to protect their jobs, homes, and businesses. Their opposition predominantly consisted of the homeless, chavs, immigrants, and other such unemployable persons as there were to revolt against the unfair government that they claimed oppressed them.

The police officers on the other hand, came from all across the south-eastern region and the various towns and cities that comprised it. They fought for justice, and many of them were either current or former military soldiers-turned-mercenaries as the NES selected their forces from the best of the best.

Breaking free of the docks, Andrzej took a right off the main road leading into town and ran through an alley towards the hills. There was an old fence but it couldn't contain him and the handful of his fellows as they hopped the fence and ran from any pursuers through the heavily forested ascent. The sounds of violence and sirens faded into the distance behind them as they made their way further up the hills towards the cliffs that overlooked the ocean and after twenty minutes of sprinting and climbing when it became too steep, they found themselves a shelter to hide away in the form of an old bunker from the Great War. The entrance was from the rear and it overlooked the ocean; there was an opening for a machine-gunner's nest and it overlooked the horizon where Legiole rested somewhere on the other side from which they'd just come.

Andrzej and Tomáš had survived their journey and managed to stick together through the whole ordeal, though only three others from their lot had escaped with them. Their companions were a bigger, well-built lad their age from Gregovia and the Ishtanian man with his daughter. Their names were Yuri, Slava, and Maria respectively. Though they were free of the riots and safe for the time being, they had no food and so they were forced with the decision to either hunt or trap what they could of the wildlife in those woods or wait until the riots passed over and scavenge whatever they were able to in the town. Slava was an experienced hunter in his own country, having grown up on a farm as a youth; Yuri also came from a small farming town in Gregovia where food was hard to come by, and so both were trained in the arts of survival. Andrzej and Tomáš grew up within the capital of their homeland during the rise and fall of communism and so neither were any more than street hustlers from the city, unlearned in the art of scavenging due to a lack of necessity.

Ever since they'd arrived in the country, nothing but chaos and madness had greeted Andrzej and his gypsy companions. Hiding away in the bunker, they'd taken to scavenging and looting as they could. Dover had fallen to the anarchist insurrection and military forces waged a war against the people, killing any who rebelled and deporting the immigrants as they found them. Life in the town was comparable to a concentration camp or life under a fascist regime and Andrzej wondered to himself what he'd run away from. At least in my own country I was free; this place is even worse, he thought bitterly between bites of a stale loaf of bread they'd managed to score from a dumpster dive nearly three days ago. The bread itself had expired on 29/6/93 according to its label, though he could not read the writing as he only spoke Alvarian and Voskan.

Slava was comforting his daughter as she cried, asking him why her father had brought her to this place. They were all asking themselves the exact same thing, though Maria was the only one to voice her thoughts aloud. Yuri was somewhere in the woods, hunting with a spear he'd carved out of a tree branch after growing sick of the stale breads and pastries. Andrzej was contemplating making another run into the town to see what he could find or steal from the shops. At this point the caravan had nothing left to lose but their lives, and so they might as well enjoy what was left of them. He was in a rather sullen mood, having traversed thousands of miles at the cost of the lives of his friends that weren't able to make the trip and without a single thing to show for it. Indeed, he would have been better off in the streets of Alvaria.

Instead, the young Alvarian man found himself squatting in destitution and dying for a cigarette, wishing beyond all else that he'd never made the trip. He laughed at the thought that those racist Brebon men could call him and his lot dirty immigrants ruining their country when it was their own people making it such an awful place to live. Even in the times before Amverin had killed his dictator, he'd never been forced to live such a lowly existence. Where are the welfare benefits for the immigrant families? Even these jobs we're supposedly stealing? I thought this was one of the richest and greatest empires in all of Aerbon... It seems like an intolerable shithole to me, Andrzej thought to himself as he prepared to make the trek into town. Their supplies were diminishing and he couldn't bear to sit around waiting for Yuri to save them another moment longer.

"Where are you going?" Tomáš asked him in their native Alvarian tongue as his friend suddenly made to leave.

"Town. I'm sick of this" was Andrzej's curt reply.

Not wanting to be left out, Tomáš readied himself as well and, despite Andrzej's objections, made the descent into town alongside his only remaining best friend. Together they trekked through the woods as they made their way down the hill in the general direction of the high street. Without speaking, they both prepared themselves for what they would experience upon re-entering the town; things had taken a turn for the worse since their arrival over two weeks ago. Soldiers marched through the streets openly brandishing their weapons whilst the townsfolk brutally resisted them. Every day they'd spent in the country so far, protesters could be seen carrying signs and fighting the militarized law enforcement, and even fighting amongst themselves. The police demanded the papers of any they came across who did not fit the image of a Brebon citizen and even took non-legal residents caught in violation to what Andrzej and Tomáš assumed to be deportation camps. They'd seen it with their own eyes on their brief trips into town, trying to make their visits as short and far between as possible.

As things were, the town was divided into a series of zones with military checkpoints separating them and small groups of patrols maintaining order in each. The pair of illegal immigrants tried to blend into the setting and join the crowds of people that walked the streets whilst seeking out a local newsagent. It was dangerous for them in those streets as they looked foreign and being unable to speak the Common Tongue didn't do them any favors. Spotting a homeless man, the two took a look around to make sure there were no nearby patrols to see them as they took advantage of the opportunity fate presented them. After seeing that the coast was clear, Tomáš jogged towards the man and smashed his fist into the side of the man's head whilst Andrzej stole the cup filled with coins before the pair turned and fled. A handful of people called out after them at the sight of the heinous act, though they ignored the shouts and ducked through an alleyway into the neighborhoods that rested atop a hill in the northwest end of town.

Once they were far enough away from the scene of their petty crime, Andrzej poured the coins into his hand and counted out $7.48. Returning their attention to finding an Eastern Aerbonean newsagent, they spotted such a store not far up the road in one of the more rundown neighborhoods after passing a couple of the NES patrols that were scattered throughout the area. They avoided the unwanted attention of the soldiers and quickly made their way within the safety of Chekov's Corner. It was basically a Voskan general store, though between the two of them, they spoke enough Voskan to purchase a pouch of tobacco, rolling papers, and a bag of rice. The packages were labeled in Voskan and it was a comfort for them to see a language that was at least familiar to them.

Before leaving, the cashier spoke briefly with the destitute immigrants, asking them what their status was within the country. After discovering they were illegal, the shopkeeper told them to wait a moment whilst she went into the back-room of her small shop, grabbing a handful of provisions for them to take along. Putting a 750ml bottle of Voskan vodka into their rucksack along with a spare 25g pouch of tobacco and some bread and meats, she told them that it was her duty to help them in response to their thanks. She said that the fortunate were always expected to help those with less, and so she sent them on their way after warning them to beware the police in the streets. After receiving the goods, Tomáš and Andrzej felt guilt gnaw away at their consciences as they made their way back the way they'd come. They took the bottle from their backpack laden with food and knew what they had to do...

As they approached the homeless man from earlier with the bottle in their hands, he flinched upon seeing their approach, fearing the return of his attackers. They rushed towards him and took him by the shoulders, pressing the bottle into his hands stammering as they attempted to apologize to the downtrodden Brebon man in broken bits of his language. They also offered him some bread and meat from what they'd been given by the kind Voskan woman who'd taken pity on them. Though they were not learned in the Common Tongue, he understood what they meant to say and took the bottle as acceptance of their apology. The bottle was worth roughly fifteen stone alone, and so they'd returned to him with more than double what he'd managed to save in the street that day. He took the bottle from them along with the food supplies and shooed them away before they attracted the unwanted attention of a patrolling NES squad in the area.

Feeling that they'd restored some of the negative karma they'd brought upon themselves, the boys made their getaway and slipped out of town through the same alley that they'd taken into town. They cut through a back garden on the other side of the alley and hopped the fence that separated it from the foot of the hill they had to ascend in order to return to their hideout. Though it was an arduous climb, they found the bunker with little difficulty and returned with their goods to an astonished Slava and Maria. The men took a delight in the acquisition of the 25g pouch of Voskan tobacco and meats, opening the initial 12.5g pouch that Andrzej and Tomáš had purchased with the ill-gotten funds. Each of the three men rolled themselves a decent cigarette whilst Maria munched away at a Voskan pastry.

After another hour or so Yuri also returned, bearing a fox and a couple of rabbits and squirrels he'd managed to catch. Upon his arrival, the Eastern Aerbonean farm-boy went about skinning the fox so that its meat could be hung to dry whilst he prepared the rabbits and squirrels for a stew. Andrzej came out to greet him and offered the lad an already-rolled cigarette and told him of their own score in the town. Making sure not to mention the acquisition or loss of the vodka for fear of upsetting him, Andrzej recollected their adventure and told him of the Voskan corner-store in the town. Yuri mentioned that it was a good connection to have and inquired if the woman might help them find somewhere to stay or if she even had any connections within the town. Andrzej's reply was that the police presence was far too great and that they would surely be caught and deported, stating that prison was worse than a communist dictatorship.

"Still, it would be better than squatting like exiles in destitution," the Gregovian farm-boy replied sullenly.

"Maybe, but I would rather live free than be sentenced to the rest of my days in a prison camp," Andrzej replied before inviting his comrade inside the bunker to enjoy their Voskan delicacies.

—◆—

Kelson Hayes is a British-American author and philosopher, born on 19 October 1994 in Bedford, England. He is most notably the author of *The Art of Not Thinking*, but his other work is predominantly centered around his fantasy books comprising the Aerbon Series, part of the greater Saga of Urea.

Libellule

Elodie Hollant

You've always been a dancer.

You started when you were three. It was your mother's idea. She'd always wanted to dance when she was little, but her asshole of a father never let her. Realize she's been living vicariously through you this whole time, that she still tries to, but you're too different now. She doesn't recognize you. It's a weird feeling.

Shake it off.

Mother keeps a photo of soft, round-faced, baby you, chunky arms and chunky legs stuffed in a powder-pink leotard on her nightstand. You were all smiles and baby teeth. You can see her crouching reflection in the mirror of the studio you were posing in. She was twenty-something. All smiles and adult teeth. She thought you were just so cute.

Dancing was more fun then.

Move away to a foreign country you say you're from. You were much too little to remember being "American" anyway, but that's what it says on your passport.

Learn that nine years old isn't *that* little, and that it's bizarre that you don't remember that hunk of your life.

Don't try to remember it. Everyone tells you a different story.

All you know is that you danced that whole time. And it was fun.

You're ten in that foreign country you say you're from and you've started dancing for real. Dance *academy*. You go to school all day just to go to another school all evening. It was never this serious in America, but you're having fun nonetheless.

Try to remember that feeling.

The taste of it.

Its colors.

You don't have that anymore. But it's all you really want, isn't it? The taste? The colors?

Months pass, and you're eleven now and you're actually getting kind of good. Your teacher tells you this. She wants you to be the opener for that year's summer recital. Shimmer with happiness, smile with crooked teeth.

Let yourself be happy, because you won't be happy for a long time after that.

I'm so sorry. You didn't deserve that.

You tell your mother you're the first thing she'll see on stage. All smiles and crooked pre-teen teeth.

You both shimmer with happiness at the dinner table, letting glitter fall into steaming plates of rice and beans.

Turn fourteen. Look at your body in the mirror. The big, big mirror in the bedroom of the house in that foreign country that's your home now.

Fail to understand the hips, the thighs, the belly, and the breasts. Fail to understand why everyone looks at them.

Why people think it's okay to touch them. To touch you.

This is still something you don't understand.

Cry as you write this.

Allow yourself to cry because you're alone in your dorm room.

Fourteen was much too little for that.

Go to dance class and stare at your chunky arms and chunky legs stuffed in a black leotard in the mirror of the studio you're practicing in.

Your mother doesn't find you cute anymore. *You'd be so much prettier with a flat stomach*, she says. She doesn't remember this, yet you never forget it.

At least you're a good dancer now. A grade three. G3s are usually seventeen. Dancing is still good. Still fun. Although when you look in the mirror, you feel sick to your stomach.

Look away, look away, look away.

Don't eat dinner tonight. You don't need it.

Turn sixteen. Your mother asks what's the matter with you. Tell her nothing, snatch your dance bag from the back seat and race down the twenty-eight steps (1.4 calories burned) to get to ballet class. You're dizzy by the time you reach the bottom.

Hyperventilate to keep from passing out.

Your teacher asks if you can hang back for a minute.

You do.

She stands, tall and lithe. Belly hollow, caving at her ribs. You're jealous. This jealousy makes your stomach hurt so badly, you can't look her in the eyes. Look at the wooden floor. At the dents you left with the box of your pointe shoes.

Your head aches. It pinches at your left eye. Ignore it.

She asks you if you want to audition for Joffrey.

Say yes.

Your teacher beams, and hands you a thick pamphlet of guidelines, instructions, and requirements. Black leotard, low bun, must be at least sixteen years of age, blah, blah, blah. But you read this bible cover to cover whilst climbing up the twenty-eight steps (4.76 calories burned). You sit in the car and try to read it again.

Punch yourself in the stomach to stop it from growling.

Your mother asks if you're hungry.

Say no.

Your mother drives you to the audition at 9:00 a.m. You didn't eat breakfast.

I get nauseous when I eat in the morning, you said to her, and it's a lie.

You just look thinner in the morning. This is important to you.

Break a leg, your mother tells you. She's trying to adopt stage speak. For some reason this annoys you. Fight the urge to roll your eyes and say thank you instead. Walk into the American audition hall, where all the dancers are pale and thin. Become aware of your curves and the color of your skin.

You've never felt black until now.

The other girls look at you weirdly.

Look down at the wooden floor.

Tell the receptionist your name. She looks at you, then at her sign-in sheet.

You don't look like what I was expecting you to look

like, she says, and she laughs like this is a funny joke. Laugh politely. Be nice. Make a good impression. Be charming.

These are all things your mother told you before getting in the car.

Like she knew you'd have to be extra shiny to catch their eye.

You smile and contemplate slapping the apples of your cheeks so that they flush.

She smiles at your polite laugh.

Tells you that you're beautiful (for a black girl).

Pretend this is a compliment. Pull a *Thank you so much*, from your ass, and walk into the studio, holding onto your pointe shoes so that you don't just fucking whack her in the head with them.

Avoid all the curious glances from the other dancers and pretend not to notice you're the only black girl there. Take a deep breath and a place at the barre. Let the cool metal quell the heat blistering your palms.

The music begins, and you dance. Remember your technique. Point your toes so hard that your calves burn. Plié as deep as you can and ignore the tremble in your thighs.

Drift like a leaf falling to the ground. Flit about like a dragonfly.

That's what your dance instructor used to call you.

Her dragonfly. And in French (because that's the language spoken in that foreign country you say you're from), *sa libellule*.

Finish the audition. It wasn't as scary as you thought. It was just like a regular ballet class. You did exceptionally well. The instructor told you this. He asked for your name. When you gave it to him, he smiled and wrote it down on his clipboard.

You're so graceful for someone so curvy, he says. This makes the budding flame of excitement extinguish. Two wet fingers pinching either side of a candle wick with a pitiful sizzle.

Smile. Be polite. Pull another *Thank you so much,* from your ass.

Your mother picks you up from the audition at 12:00 p.m.

"How did it go?" she asks.

Tell her fine. Turn up the music on the radio so she doesn't hear your stomach growl.

She asks if you're hungry.

Say no.

Months pass. You get an email from Joffrey. You get in. Shimmer with happiness and tell your mother.

She tells you that you can't go.

Ask her why—dully, flatly.

You didn't get a scholarship, she says.

You never learned the real reason she said no. Hold this grudge. Think about where you could've been if she said yes. Think about it all the time. Think about it until regret burns your cheeks and lodges a lump of coal in your throat. Drink sparkling water (0 calories) to dissolve it.

Okay, Mom, you say.

Your head aches. It pinches at your left eye.

Your stomach h.urts. The last time you ate something was two days ago. One tablespoon of peanut butter (95 calories).

Go to your room. Take a shower in the dark so you don't have to look at yourself.

Dry off and shiver. Pinch your inner thigh when your stomach growls.

Curl up under the covers and look at pictures of skinny white girls on Tumblr with tears in your eyes. Think that you might've gotten that scholarship if you looked like them.

Know deep down that if this continues, you're going to die.

This doesn't scare you yet.

Check if you can feel the sharpness of your collarbone. Make sure your fingers still touch as they wrap around your wrist.

Go to sleep and hope you don't wake up with a headache again.

Try to convince yourself dancing is still fun.

═◆═

Elodie Hollant is an aspiring writer pursuing their BFA at Pratt Institute. They're from Haiti, and travel frequently between Port-au-Prince, Fort Lauderdale, and Brooklyn to visit their family, shoot film photography, and eat French pastries. Their interest in writing began when they were just six years old, when their mother read a chapter of *Charlotte's Web* to them each night before bed. E. B. White's ability to foster sadness in baby-Elodie (who was, and still is, terrified of spiders) toward a dying Charlotte inspired them, even at such a young age, to explore different relationship dynamics and express all the emotions they've ever felt.

Heat Stress

Claire Ibarra

It was an Indian summer almost as hot as that record-breaking year when coyotes came out of the wilderness in droves looking for reprieve. The animals went crazy from the heat, and in some cases gnawed their way through screen doors and broke windows to get indoors. Others ran in front of moving cars to end their misery.

Now along the outskirts of Moab, the Canyon Lands in the distance shimmered like a mirage in the scorching heat. The dark reds, yellows and oranges of the surrounding desert merged into a single flame, and Kiran felt like the hot winds were incinerating her spirit. It was a cleansing baptism of fire, turning her insides into dry ash.

Kiran drove along a wide dirt road until she reached the state park entrance. She pulled up to the stationhouse and a stout-bellied ranger walked out.

"How long?" he asked.

"We'll be camping for two nights."

"Your pass will be good for a week," the ranger said as he approached the car.

While Kiran asked him questions about fresh water,

bathrooms, and trails to the Arches, Sam and Zadie began to argue.

Zadie yelled at her brother, "Why did you take your shoes off? Your feet stink like a dead animal."

"Shut up. It's because these sandals are plastic. It's not my fault Mom's so cheap," Sam responded.

Sam was sprawled out on the backseat, but when the ranger tapped he scooted upright and rolled down the window.

"Looks like you're the man of this small expedition. You gonna look out for these gals?" the ranger asked as he leaned inside the window.

Sam rubbed his bare knees. The air conditioning was sucked out in an instant, and his legs were already slick from sweat. "Yes, sir."

"Good. Now, I should warn you all, this heat can be dangerous. You have to make sure you have plenty of drinking water—there are faucets located throughout the grounds. I've highlighted them on this map. If you go hiking, well heck, I'd just rather you didn't."

Zadie put her feet on the dashboard and her long, slender legs scrunched in the tight space. "We came to see the famous Arches. It took us plenty of time to get here," Zadie said.

"You can drive right up to them. No need to hike the trail—I don't recommend it in this weather. Even the wildlife tends to get loony when it's this hot."

"Don't worry, we'll be careful," Kiran interrupted. Kiran was starting to get irritated; she had had enough of controlling men to last a lifetime. "Let's go, kids," she said. Kiran slowly pulled out, forcing the ranger to take a few steps back or be dragged away with the car.

"What a jerk," Zadie said as she twirled her long hair into a bun, looping and tucking the ends tight.

They drove through the grounds, and Zadie began reading from the park guide, "It says here, we can see Devils Garden and Fiery Furnace; and here's another, Dark Angel. My God, this place is hell." Zadie laughed nervously.

"I came here with your dad once," Kiran told her kids as they made their way along the snaking dirt road. Memories of Doug began to spark and flicker like lit candles in the dark. Kiran saw his image illuminated in her mind's eye.

"But Dad told me he's never been west of the Mississippi," Sam corrected her.

"Not John, I mean your real dad." Kiran was afraid that Sam would forget his father. Sam had been only five years old when Doug crashed his small plane in the middle of an orange grove. She kept photos around the house so the kids would remember his face.

"Daddy was here. When was that?" Zadie asked.

Zadie was a few years older than Sam, so Kiran hoped her daughter could still recall Doug's boisterous nature, his soft burliness and deep, reassuring voice. "We came here before you were born," Kiran said.

Now all three were quiet, and the tires crackled over the dry, sunbaked earth. It sounded like the ground was ripping open underneath them, and Kiran imagined falling through a crack of the earth, into a fiery abyss, and she shuddered.

"Here's a good spot. What do you guys think?" She pulled into a site surrounded by large reddish boulders and a few small trees with dry leaves. It looked tidy and fake, like a campsite at Disney. Kiran began to question why she was there, as she did when arriving at every new destination.

They had just spent a week in Colorado, now Utah, and after that she had thought maybe they would head south to Arizona. So many places, sometimes it felt like they were on the run. In some elusive way they were. The summer had already come to an end, and they hadn't even reached California yet.

"Yeah, it looks good, Ma," Sam said in an easygoing manner.

"Wait, how far are the bathrooms? I won't trek to go pee," Zadie whined.

"They're around that bend. The bathrooms are the blue square on the map," Kiran said as she watched a Jeep pull into the campsite next to them. Three young guys climbed out and began unloading the bags strapped to the roof. Kiran noticed they were good-looking. They had longish hair and scruffy chins.

Zadie stared out the window, then suddenly opened the door and jumped out. This was her opportunity. She walked around the car, so she would be in full view. She stretched forward and backward, touching her toes and leaning back—while her long, tan legs glistened with sweat. Her bun had come undone, so her thick mane of dark hair hung down her back.

It didn't take long for the guys to nod and smile at each other like they had just spotted a rare species in the wild. Maybe they had; Zadie was that beautiful and she knew it. There was a time when Kiran got the same reaction from men. Now Kiran admired her daughter.

Sam got out of the car and moaned, "My God, this really is hell. I can't even breathe, it's so hot." His t-shirt was soaked in the armpits, and it clung to his scrawny frame. Kiran worried that the heat would make Sam's acne worse.

Kiran felt the heat singe her own skin. Sweat dripped down her back, a slow trickle that caressed her spine and almost titillated. It had been that long, so long ago that a drop of water mimicked a human fingertip, a human stroke. She glanced at one of the young men as he strolled across the dirt road, checking out the area. The camper noticed Kiran watching him.

"Hey there, neighbors. Looks like we're the only ones braving this heat wave," he said.

"We must be crazy," Kiran replied as she began to help Sam unload.

"Where you guys from?" the young man asked as he took a few steps closer. Kiran rapidly assessed that he was well built, with reddish hair and blue eyes.

Zadie jumped into the conversation. "We're from Orlando, Florida," she said.

"Orlando? You mean Walt Disney's home turf? Do people actually live there?"

"Of course people live there. It's a real city, you know," Zadie replied. She had heard this reaction often while driving across the country, usually from waitresses in small-town diners and clerks in rundown souvenir shops. Many of the families they chatted with at motel pools had been to Magic Kingdom but didn't notice the suburban sprawl beyond the gates.

"What are you doing all the way out here in the Wild West?" he asked, walking right up to their car and leaning on it.

"Hey, Jim, get over here and help with the tent," one of his buddies called, jogging over. "Sorry to interrupt, ladies, but this is a classic Jim move, checking out the hot chicks while I do all the work." The friend noticed Sam for the first time. "Oh hey, sorry, dude. I didn't see you."

Sam muttered under his breath, "That's okay." His acne was inflamed bright red and his stringy hair was plastered to his forehead.

"You can't blame me; I'd be an idiot to ignore these beautiful ladies," Jim said while looking directly at Kiran.

Kiran was single now, but she had no confidence flirting. Maybe if she were ten years younger, she would have enjoyed the banter. John, her second husband, took off with a woman ten years younger than her. Kiran caught him and the woman, a teller, holding hands and kissing in the parking lot of the bank where she worked. She wasn't even that surprised.

Kiran felt a rush of adrenaline as she locked eyes with Jim. She felt nervous, yet excited at being watched by him. Zadie flipped her hair indifferently; she was used to the attention. Then Kiran noticed Sam struggle, trying to be cool while suppressing the discomfort of strangers in a desolate area hitting on his mother and sister.

"We'll catch you later. Maybe we could have a beer," Jim said as he walked away.

Kiran wondered if it was a real invitation.

The three worked to pitch the tent and set up the sleeping bags and stove. Kiran rummaged through the ice chest. She took a piece of ice and let it melt on her forehead. She felt slightly nauseous, but soon they were sitting at the picnic table, eating pasta and tuna doused with salad dressing. It was too hot to build a campfire, so after they ate Sam and Zadie played backgammon while Kiran pretended to read a book.

She worked to collect her thoughts, review her plan. Here they were in the middle of nowhere, a beautiful yet broiling middle of nowhere; a nowhere with Arches formed of sandstone, wondrous pieces of God's handiwork plopped down straight from heaven; a nowhere with an expanse of canyons so impressive Kiran had cried the first time she saw them. Doug had stood at her side, wrapped his arms around her and cried too.

The memory flickered.

She had been able to convince the kids that a cross-country drive for the summer would be a decent family vacation, camping in state parks, visiting such Americana marvels as Graceland and Dodge City. What else could she have done with their real father dead and their stepfather having run out on them for another woman? It was the only thing Kiran could think to do, run away and leave it all behind. She had taken a leave of absence from the bank and locked up the house, the same house where she and Doug had planned to raise a family. She now remembered the nights when she had reached across the bed to caress Doug, only to wake up and find John there instead.

Kiran hadn't calculated the time it would take to drive home. She didn't want to go back to a place tainted with so many memories, and she wanted a fresh start. Whenever the kids brought up the fact that school had already started weeks ago, Kiran drifted further into dreams of making it to California, a place where anything was possible.

Now it was dusk, and the light was pink and golden. Everything appeared to glow, but the heat was still thick and syrupy, as if Kiran had to swim through the air every time she moved. She looked up to see Jim standing in front of them. He had approached stealthily. Kiran was startled.

Lit by the glow of the sunset, his reddish hair now looked vibrant orange. His face and arms were covered in dark freckles, and when he smiled his teeth were unnaturally white. Kiran didn't find him as attractive as she had just an hour before.

"Hey there. You guys about ready for that beer?" Jim lifted a bottle of Heineken, dripping with condensation. "Come on, I won't bite."

Zadie jumped to her feet and began to bounce around Jim. "And your friends? Where are they?"

"We drove a straight forty-six hours to get here, they're wiped. They crashed out a few minutes ago." Jim flashed a neon-white smile.

Zadie slouched her shoulders and moped back to the picnic table, disappointed that the cute one wouldn't be stopping by. Sam awaited her next move.

"Well then, how about you, Mom?" Jim handed the beer to Kiran. She took it reluctantly, but then lifted the bottle to her lips. The beer was warm and bitter. By the time she finished it off, Jim had settled in and was telling stories about surfing in Hawaii and Baja.

His stories were stirring memories, and Kiran sighed

as she thought about the days she spent hitchhiking through California with her friends. She had been so young and reckless, and unimaginably free. Later she met Doug there and fell madly in love.

Kiran thought she might be able to recapture her spirit, if she could just make it there in time.

"Hey, shouldn't you guys be in school?" Jim asked curiously.

Sam began to fidget. Every day he reminded his mom that truancy was breaking the law—and he believed they were going to be busted at any moment. "Yeah, we should. Ask my mom why I'm not enrolled in the eighth grade."

Kiran's throat tightened because she knew Sam was right, not because she could hardly breathe in the stifling heat. "Well, I had this plan to get us to California. I really wanted Sam and Zadie to see it," she tried to explain, knowing how foolish she must sound to Jim and her kids.

It wasn't really California she wanted them to know and see—she wanted them to know Doug, as well as the person she used to be. But now the absurdity of her plan weighed on her, and Kiran needed to be alone to collect her thoughts. She suddenly rose and walked away, toward a dark path just beyond their campsite.

"Hey, wait up." Jim had to trot to catch up because of her long, quick strides. "You're not bandits on the run, are you? Did you rob a bank or something?" Jim called out jokingly.

"I worked in a bank. I should have thought of that," Kiran replied. She was reminded of John and the bank teller leaning up against a car with their arms wrapped around each other.

Kiran walked with her eyes on the moon. It wasn't full and spectacular, just lopsided and hazy, yet it lit the path so that she could dodge rocks and sticks. Although it was still hot and muggy, she felt less claustrophobic, like the world had expanded slightly. She could sense Jim behind her.

"You didn't need to come," she called back to Jim. Then she remembered what the ranger had said about the wildlife getting loony from the heat. Maybe it was better he was there.

"I wouldn't want you to get lost," Jim said. "It's better to hike in pairs. Anyway, I'd be an idiot to leave a lovely lady all alone out here."

Kiran couldn't think of a clever comeback. She wondered where his eyes rested: on the path, the sky, or on her. She hadn't felt desirable to a man in a long time.

Doug had made her feel beautiful every day, until the day he crashed his plane. John was the kind of man who stared at other women in her presence and was quick to notice when she gained a couple pounds. She knew he was good to the kids though.

Kiran was sweaty and breathing hard. She became more determined to reach the trail's end as the sky cleared and stars glimmered overhead. Jim had been quiet, but now he said, "I guess you have your mind set on seeing the Delicate Arch tonight."

Kiran kept walking until she finally came onto a clearing. She held her breath when she saw it. Under the lopsided moon it looked immense yet worn, sublime and flawed at the same time. Over the eons, the arch had eroded and morphed into a blazing, drastic structure, teetering between omnipotence and destruction.

"I didn't think we'd make it," Jim stood with his hands on his hips, panting and then bending backward to let out a bellowing yelp. He mimicked the coyotes howling in the distance. Kiran stood motionless while Jim began to explore, walking over the sandstone plateau in large circles around her.

"I thought if I got to California, my kids might know their father better. They were so young when he died," Kiran said suddenly. "But now I've run out of time."

Jim stopped roaming and approached her.

"I met Doug at a Grateful Dead concert. Jerry was still alive then," Kiran continued to explain in a low voice.

"You saw Jerry Garcia? I would die to have seen him play. I have some of my dad's old bootlegs. They're so awesome. Space was psychedelic!" Jim was laughing and whooping.

"Your dad's bootlegs?" Kiran looked at him mockingly. "You're just a kid, aren't you?" She calculated that she was nearly twice his age.

"I guess to you and my parents, I am," Jim said. He had lost his playful tone.

Kiran suddenly felt angry. She was annoyed with this cocky kid, but really she was angry with John. Kiran gradually came to realize during the cross-country trip that she never even loved John; she had just been lonely and scared.

Doug was the love of her life, and he died. How could he leave her and the kids like that? Kiran felt her insides constrict and ache.

"Why did you follow me?" Kiran asked. She now regretted being so far away from camp with Jim.

"Follow you? Come on, Mom, I thought I was keeping you company. I thought we might have something going."

It got darker as a cloud rolled over the moon. Kiran could see Jim's silhouette, as if he were only a dark spirit with no substance. Kiran's heart beat fiercely in her chest. She was frightened by his shadow. "I want to be alone. Maybe you should leave."

"Leave to where? You're crazy, lady."

Kiran knew she was crazy. What kind of mother keeps her kids out of school to chase some dream of California? Zadie should be going to Homecoming, taking her SATs and applying to colleges. But Kiran couldn't bring herself to turn the car around and go home. She would have to face friends and coworkers and explain John's decision to leave with the young bank teller.

Sam had needed a father so desperately, and he looked up to John. Now she would have to watch her kids be fatherless once again. She stood near the Arch and her body shook.

"Listen, I'm sorry. I didn't mean to upset you." Jim tried to approach her with concern.

"Stay away." Kiran glared at him.

"Okay, just stay calm. I can't let you walk back by yourself." Jim rubbed his elbows nervously. "Let's just head back. I'm sure your kids are worried about you."

"My kids? What do you know about my kids?" Kiran saw Jim's face more clearly as the moon reappeared, brighter and larger than before. She couldn't stand the thought of this young person judging her. He didn't even know her name. "I told you I want to be alone."

"Oh man, lady. I thought you were cool." Jim paced

and clenched his fists. "You start back, and I'll stay here and wait. Is that okay with you?"

Without answering, Kiran walked to the trail and once there she moved briskly despite the weight of the heat clinging to her back, which made her hunch slightly. Her legs felt swollen and thick, but she nearly trotted to get back to the campsite. After a few minutes, she sensed Jim behind her. His steps made a scratching sound against the dry, rocky trail. As the moon hid and it darkened around her once again, she quickened her pace even more. She remembered the coyotes in the distance and felt real fear.

Suddenly, she lost her balance. She tried to catch herself, but the crack of her ankle resounded in her ears. She didn't let out a scream, just a quiet whimper. Then she was seated on the ground, her chest heaving with tearless cries. Jim halted his steps and whispered curses, which sounded to Kiran like some kind of incantation. She moaned.

"Just leave me alone." She looked down and the ankle was swelling.

Jim stood over her and said, "Listen, I don't know how this happened, but you've got me all wrong. I'm not a bad guy, lady. And listen, I can help. You just have to trust me."

Kiran imagined coyotes circling in on them, going mad from the heat. She knew she couldn't make it back by herself; she had no choice. She lifted her arms and Jim gently pulled her up, wrapping an arm around her shoulder. She clung to him as they made their way along the trail, her leg lifted behind her. The ankle throbbed and a sharp, hot pain ran up her leg.

As they walked together, Jim began, "My mom had this friend. I was in high school, and, man, I fantasized about that woman. Ann was her name. I can't tell you how many times alone in my bed... you can use your imagination. She was older, but very beautiful and kind of mysterious. Anyway, you remind me of her."

Jim was speaking so close that Kiran could feel his warm breath brush against her cheek. He held onto her, nearly carrying her along the trail.

Kiran had thought she wanted to be desirable to a man who wouldn't die on her, to a man who wouldn't cheat. Instead, she began to imagine her life without a man in it. She felt tired, tired to the bone, and the pain in her ankle made her want to be home.

They neared the campsite, and as Kiran listened to Jim's fantasies about a woman named Ann, she thought how pathetic it all had been. She began to calculate the trip back. Her ankle hurt, but she could suddenly breathe easier, deep into her belly, which felt soothing. She realized it would take less than a week if they made a straight shot for it. Kiran decided she was ready to let go of memories and make a new home for Zadie and Sam.

=◆=

Claire Ibarra is the author of *Fragile Saints,* a novel published by Adelaide Books in 2021. Claire's poetry chapbook *Vortex of Our Affections* was published by Finishing Line Press in 2017. She received her MFA in creative writing from Florida International University. She currently lives and teaches creative writing in Colorado.

Destination

Kallista Kusumanegara

They say it will be Paradise. Time stops, but it also runs. It's beautiful. It's horrible. It's the worst place you could ever imagine. People are shredded between the teeth of giants and the poor are enslaved by the color green. They are just bones—stuck—screaming from the deepest chasms of the earth. No one can hear them. But the green is beautiful from the clouds. Dirty. White. Hot. Cold. Paradise. Soft women. Rolling hills. Barren deserts and endless ocean blue. Red skies. Rats in gutters and warm bread baskets on tables. Every kind of animal, land and sea. Children's laughter. All of the fish you can eat, blessed by the hand of a man in white. Vomit on walls and hearts on sleeves. Paradise.

A son executes his mother and sister at the kitchen table with a brand-new rifle he's been hiding under his bed for a week. He notices that, in the sunlight, the spatters of blood look a lot like thick maple syrup. He is fourteen years old. He sits down at his breakfast and cries.

A glass of milk. A revolution begins. Sweet maple leaves. Men and women dressed in the warmest gold you've ever seen. The orchestra begins to tune. Endless screaming. Angels singing.

A priest confides in his eldest niece. He has been taking an antidepressant—Lexapro—for several years now. He can't live without it. She tells him that she has been taking the same antidepressant since she graduated from high school. They laugh over cups of stale coffee, while a hailstorm passes outside the parish window.

They say it's a place where bubbling streams will teach you everything if you listen with your ear to the water. Wars are fought amongst men in pressed shirts who share the same face, the same indestructible, grinning mask. Old heroes wander the streets. They pee in dark alleys, alone. Unopened love letters. Freshly cut flowers. Trimmed dead ends. Crowded pews. Broken toddler bones. Mountains of fried bacon. Infinite images of perfection. Mothers kicked to the curb. Empty condolences. Tennis balls. Cello strings. Chicken shit. Children speaking five languages. Children flushed down toilets. Ten kinds of milk. Eternal youth in plastic bottles. Coins under dusty couch pillows. Holy vows under stone arches. People speaking, people saying nothing. Paradise.

A girl stands on an unlit street corner in the snow waiting for her next client. A man pulls up to her in a crackling red sedan. Dutifully, she bends down to his window. Her knees are naked. He extends his hand, and takes hers in it. He holds her hand, and wishes her a safe night. Snowflakes catch on his sweater sleeve. He rolls up his window and drives away. She never forgets his license plate number.

They say it's a place where everyone makes love in the daylight. Where love is measured meticulously by numbers and symbols. Where women hold drowned children in their arms. Fathers missing. Fathers coming home. Women using clothing hangers. Fulfilled promises. Lovers skinny dipping under meteor showers. First strokes on white canvases. Bodies colliding. Wet, mildew towels. Young blood. Open wounds. Fates deciphered through tea leaves. Fates dependent on daisy chains. Boys and girls crying, holding onto their sweethearts in the dark. Knowing the future. A first kiss feels like it will last forever. Until the next one. Second kisses. Third kisses. Last kisses. Dreams riding on eyelash wings. Vomit on walls. Hearts on sleeves. Endless screaming. Angels singing.

But what if they're wrong? What if lips don't exist in Paradise?

What will it be like?

What will it be like?

What will it be like?

What if it's Paradise?

One push through a blinding white.

I blink.

=≡◆≡=

Kallista Kusumanegara graduated from the University of Southern California in 2017 with a major in Design and a minor in Advertising. She is a graphic designer by day and a writer by night, and currently works as a senior designer at AUDIENCEX. She lives in Los Angeles. "Destination" is her first published work.

Lifted

Patti Larsen

Jenny twirls a long brown curl between her fingers as she gazes through the dusty glass. The sign over the door reads "Curious" and makes her skin itch. In a good way. Chances are the place behind the dirty windows, with the thick curtains holding back the light and the half-peeled name sticker above eye level, is the perfect place to alleviate her crushing boredom.

"I'm in here, sweetie." Jenny turns to half-heartedly wave at her mother. The rundown indoor mall has seen better days, but Mrs. Arthur insisted they try it out. "Great deals," she said and grinned at Jenny in the car on the way here. "Heard Penny Walsh got a knockoff Prada purse for twenty bucks."

It was either shop with her mother or hang out in her room and pretend to study for midterms. Jenny would rather be in Aspen with her friends, but her parents refused to foot the bill for the trip. So she's stuck here, staring through dust and grime, trying to decide if opening the door is worth the effort.

It's the first place she's found that could offer some sport. If only Connor was here. He'd be her wing man, just like always. But her boyfriend is gone, family trip, she guesses, like everyone else, though he didn't bother to tell her he was going.

Jerk.

Jenny slips her pink-clad phone from her pocket and texts Amber, knowing already from three unanswered messages Connor is ignoring her. He better not have dumped her. Not this close to prom.

Heard of Curious?

Her fingers tap against the side of the phone as she bites her lower lip and waits.

Ew. Amber's reply makes Jenny grin. *What RU doing there?*

Mom. It's the only response required.

Get me something. It's their code. Jenny slides the phone back in her jeans pocket and rounds her shoulders forward, taking a breath. Amber always says shoplifting is a mental game. Good lifters look ordinary, relaxed, almost bored. Even a hint of anxiety and you're toast. Connor's aces at it. Again, she wishes he was here and not being an asshole.

Jenny takes one look over her shoulder, spots her mother squealing in over-enthusiastic excitement, a giant pink bag in her hands, and makes up her mind.

Air displaces as she pulls open the door, a waft of fresh passing her, replaced swiftly by exiting stale, carrying a heavy scent of second-hand-store stink and mold. Jenny hesitates, knows she has to commit or leave as the bell over her head lets out an irritating jangle. A shiver from her phone and she's moving inside, letting the door sigh shut behind her.

It's dark in here, crowded. The heavy curtains are black velvet, dusty and oppressive. Jenny looks right and left at the window ledges, filled with what look like antique toys. A little wooden doll in desperate need of a paintjob stares at her as though afraid, eyes the only part of her that seem real. Too real. Jenny shivers, hand reaching for her phone.

What's it like?

Amber. Her fingers fly over the keys as she nervously looks around. So much for calm.

Creepsville.

Something 4 Brit 2.

Jenny inhales. Two things? She's only ever lifted one at a time before, and never alone. It feels weird not to have Connor or one of the girls at her side, watching her back. But she can't say no. This is Amber she's texting. If Jenny ever wants a chance to go to Aspen, or to have a social life, she has to do as she's told.

Makes her wonder if maybe Amber is the reason Connor isn't answering. Soft panic clutches, pulls at the air in her lungs. Has she done something to offend without knowing it? Amber hasn't shown any indication, but she's been gone since Thursday. And so has Connor.

She could ask, but that would look weak. Better to do what she's told and just hope it's enough.

Done. Once more the phone disappears. Jenny's sneakers make no sound on the old, stained floor, peeling edges of industrial tile stopping her toe, making her trip. She catches herself in time, hands grasping the edges of a rack, jarring the contents into a musical rattle. A tiny giggle of anxiety escapes her as a round-bottomed boy clutching an anchor, on a shelf at her eye level, bobs front to back, front to back.

Jenny steps away, coughs softly at the dust she's disturbed, the faint light of a handful of active fluorescent bulbs already giving her a headache. The smell of old and decrepit is everywhere, engulfing her. She's half tempted to leave, no matter Amber's request and Connor's absence. Surely she can find something at the corner market for the two demanding girls.

Something moves, a subtle sound freezing Jenny in place. She eases sideways, peering down the aisle between a glass case and a long rack toward the back of the store. An old-fashioned cash register sits at the edge of the back counter, light reflecting from the case front, blocking her view of what hides inside.

The place is aptly named. Curious, she eases further down the aisle, eyes wandering around the shelves stacked with painted wooden plates and cases lined with old chess boards, ancient-looking knives and guns and a dented collection of trumpets. Resting on the top of the counter on her left is a little violin, a tiny replica, complete with strings and a bow, sitting inside a perfectly crafted case.

Jenny's nerves leave her the moment she sees it. Perfect. Amber is obsessed with her violin right now. She'll love this, and it's the ideal size for an easy lift. Jenny's tense shoulders relax and she forces a vapid expression as she saunters to the counter and leans against it. Looks around like Amber taught her, yawns. Checks her phone with her right hand. While her left hand drifts up and sideways, fingers tenting over the tiny violin.

She screams as something sharp jabs her in the ribcage. The little instrument in its case flies from the countertop and lands on the floor, skittering under one of the racks. Jenny turns, heart in her throat, free hand clenched to her chest, to find a tiny man standing behind her.

She almost screams again. He might be small and thin, barely taller than her shoulder, but there is a look of pure evil in his icy gray eyes, in the set of his thin lips, the paleness of his ashen skin. Folds of wrinkles hang everywhere, save for the shiny, bald center of his head, only a wispy ring of white hair clinging to his white scalp.

His hand is still raised, one fingernail extended. It's sharply filed to a point, longer than her mother's, for shit's sake. Did he really just assault her with it?

"Children," he says in a soft, harsh voice. "All the same." Before Jenny can lie in protest, his arm jerks upward, finger now pointing elsewhere. Her eyes follow without her permission to a sign hanging from the end of the shelf in front of her.

No Stealing! Guilty Parties will be Lifted!

She almost laughs, it reads so absurd. How can a person be lifted?

He glares at her. "Understood?"

Jenny nods, shrugs. His arm drops, eyes narrowing. She's certain he's going to speak again, but instead he grunts at her and stomps past. His feet make loud clomping sounds on the floor, though he's truly tiny, narrow shoulders hunched inside a yellowed shirt, suspenders holding up his bagging pinstriped pants over a non-existent ass. It's tempting to taunt him and, were the girls with her, Jenny has no doubt Amber and the others would make it a point to make his life miserable.

When they get back from Aspen, they'll have to come back, with Connor. If he's still hers by then.

Jenny's hand explores her ribs, temper flaring now he's moved on, focusing her frustration on the old man. She watches him shuffle his way behind the counter, hoisting himself up with another grunt onto a stool. He unfolds a newspaper and promptly ignores her.

Asshole. She shifts to the right, eyes settling on the little violin. He didn't even pick it up. Anger makes her daring, sneakers squeaking slightly as she crouches and fishes the small instrument and its case out from under the rack. It's undamaged, at least. But now she can't take it. Instead, she makes a big show of putting it back inside the tiny case and dusting her hands off.

So there, Mr. Jerkwad. See how you like that.

He doesn't seem to notice. Jenny turns, determined to leave. Forget this place for now. Amber will know how to deal with this guy. Maybe a brick through his front window in the middle of the night. A couple of the other guys Amber hangs with have been known to be open to such ideas.

But her phone buzzes at her just as she turns away, and, like a compulsion drives her, she looks at the screen.

Better B good, J. Ur standing depends on it.

Jenny shivers, her heart skipping a beat. Amber's giving her an ultimatum? So this is about Connor. Has to be. Damn it, what did she do?

Missed the trip, Amber's next text says with cold calculation. *Ur out. Unless.*

Unless Jenny lifts something worthy.

Coolest ever. Her nervous fingers type the words. *U'll see.*

Amber doesn't respond. But Jenny's cold sweat doesn't go away. She glances toward the end of the counter, at the rustling paper as the store owner turns the page, but continues to ignore her.

She has no choice, now. And he's not even looking. This will be super simple. Child's play, even. Her eyes go to the sign. Guilty Parties will be Lifted!

Whatever.

The violin in its case finds its way into the pocket of her jacket. She's almost to the door when she remembers Brittany and Amber's second request. A quick snatch and she's the proud owner of a crystal swan with a rose in its beak.

She could be brave and find something for Connor, too, but she just wants out of there. She's expecting another poke in the back as she reaches for the door handle, the owner on the phone calling the police. Something, anything. But only silence greets her as she pauses and turns back. He's still there, behind his paper.

The idiot.

"Thanks," she calls out, buoyed by her victory, the rush of satisfaction she gets from stealing rising at last. Screw him. "Have a great day!"

Jenny laughs to herself, under her breath, already planning the grand reveal in her mind as she hands over the little violin to Amber and is in her good graces again.

The bell clangs its ugly song, her foot passing the

threshold as a giant flash of white light flares in front of her and everything goes dark—

—=◆=—

Jenny opens her eyes, mouth dry, throat parched, but unable to swallow. She groans, but no sound emerges from her chest, only silence, muffled and still. She sniffs. Again nothing happens, and she realizes she can't smell anything. One hand tries to rise, fails.

Frozen.

Panic takes her, shakes her, but only on the inside, where her soul lives. Her body is immobile, rigid, out of her control. For a long moment, Jenny sobs in the silence of her head, begging someone, anyone, to help her.

A dream. It must be. That's it. She must have passed out or something, and now she's dreaming. If only she can make herself wake up.

Just wake up!

She squeezes her eyes shut. Opens them. Nothing. No change. Still held by whatever force contains her, Jenny breaks down and weeps in the quiet spaces of her mind.

It's a long time before she pulls herself together enough to try to understand. Her eyes are movable, at least, if the only part of her that is. There's glass in front of her, a thin layer of dust over it. Is she outside the store, looking in? She can see just a hint of something red under her feet, and, to her shock, another person on her right periphery. She's not alone. Relief floods her, though she's not sure why having someone else there makes such a difference.

A sound perks her, draws her full focus. She knows that chattering, unhappy sound. The bell at the front of the store. But it's distant, muffled, as though coming from far away. Jenny squints into the light as the door closes and a figure approaches.

Jenny sobs again, but this time in happiness. *Mom!* Her mother hurries forward, toward her, but something is wrong, horribly wrong. Why is she getting bigger, so big Jenny can't see all of her suddenly, eyes only able to reach to the top of the ugly pink bag, the fold of her mother's coat pocket?

"I'm looking for my daughter." Her mother's voice sounds hollow. Where is she? Jenny strains, struggles, but is unable to break free of the prison her body has become, screaming for her mother, throwing everything she has at whatever keeps her still. And fails.

"I'm afraid there hasn't been anyone in here all morning."

Jenny stills. His voice is kinder with her mother than it had been with her, but she is well aware who speaks. The damned shopkeeper. What has he done to her?

"I thought I saw her come in here." Mrs. Arthur sounds confused, hesitant.

"I'll certainly keep an eye out for her," the shopkeeper says. "Do you have a number I can reach? In case she shows up?"

"No, that's all right." Her mother's tone shifts to anger. "She's probably decided her friends are more fun than I am."

No, Mom, please. Jenny weeps as her mother turns away. *Please, come back!*

"Have a pleasant day," the shopkeeper says.

"You, too." And Mrs. Arthur is gone.

Jenny pants in her head, wriggles and wiggles and fights until she has nothing left. Her ears pop as something moves above her, the feeling of vast emptiness replacing the muffling claustrophobia. A shadow falls over her as she rises, lifted into the air, turned slowly around. Toward his grinning face.

"Well now," the shopkeeper says, eyes giant, nose almost poking her as he examines her. "A violin, is it? Did you used to play?" Jenny catches her reflection in his glasses, horror choking her. She's dressed in a frothy black gown, a violin in one hand, bow in the other. But she looks plastic, like a figurine of some kind. With a crystal swan, a rose in its beak, at her feet. "No matter," he says, turning her around, fingers setting her back inside the case. "Can't say I didn't warn you, girl." Now she understands. He's left her on an angle, enough to see the lines of other figures, row upon row, watching her with their rigid, plastic forms and terrified human eyes. "You're a lovely addition to my collection."

Shock makes her mind break. Because she's found Connor. Not on a trip after all, not ignoring her texts. He's there next to her, where he will stand in perfection forever, a sparkling silver tiara in his hand, held out toward her in an eternal offering of adoration.

His eyes beg her to help him. But she's already falling into her own madness.

Jenny's mind wails its horror on and on, into despair and darkness, as her perfect doll body cradles the violin, the silent crystal swan waiting for her to play.

⇒◆⇐

Patti Larsen is a *USA Today* bestseller and international, multiple-award-winning writer with a passion for the voices in her head. Now with over 160 titles in happy publication—and many more pending, making sleep impossible—she lives in beautiful Prince Edward Island, Canada, with her pug overlord and overlady, four chonky cats and Gypsy Vanner princeling, Fynn. You can find her at pattilarsen.com/home, on stage with her improv troupe, Side Hustle, or at the beach.

Pareidolia

Conor Marko

Someone should help her.

Not that it will make a difference if anyone does. On this lonely stretch of mountain highway, during the early stages of a snowstorm, there are likely no witnesses that will stumble upon this scene anytime soon.

Except you.

It's your fault, really. Not the accident, but the fact that you're seeing it. You should be moving into your new apartment now, back in the city you grew up in. But, somehow, you forgot your mirror at your old place. Technically, Morgan forgot it. You weren't responsible for packing it into your tiny car, and Morgan didn't really care what was in there, as long as you were out before the new tenant arrived. You didn't want to turn around under the brewing storm above, but the stupid mirror was quite expensive, and your new apartment is not furnished at all. Once you realized you weren't sure it was there, you were convinced that Morgan had forgotten it. Turning around to go get it was the most sensible option. It would be faster than unpacking your entire trunk just to find it.

You have no idea what caused the accident, but you can guess. Between the steep incline of the road, the sheet of snow on the highway, and the sharp bend just beyond, little is left to the imagination. The woman's car is wrapped around a thick aspen tree in a twisted steel embrace, and the windshield is completely blown out. There's glass everywhere, all along the road, and the front tires are completely deflated.

But it's the driver of that car, the woman herself, that you find yourself fixated on. She lies in the snow, mangled and broken, but alive. Her face is contorted into a raging, gasping snarl, the fight for her life clearly etched between her chipped teeth and bleeding forehead. The contours of her face are sharp, angular, but changing constantly as she pants through cherry-red lips. She is lying some distance away from the totaled car, but you don't know how she got there. She may have been thrown through the windshield on impact. She may have crawled that far. You aren't certain.

What is certain, though, is that she will die. You're no doctor, but you can see that her body has fared far worse than her face. The snow around her is stained a heavy crimson, becoming darker by the second. Three of her four limbs lie in unnatural, sickly angles, and with her good arm, she props herself up on her side. The eyes staring at you are partially obscured by her long matted hair, but you can see that they house imprisoned emerald irises, pleading with you to intervene.

No call to emergency services will be quick enough to get to her. No amount of training from that CPR course you took last year will make a difference. Her fate is sealed.

And that's when she opens her mouth again, not to breathe, but to speak. She coughs once, twice, then utters a word that cuts deeper than the horror of witnessing this tragedy—

She calls out your name.

Your mind races and your heart beats even harder than before. How did she know that? You look again at her sharp face, those high cheekbones. She's a stranger. A complete, total stranger. You've never seen her before, you're sure of it. How does she know you?

While your mind is swimming, spiraling, your body is acting. You step away, over a twisted length of metal, backpedaling until your hands make contact with your car. You stumble around back to the trunk—it was only held down by a loose rope because the trunk was too full to close completely, and it flung open when you slammed the brakes upon seeing the car crash—and tie it down again with shaking hands. She calls out again, but you can't make out what she says this time. You just find your way into the driver's seat, spin the car around, and peel away from the dying woman who knows your name.

$$\Longrightarrow \diamond \Longleftarrow$$

It is less than half an hour before the apartment becomes an unbearable hell. There isn't even time to unpack anything. The walls are immediately suffocating, the ceilings too low, and the floors crooked and uneven. The hot air coming through the vents sounds like distant screaming. On top of it all, there is the overwhelming, insatiable urge to get out. The apartment that looked so cozy, so homey during the property viewing, now feels like the setting to a horror flick. Nothing good will come of being here, not now. There has to be some other place in this familiar city that won't be so oppressive, so damning.

One such place comes to mind, and it's not long before you are in the old, familiar coffee shop, with Priti at the other end of the table. A lot of long nights were spent here as teenagers, feverishly studying for those high school exams that seemed so important at the time. Even though those days have long since passed, she seemed excited to meet here again. This building is just a nondescript coffee joint to some, but to others, it's like a home away from home. "You know, I always pass this place on my way to work," Priti says, a cappuccino in her cupped hands. "And I think to myself, 'I should go in there again.' But it wouldn't feel right, going in alone. But now you're back, and, well, it feels good to end up here again, after all this time."

"I know what you mean. Thanks for coming at such short notice."

"Of course! I feel like we haven't seen each other in so long!" Priti smiles. Her lips part into a thin smile, reminiscent of the way they would when she figured out the answer to a tough math problem. "When's the last time we saw each other in person, and not over a video call? A year? Maybe more?"

"Something like that, yeah."

Her smile fades, but her contentedness lives on in the soft crinkles around her eyes, the soft curves of her eyelids. Steam rises from her drink, dissipating into the air around her.

"How have you been?" she asks. "When did you move back from Morgan's?"

"Just today, actually."

"No way!" Priti smiles again, but it's a wide one now, the one that she made when she found out she was going to college. She had dimples back in high school, but they seem to have faded now, filling in as her face filled out.

"Yeah. It's just a few blocks from here, on, uh… 34th street."

"We should go see it after! I bet the place looks great," she says.

"Hah. Not really. We, uh, probably shouldn't go there just yet. I need to, um…"

Priti cocks her head. She cut her hair short recently, and it barely reaches her shoulders. Most of it is hidden under her beanie.

Then she puts a hand to her face, her cheeks turning pink. "Oh, shoot. You just got here, I shouldn't be inviting myself over like that. You probably haven't even unpacked yet. I shouldn't be so eager."

"No, no, it's fine. But you're right, I haven't even taken everything out of my car."

"That same old car you had in high school?"

For a while, the conversation continues about the car, and what Priti's been up to recently. What mutual friends have gotten married, or graduated, or both. Priti finishes her drink. The other one at the table remains untouched. She continues to talk, but it's to a distracted audience. There is a figure at another table, just behind Priti. The body is obscured, but the face is visible. The features are unmistakable, and that feeling of impending doom is back.

"I saw someone die on my way back here."

Priti freezes upon hearing it. Even her mouth stays put, slightly open, and the muscles in her face clench and unclench, as if unsure how to react. Eventually, she blinks a few times and quietly asks, her lips barely parting, "What did you just say?"

"I... saw a car accident. EMS hadn't arrived yet. The car went off the road and hit a tree."

"Oh my god." Her expression is something between sympathetic and shocked. "I don't even know what to say..."

"The driver, they got thrown out of the car, I think. They were on the ground, and—"

"No, no. Please, stop. I can't. Not here." Her lower lip quivers, but she composes herself and takes a breath.

"I'm so sorry you had to witness that. That's awful, it really is. I feel like I'm going to cry... I don't know how you're staying this calm about it."

"She said my name."

At this, Priti's expression changes. Her mouth closes and one of her eyebrows raises, ever so slightly. "Was it someone you knew?"

"No, it wasn't. It was a stranger, and they... well, they look like the person sitting at the table behind you. Exactly like them."

Priti doesn't turn around. "Am I missing something here? Is this a joke?"

"No, it's not. She..."

But the figure behind Priti has changed. Someone still sits at the table, but the features are different. Maybe it was just the lighting. It's a woman, still, but not the driver. Definitely not the driver.

The crinkles around Priti's eyes are back, but they aren't there from smiling, anymore. Her eyes are narrowed, pupils dilated. Something in the way she is regarding you makes it seem like she suspects something. That, in turn, makes you suspicious of her. That oppressive feeling is starting to get even worse than it was in the apartment. Time to leave.

⚊◆⚊

The clouds above the town roil and spit, the snow turned into freezing rain. The dense columns block out the sun, and it seems a lot later in the day than it actually is. People take shelter wherever they can, going to great lengths to avoid being pelted and stung. Cars inch through the slush, sliding through intersections and skidding around corners. It is doomsday.

In the town's largest supermarket, the lines are backed up. Each till has several shoppers standing single file in front of it. You're one of them. After making a less-than-graceful exit from the coffee shop, and Priti's questioning glare, you figured grocery shopping was a safe option. After all, you haven't eaten anything today. Returning to the apartment makes you feel nauseous, but maybe that's just your hunger pangs. They'll go away once you get something into you.

Besides, being an anonymous person in a crowd has you at ease—at least, more than you were at the coffee shop, or apartment. No one knows you here, no one can identify you. And as long as you don't look at anyone, you can't mistake them for someone else.

A couple is behind you, waiting to unload their shopping cart as the conveyor belt jerks ahead. Though you don't mean to listen in, their conversation carries over as you wait for the cashier to scan your things.

"...said he had to cancel for tonight. The road he normally comes in on is completely closed down," the woman says.

"Then why are we buying all this stuff?" the man asks. He has a gaunt, scruffy face that looks like the old neighbor next to Morgan's house, a retired police officer.

"Well, he said he could come tomorrow."

"Oh. Alright." He examines one of the cans in their cart, squinting at it from behind his horn-rimmed glasses, before placing it onto the conveyor belt.

"Yeah," the woman says. "He said they closed it because of an accident. Really bad, apparently."

"Well, in this weather, I'm not surprised." His nose is crooked, seemingly almost too big for his face. "Hope everyone's okay, though."

"He told me that someone died in the crash."

"Oh no."

"Yeah. Someone from around here, too. I really hope it's not someone we know. That would be awful."

"Does it matter if we know them or not?" the man asks.

"I—what do you mean by that?"

"Either way, someone's dead. If we're not grieving, someone else is. It's equally bad."

"I guess. It would just feel a lot worse if I knew them."

"Worse for you. Better for someone who doesn't know them. Same amount of grief in the end."

"You have a weird way of looking at things," the woman comments. She goes to place a loaf of bread on the conveyor, revealing the shape and detail of her face. Familiar.

"Isn't that why you married me?"

"Oh, please— Hey, where are you going?"

But you've seen enough. The woman calls after you again, but you're already halfway out the door, groceries left behind, sitting idly as you plunge into the driving rain.

≡◆≡

"That's a hell of a story," the man says. His features are uncertain in the dim light of the bar, but that's ideal. It's comforting that the light is too dim to make out each other's faces. In absence of expressions, of intimacy, of knowing, a stranger is the easiest person to talk to, right about now. You struck up a conversation with him not long after stumbling into the establishment, cold and wet. He listened quietly while you told him about what happened today, down to the last detail. He never asked questions, never interrupted. Just listened.

It might also be the alcohol. The man has been drinking for a while, judging by the empty glasses around him, and you've just finished your first drink. Another is on the way.

"But—and forgive me if this sounds a bit crass—that's the way things go," he continues. "Things happen, you don't have a lot of control over them. You don't have *any* control over them." Outside, the rain has turned back into snow, and it's starting to get even darker out. The bar is quiet, but it won't be long until people start trickling in for happy hour.

"I can't stop thinking about it, though. I'm reminded of it all the time. Everything I see just puts me back there, mentally."

"Do you think you're reading into it a little deeper than you should?" he asks. Drinks arrive, and he takes his.

"How can I not read into it? It's everywhere I go. I keep seeing signs."

"And that's what you're misinterpreting. What's that phrase again? You can't do... no, you can't see... Oh, I know. You can't see the forest for the trees. That's the one." He leans back, probably looking impressed with himself.

"I don't think so."

The man huffs. "Alright. Look. You give me an example of something you think is a 'sign,' and I'll tell you why it's not. I'll buy you a drink every time that I'm wrong. Go for it."

"Well... that conversation I overheard earlier. Of all the things they could talk about—the crash?"

"You don't even know that was the crash you saw. You've seen the weather recently? And the state of the roads in and out of this town? It'd be a miracle if there was only one fatal crash today. You said you were local, didn't you? You know that as well as I do."

"Alright... But what about the faces? I saw her face twice today. There's no way."

"Oh, come on. That's just statistics. You go to crowded places, like restaurants and grocery stores, you're going to see similar-looking people. Especially if you're primed to look for certain features. Distinctive ones."

"You a psychologist?"

He laughs. "Right now I am."

"Fine. Then explain the name thing. There's no way you can explain that away with stats or coincidence. There's no way she knew my name."

The man nods his head slowly, a bobbing shadow in the darkness. "That is a weird one, I will admit... But hold on a second. What was your name, again?"

You tell him your name.

"Ah..." He repeats your name a few times, each iteration becoming more and more garbled, until it starts to resemble a completely different word entirely. Eventually, it sounds like a vague cry for help, an awkward phrase that sounds only tangentially close to your own name.

"...right. I can't say I'm convinced."

The man sighs. "Look. You saw something awful. It's terrible that you saw it. But that was your only role in it. The rest was out of your control. Even if you tried to save her, nothing would have changed. Maybe you've got some weird form of survivor's guilt, maybe you think you're responsible. You'll screw yourself up thinking about it like that. It's already screwing you up. You sound like someone going through a breakdown. Like a trauma response. Something of that nature."

Now he shifts in his seat, and the light reveals his face more clearly. You see his creased forehead, the groomed beard, and the piercing in his left ear. He regards you curiously, the wrinkles of his face casting minute shadows. In that moment, the boundary has been crossed. There is no longer a sense of strangeness in the air, of anonymity. It has been replaced with something far worse, far more condemning.

"Are you feeling alright?" he asks, a level of concern evident in his voice.

You shake your head, eyes wide. You throw cash onto the counter next to your untouched drink and run out of the bar.

—◆—

Nighttime. Shivering, tired, and alone, there is only one place left for you to go.

You stagger back into your apartment, immediately feeling boxed in again. You've given up. Between your pounding heart, your racing thoughts, you are resigned to the fact that this will never go away. The fates have cast their die for you, and this is how they have landed.

After what feels like hours of staring at the empty walls, you wander over to the windows. The snow is coming down heavily, streaking the glass and obscuring your vision. By tomorrow, it might be a foot high. It could be a dozen. You hope it's a hundred.

Your phone vibrates from your back pocket. Taking it out, you accept the call, recognizing the name.

"How's your new apartment?" Morgan asks. "Say that it's awful so that you can move back here. I'm already sick of the new tenant."

"Really?"

"Yeah, really." Morgan goes off about the new tenant's strange quirks, which seem numerous despite it only being a few hours since they moved in. You're just glad to be talking about something other than yourself.

That isn't to last, though. Eventually, Morgan asks the

dreaded question: "How about you? Your day going any better?"

Steeling yourself yet again, you go through the details of your day. Morgan reacts much like Priti when hearing about the accident itself, then falls silent as you move on to talk about seeing Priti again. You're talking about the conversation in the grocery store when you're cut off.

"Hold on, hold on. You stayed until the ambulance came, right?"

"Uh, no, I... I left right after she said my name. I freaked out and drove away—"

"What the hell is wrong with you? A woman was dying in front of you, and you didn't help them? What were you thinking?"

"Morgan, they were going to die!"

"That doesn't matter! If someone's lying there, injured, alone, you can't just... I don't even have the words for this. Did you even call the police?"

"I—no, I didn't. It was out of my control! She would have died whether they were there or not. It makes no difference!"

"That's a load of garbage and you know it," Morgan seethes. "There is something seriously messed up in your head. Just leaving the scene of an accident like that—"

"I had no part in it!"

"Doesn't matter. Not a bit."

This conversation isn't going the way it should be. Morgan is probably seconds away from hanging up, and that means being alone in the apartment again. The harder you breathe, the harder it seems to get any oxygen in. It's like the air is being sucked out of the room.

You're grasping at straws. "The—the mirror, Morgan. I forgot my mirror at your place when I left today. The big one. Is it still there?"

"What? What does that have to do with anything?"

"Just— Please, answer me."

Morgan groans. "No, it's not here. Why would it be?"

"Because that's how I saw the accident. I realized you didn't pack the mirror, and I turned around to go get it."

"Yes I did. You were busy packing your other bags, but I put it in there, behind your box of clothes."

"I don't remember that at all. I believe you, but... Why didn't I find it in my car when I got to my apartment?"

"How would I know? Are you trying to distract me here? Seriously, you did something really irresponsible today, I'm not just going to let it go!"

Morgan continues to berate you over the phone, but you sink down onto the floor, no longer listening. The apartment feels spacious and breathable. That stupid mirror, the root cause of all of this, must still be in your car, buried beneath the piles of junk you crammed into it. It's that damned mirror that caused you to turn around, to see the accident that has been messing with you all day. You'd been blaming the mirror—blaming yourself—for all the trauma you'd been put through today, but really, it had nothing to do with it. Just a weird twist of fate. Completely out of your hands.

⇒◆⇐

Unbeknownst to you—or maybe, buried by snow and ice and dirt, in a deep recess of your mind, it is known—there is a broken metal frame still sitting behind a tree, missed by the cleanup crews. It is twisted, scarred from being hit by freshly pierced tires, tires embedded with shards of something clear and sharp. The metal no longer resembles its original shape. But from a certain angle, combined with a few haphazard shards of glass that were also missed, it almost seems to resemble the form of a human face.

≡◆≡

Conor Emerson Marko is a writer and musician based in Hamilton, Ontario, Canada, and is heavily influenced by the many unique and vibrant personalities he has encountered during his time there. A graduate of the Chemical Engineering and Bioengineering program at McMaster University, he is fascinated by the inner workings of the human body and mind, seeking to express them through artistic media. His first publication, "Pareidolia", explores not only how influential our mind's perceptions of events are, but how fragile as well.

Apartment Complex

Vivian R. McInerny

Mom was not happy about the move. I promised her she wouldn't have to pack or carry a thing. She didn't. I slung her suitcase-sized brown purse over my right shoulder and was struggling to balance two cardboard boxes of cheap glassware in the elevator when we ran into Rachel from 17C. I made introductions between floors.

"Mom finally agreed to move in with me," I said. Rachel had heard the whole saga.

"Welcome," she said, a bit too enthusiastically. "I hope you'll be happy here."

Mom just stared at the numbers clicking off the floors whizzing past. It had taken three years to convince her to sell the old house, and Mom made sure everyone knew that she was miserable about the decision. But it had to be done. Even if I could make the drive to Heuertown every weekend to do yard work and clean her house, there was still the rest of the week when she was alone. I tried to hire help. The people never lasted. Mom wouldn't even consider a senior community.

"Assisted living?" she sneered. "Sounds like an iron lung."

But the day the owner of The Stage phoned to say Mom was at his bar trying to order a beer for her dog—a collie we'd put down a few months earlier—the move was no longer up for debate. I put her house on the market. The realtor suggested it would show better if we decluttered. I asked my siblings if there was anything they wanted, hoping one of them might volunteer to fly home and help out. My sister wrote back, "It's all yours!" She included a link to eBay. My brother never even responded.

The elevator stopped at the fourteenth floor.

"This is us," I said as the doors opened.

"There was no thirteen," Mom said.

"A lot of buildings don't have a thirteenth floor," I said. "Some people are superstitious."

"Call it anything you want," Mom snapped. "This is the thirteenth floor!"

Rachel held the door and mouthed good luck. I exited carrying both boxes while trying to usher Mom out with my elbow not weighed down by her gigantic leather purse.

I'd moved Mom's old bed and nightstand into what had been my home office. Her recliner took up most the living room. The red carnival glass I put on a windowsill by the kitchen sink. The afternoon sun cast pretty ruby shadows across the countertop.

"If that fades…" Mom said, leaving the thought to dangle like a vague threat.

I made tea. It was too hot. The wafer cookies from Petite Eats I served tasted like dog biscuits. Later, I took her on a full tour of the building. I showed her where to pick up the mail in the lobby, and gave her a duplicate key for the box. We toured the laundry room in the basement. I told her where I kept a stash of quarters for the washer. The dryer took dollar bills. We went up to the rooftop. There's a spot where she could grow container tomatoes come spring. The view is spectacular. We stood for a while looking out over the city as dusk fell, watching the other high-rises light up against the night.

"Everyone's stacked on top of each other," Mom said. "We're like caged chickens in a Chinese street market."

A couple weeks before Halloween, the super posted a notice in the lobby about trick-or-treating etiquette. Next to it was a large Manila envelope filled with cutout paper pumpkins. You were advised to tape one to your door so kids knew they could knock for candy. Rachel called it reverse pumpkin Passover.

On the way home from work, I stopped at the store to pick up a few things and threw in a couple bags of fun-size Snickers. Mom thumbed through her mail order catalogs while I put away groceries. I'd never known her to order anything.

"Apples don't need to go in the fridge," she snapped.

I left one on the counter for her even though she couldn't eat apples because of her teeth or lack thereof. The bags of candy I shoved back on a high shelf of the far cupboard so I wouldn't be tempted.

"You better hope some kid with a nut allergy doesn't come trick-or-treating at your door," Mom said. "I read in

Good Housekeeping about a boy flying to Oklahoma to see his divorced dad, and when the stewardess handed out the snack packs of peanuts, he died. It said so in the magazine."

"That's a shame," I said, putting away the cereal. I'd forgotten toilet paper and toothpaste.

"He died dead, just like that, because of nuts in the air."

The next day I stopped at the mart to grab the essentials and bought a bag of Tootsie Pops, too.

Things were getting tense at work. Corporate denied rumors of layoffs, but everyone was jumpy. Some idiot in Printing and Distribution circulated a cartoon of a suit in a guillotine with the basket beside the victim labeled Department Head, then acted surprised when he was sent to H.R.

My office has a large window overlooking the cubicles. I closed the door but kept the blinds open.

"Have a seat," I said, trying to keep it casual. "It's Rick, right?"

"Richard," he said coolly.

The cubes were doing a lousy job pretending to work. My body language all but shouted nothing-to-see-here-people. I smiled, offered coffee. Cream? Sugar?

"Richard," I said, "tell me what's going on?"

He said he had nothing to say which I've come to learn is code for I am a dam of complaints ready to burst. Two sips into his coffee—cream, no sugar—Richard sprang a leak no Dutch boy's thumb could plug.

"There's this woman in my department," he said. "She wears way too much perfume; a cheap, nasty fragrance."

He asked her, politely, to please refrain.

"And she just rolled her eyes."

He developed a rash, "an allergic reaction." He's sure the perfume was to blame. His manager, who he referred to several times during the conversation as my less than super-visor, did nothing to help.

"She just tells me, 'Focus on the job, Richard. Focus on the job.'"

He did a spot-on imitation of her. I smiled. I shouldn't have, I know, but I did. Richard looked pleased with himself and added in a conspiratorial tone. "She's turned everyone in the department against me."

Richard told stories. He shared secrets. He had theories. I let him rattle on, every once in a while murmuring an encouraging I understand and sure or that must be very frustrating for you. After a while, I asked him what he needed to do his job effectively. Oh, Richard was chock full of ideas. We had to fire the perfume woman, obviously, and take a closer look at his supervisor's performance. He requested a different cubicle, one closer to the window. He needed to telecommute on Fridays and occasionally on Mondays, too. Oh, and he was overdue for a raise.

I took notes. After each of his demands I asked if he was certain that this particular staff change, cubicle move, raise or what-have-you was really necessary for him to get the job done.

"Absolutely essential," he insisted.

I put a bold check mark by each itemized grievance, summarized everything we'd discussed, and drew the meeting to a close.

"I wish we could accommodate you, Richard," I said in a tone that was all humble regrets and apologies. "I really do."

He crossed his arms and his face contorted into a smug I-knew-you-would-do-nothing expression.

"Unfortunately," I calmly continued. "At the present time, the company cannot afford to make the kind of changes you require to be successful at your job."

Richard looked pissed. He still wasn't getting it. Time to hammer it home.

"We need someone who can do the job under current conditions. I'm so sorry, Richard," I said rising to stand. "You will be missed."

I extended my hand across the desk in a gesture of professional finality. Richard looked stunned. The skin of his face turned a lighter shade of pale. I could practically hear the gears and cogs of his brain clunking to WTF mode. Keeping my eyes locked on his, I let an awkward silence hang in the air along with my outstretched hand. Seconds passed. Nothing. I stood firm. Finally, Richard made the slightest move, resigned to surrender a handshake.

Just then my office phone rang. I ignored it but the spell was broken. It rang a second time, my direct line. I glanced at the flashing caller ID for a split second.

"I'll let you get that call," Richard said, excusing himself.

"It can wait," I insisted, but he was already out the door. I watched him scurry through the maze of cubicles while I picked up the phone.

"Hi, Mom. Everything okay?"

"Where did you put my pills? I can't find them. I'm supposed to take one now and you've put them some place stupid."

Halloween night, we had about a dozen kids. Mom followed me to the door each time, but stood back and said nothing. We had a couple super heroes and three fancy princesses in a row. I greeted the pirates with an Argh! I offered to get dog biscuits for the little boy dressed in a furry Dalmatian costume. He shook his head so furiously ears flapped all over his face. Most the kids were shy at first but responded with sing-songy thank-yous after some prompting from parents. I recognized the twins from my floor, two boys, maybe five years old, dressed as Bert and Ernie from *Sesame Street*. Their mom wore a Big Bird costume. I let them choose extra candy from the bowl.

"Did you see that one kid?" Mom asked before the door clicked closed. "A giant yellow chicken!"

I stopped for Chinese on the way home from work on Thursday. Dry-sautéed string beans, two spring rolls, rice, and one Kung Pao chicken. Hung Lo on the corner wasn't great food, but it was cheap and close. It took three minutes to walk back to my apartment with take-out and an hour if they delivered. Don't ask me why.

I ran across the lobby to catch the elevator. The doors were closing. I swung the plastic bag through to trip the sensor, and when the doors parted, I slipped in to find an embarrassed Rachel pressed against the back wall.

"You're pretty fierce with a Hung Lo bag," she said.

"Sorry, but you know how slow this elevator is."

"I was half-hoping the door would close, you'd drop the bag, and I'd get a nice meal in the deal."

"You obviously haven't eaten at Hung Lo's."

She laughed. I hadn't seen her for a while and said as much. She mumbled something about being busy with work.

"Sure," I said. "Work's a bitch."

She agreed that it was, in fact, a bitch, and then we still had a couple more floors to go. By the time I said goodbye and got out on fourteen, the whole elevator reeked of greasy chicken and white rice.

I found Mom sitting in the dark in the kitchen. I flipped the light switch.

"You feeling alright?"

She hardly registered my presence.

"Chinese," I said. "Do you want to try chopsticks tonight?"

No response. I set the table, putting each item down with a deliberate clunk. Plates. Glasses. Knives. Forks. I stuck serving spoons in the paper cartons and called it good.

"Would you like a glass of wine?" I pulled an open bottle of white Zinfandel from the fridge. Mom rarely drank, but I definitely needed something so poured us both glasses. That morning, one of our department heads went to the ER thinking she was having a heart attack. She wasn't, but I spent the rest of the day dealing with the aftermath. Everyone had a story about being worked to death.

"So, how was your day?" I asked Mom.

"Ellen is no Oprah!"

Before I could come up with a proper response to that comment, Mom was explaining the plot of a movie, or maybe it was a documentary, she'd tuned in halfway through so didn't know the title and her storyline recollection was a bit spotty. Mom habitually channel hopped. As far as I knew, she'd never seen any show in its entirety, but that didn't stop her from complaining about the parts she did happen to catch.

"That actor Montgomery Clift," she said. "He played a priest."

Everyone used to say Dad looked like Montgomery Clift—and some whispered that Dad shared the same secret—so I guessed the movie might have left Mom feeling sad. She bit into a spring roll. Grease dribbled down her chin. I wiped my own chin, hoping she'd mimic me. She didn't. Instead, she helped herself to white rice and green beans. She said the priest struggled with his sacred vows, a doctor at a hospital was having an affair with one of his patients, and there was a lot of sparkling jewelry, mostly rubies and sapphires. Mom talked about television the way she watched it, jumping back and forth until my head hurt. I downed my first glass of wine in about ninety seconds.

"Mom," I finally interrupted. "You've got something on your chin."

She swiped at her face with a paper napkin and got up from the table in a huff. Lately, it seemed any little thing might set her off.

"Come on, Mom," I pleaded. "You've hardly touched your dinner."

"You know I don't like chicken!"

She went into the living room, turned on a sitcom, and cranked the volume full blast. There was no point asking her to turn it down. I helped myself to seconds and drank the wine I'd poured for Mom. I could hardly hear myself think through the canned laughter. Everything was hysterically funny until it abruptly wasn't.

I stuck the leftovers in the fridge even though I'd probably throw them out in a couple days. The cellophane-wrapped fortune cookies went into the cupboard with all the others. I loaded the dishwasher. Mom paused on a game show.

I opened another bottle of wine. The first had been half-empty. I sat at the kitchen table and drank the second bottle to the halfway point. I flipped through Mom's Eddie Bauer catalog. Khaki pants never looked that good in real life.

About ten o'clock I found Mom asleep in the recliner, still clutching the television remote. I draped a ratty Afghan over her, one she crocheted back when she still did that sort of thing. The light from the screen softened the lines of her face and she looked almost happy. Then a commercial came on. A mop appeared to be stalking a woman. Mom looked lurid in the light. I reached beneath the blanket, slipped the remote from her hand, and clicked to Off. The only sound was the shuffle of our upstairs neighbor walking slowly across our ceiling.

It snowed the second Saturday of November. I'd been out late the night before and woke to the sight of big flakes falling slowly past my bedroom window. I wrapped the duvet around me like a robe and padded into the kitchen.

The place was a mess. I'd been a last-minute sub at an auction for a charity my boss supposedly supported, but never found time to attend. Mom had spent a rare evening alone. Dirty pots and pans sat on the stove. Her dishes remained on the table. I'd bought frozen meals for Mom but she hated microwaves, said they "made the food radioactive."

I ran some water and left everything to soak. I put a mug in the microwave for tea. When it dinged ready, I stirred in a package of instant cocoa instead.

I found Mom in the living room staring out the window.

"Pretty, huh?" I said.

I held the mug in both hands for warmth even though the thermostat was set at seventy-three since she'd moved in. I took a sip. It tasted of marshmallow-flavored cardboard.

"You sure you don't want any?"

She ignored me. We stood side-by-side watching the dirty gray sins of the world erased by white.

"Flat roofs," Mom said. "They can't handle the weight of all this snow. "

I dumped the hot chocolate into the kitchen sink. The dishwater grew murky. I turned the tap to scalding hot and added lemon-scented dish soap. The window above the kitchen sink steamed over. Condensation formed on Mom's fancy red stemware. I picked up a glass still dripping with bubbles, closed my eyes and tried to imagine the color dancing across my soapy skin.

=◆=

Vivian R. McInerny is a journalist and writer of fiction. Her short stories appear in several publications including *805 Lit+Art*, *Buckman*, *Dunes Review*, and *Locavore Lit LA*, used in the Los Angeles high school curriculum. Houghton Mifflin Harcourt published her first children's book in 2021. She's working on a collection of essays about traveling overland from Europe through Iran, Afghanistan and Pakistan to India at age eighteen.

Fake Meat

Madoka Mori

When it first started he thought it might be Alzheimer's, or the signs of the onset of Alzheimer's.

I'm too young to get Alzheimer's, he told himself. He was thirty-seven. *Is that too young for Alzheimer's?*

He looked it up online, whether thirty-seven was too young for Alzheimer's, and found some sources saying it was, some saying that no, it wasn't. He wondered how to phrase it. Too young *for* Alzheimer's? Too young *to get* Alzheimer's? He was reasonably certain that *catch* Alzheimer's was incorrect; it was not a cold.

It was this uncertainty which led him to wonder about the Alzheimer's in the first place—a lack of confidence in what he was saying, an absence of trust in the very words he used. Did these words mean exactly what he thought they did?

He worked in marketing, and was used to expressing himself fluidly and well. Now he stumbled over words in meetings, stammering as he tried to expand his point. Where he used to be succinct and glib, he was now long-winded and uninspiring.

Was he just getting old?

≡◆≡

He traveled often for work. His company was a major producer of food flavoring chemicals, with branches in every continent except South America. The big topic in flavorings these days was artificial meat and meat-like products: it was shaping up to be a sea change in the way people ate food, and kept him moving from one region to the next to ensure that all elements of the corporation were pushing in the same direction, except when the particular demands and customer demographics of that region meant they must push in a different direction, or push softer in one aspect, or harder in another, or both.

"We have a strong historical tradition in soy," said his counterpart in the Japanese office. "Consumers do not need to be persuaded to accept it here, as in other markets."

"Yes, I know," he replied, blushing furiously, "that's what I'm here for. Why I'm here. To ask you about—about the acceptance of soy. How to replicate it in other markets. Replicate its... acceptance." He had told them that at the start of the meeting. In his introduction. Hadn't he? They were already forty minutes into the meeting. What had they thought he was talking about?

The meeting seemed a disaster, and he the cause of the disaster, but the follow-up email chain from the Japanese marketing department expressed gratitude and enthusiasm. Or at least, he thought it did.

≡◆≡

He wasn't sure what emails meant anymore. He read and re-read the text of emails from his manager and colleagues, trying to glean points of hard information, but the more closely he read the emails the less sense they made to him. Each word was one he knew, or thought he knew, but when assembled into the specific context of their origin sentence their meaning became shaky, like a wall of ill-fitting bricks. He felt that if he could just find one sentence that gave absolute, concrete information then it would provide context for the sentences immediately around it, which would then pass on their context outwards in a ripple effect and the wall of ill-fitting bricks would shift, all falling into place, having only needed a tiny nudge. He combed through the emails, out of frustration looking up each word in the email in turn, but they refused to solidify into anything objective. It was like navigating in heavy fog.

—◆—

He was terrified of his confusion being discovered. Terrified. At any point, he felt, someone would rise up in a meeting in Singapore, in Frankfurt, in San Diego, and say: "You don't know what you're talking about." Someone in an email chain with the C-suite cc'd would ask a question point-blank to which he had no answer; or worse, one where he could not even parse the meaning of the question. He would be fired, he was sure of it. He would have to confess to his slipping grasp on speech, and would be forced to the doctor, where he would be diagnosed with Alzheimer's, or a brain tumor, or dementia.

Unable to ask for clarification directly (and anyway unsure of being able to word such a request correctly), he instead sent vague reports of success and yet-vaguer requests for feedback and clarification. He combed through previous emails that he had sent, emails to previous colleagues in previous projects, copy-pasting fragments into something he hoped resembled sense.

The replies were blandly encouraging, and devoid of meaning.

—◆—

Life followed a pattern, which pulled him along without his permission or input. An itinerary would be sent to his company email account with a flight number and the name of a hotel. He would take a taxi to the airport at the given time and board the plane. On the plane he would sleep and eat unmoored from normal timekeeping. Breakfast as the sun burned hotly through the porthole window. Lunch while looking out at the twinkling lights of a nameless city at night far below. He ate and slept, slept and ate, and woke without knowing how much time had passed while he was asleep, or how much was left until arrival. Did it matter?

Arrival in the destination airport was a coin-toss. Customs and Immigration (sometimes there was Immigration, sometimes not; he was never sure which it would be until he arrived) would often just require him to hand over his little sheaf of travel documents and stand there quietly. But occasionally they would ask him questions.

"Business trip," he would say lamely, gesturing at his documents spread out on the counter in front of him. Their words slid around him like a shoal of quicksilver fish around a diver. He examined their faces: bored and annoyed, mostly. If more bored, he would get his passport and itinerary pushed back into his hands with a roll of eyes; if more angry, then he would be forced to explain himself and his purpose more.

"Business trip, a meeting," he said, close to tears. He tapped on the itinerary where it lay in front of the immigration officer, "my hotel."

From the airport, a taxi to the hotel. He stumbled when speaking to taxi drivers. He had entered a taxi a few weeks ago (or was it a few months ago?) and had gotten stuck trying to tell the driver the destination hotel. He tried his smattering of Spanish, of French. The driver jabbered at him in return, until—giving up on niceties—he had thrust the print-out at the driver, pointing to the name of the hotel. The taxi driver nodded brusquely, muttering under his breath. As they drove, he recognized the buildings. He was in London, and the driver had been speaking English.

Since then he stopped talking to the taxi drivers altogether. The night before departing his hotel he prepared six copies of his itinerary in six transparent plastic loose-leaf folders. One for each taxi between hotel and airport, one for checking in to his flight, one each for customs and possible Immigration in the arrival airport, and one for the front desk clerk when he checked in to the next hotel. He found that if you walked up to the person with confident body language but an apologetic face and handed them the folder, then they would ask few to no questions and simply go about the task of helping him move from one stage of his journey to the next. He was surprised at how grateful he felt to be spared this minimal amount of human interaction. He slid through the world with increasingly less friction.

=♦=

He tried bringing the same strategy to his work. He started meetings by writing vague platitudes on the whiteboard and then gesturing for discussion. *Demographic Limitation* he wrote in one meeting, *Externalize / Glean* in another. He slashed the board into quadrants and then let the meeting run its course. If he was asked a question he would stare out of the window, a pantomime of pensiveness and deep thought. Usually the room could only hold this silence for a few seconds before someone else would suggest an answer on his behalf, to which he would nod sagely, and the meeting would continue. He felt that he was getting strange looks. He felt that there were awkward pauses.

But he could no longer tell for sure.

=♦=

It was after one such meeting in Cape Town, or Vancouver, or Hong Kong, and he was in his hotel room. The television was on. Blobs of color moved about on the screen, there was music or maybe laughing. He was sitting on the bed with his laptop on his knees, scouring his email inbox for sentences to copy-paste into a report for his manager when the phone rang. He froze. People didn't call him in hotel rooms, ever. They sent emails.

Perhaps it was a mistake. He waited, barely breathing, until it stopped ringing. Then he took the receiver off the cradle.

After an indeterminate time there was a knock at the door. He held very still, and wished that the television was off. If the television were off then he could pretend not to be here. The knock came again, with a voice attached to it. Was it saying his name?

He opened the door to find a person in hotel uniform. It was a man, he thought. Words tumbled from the uniformed figure, too fast to parse. He thought his name was among them.

"No thank you," he said to the hotel uniform. He made what he hoped was an apologetic face. "No, thank you." He made to close the door, but the uniform rested a hand flat on its surface—the door's—to prevent him from doing so. More words. He thought among them was *check out*.

He was sweating now, clammy moisture sticking his shirt to his back. He had not received his itinerary yet. Or had he? Was he supposed to leave? He longed for a print-out of his itinerary to press into the man's hands, or perhaps it was a woman. They were standing in the doorway, looking at him. Their expression was impossible to read. They spoke again, softer now. It felt like it was a question.

If he could check his laptop then maybe there was a new itinerary there. He could make print-outs of it and this problem would be fixed, or at least this interaction would be over. But he didn't think there was an itinerary, or he would have seen it. Or maybe he no longer recognized them, the itineraries, when they arrived in his inbox.

The person in the door spoke again; more questions perhaps. They could be asking for his name, or his itinerary, or where he was going next but it did not matter for the man was not sure that he knew.

—⟫◆⟪—

Madoka Mori grew up in Singapore, South Africa, and the UK, which is pretty wild when you think about it. Having received her degree in Comparative Literature quite a while ago, she is relieved to finally put it to some sort of vague use by writing fiction. She enjoys reading, cooking, and going for walks—causing frequent comparison to hobbits—and dislikes corporate culture, packs of suspect youths, and talking about herself in the third person.

The Kneeler

George Murray

10:30 p.m. and James Morse is at the bar of the Mohegan Sun Resort and Casino, sipping a glass of scotch that would have been far too expensive for him even if he wasn't $200,000 in debt. That's no problem, though. The debt was from out west, built up on the Strip at Vegas and then, when Vegas got too expensive, Reno. Now he is back east, casting bets at Reservation casinos under the name "Morton Quailey." His bookies gave up chasing him months ago. Last time they got close was at the Kansas Star Casino in Mulvane, where James had paid off the valet to send them after the wrong car. The time before that was in a speakeasy in Billings, Montana, where James had paid an unsuspecting rube half a grand to swap clothes with him. Before that, Salt Lake City, where James had mussed up his hair and convinced a cop that the guys after him were muggers. That one wasn't even a lie.

A lesser man might have given up by now, thanked his good luck for leaving him with two good knees and a skull unmarred by bullet holes before settling down and getting a real job with a new identity. James is not a lesser man. What's the point of being $200,000 in debt if you're not going to have fun with it?

James has his chair turned so his back faces the bar, and he watches the stage with amusement as a blacked-out college kid stumbles through an off-key rendition of "September" by Earth, Wind & Fire. He is singing at a faster tempo than the karaoke machine, so every line or so he has to pause to wait for the lyrics to pop up. When he whines out the final "ba-dee-ya", the crowd applauds, led by the singer's cadre of frat brother friends.

The college kid stumbles off stage and is replaced by a middle-aged woman and "We Didn't Start the Fire." James watches the kid join his friends and thinks back to when he was that age, training as an opera singer in Vanderbilt. He and his friends would go out to The Maple Bar on Thursday nights when they had the karaoke machine up. James would get a shot of whiskey—later two shots, by senior year he needed four—to get a good buzz going, and then he would saunter up to the stage and bring the house down with a performance of "My Way" that put Sinatra to shame. Brian Martino, his roommate, hated it. "It's a dirge," he would say. "You destroy the mood every time you sing that." James would retort by saying that hey, tell that to the old guys that buy me drinks after I sing, but secretly Brian's words confused him. To him, "My Way" wasn't a dirge, it was triumphant, a statement of victory.

Brian had followed James to Vegas, where they tried to find work as in-house performers. Brian's career worked out; three years out of college he was hired by Caesar's Palace. As far as James knew, he was still there.

By the time James lifts himself from his thoughts he realizes that he has gone up to the guy manning the karaoke machine and put his fake name and "My Way" in the queue. He has a moment of doubt—he hasn't sung in years. He doesn't even know if he's still good at it. He is about to go back and tell the karaoke man that he changed his mind, when he notices that someone is sitting next to his empty stool, staring at him with a friendly grin.

"Hey, James."

"Brian? Holy shit."

Brian stands and they exchange a curt, manly hug. James calls the bartender and orders drinks for the two of them, on his tab.

"Let me cover them."

"No chance. Put that wallet away."

Brian does as he's told and the two sit back down at the bar. It's been ten years, but Brian looks like he hasn't aged a day. James tells him so and Brian laughs.

"So how's Caesar's Palace treating you?"

"Haven't worked there in years."

"You're kidding."

"Nope. Lost my voice for a few days, by the time I got better they had replaced me."

The bartender slides them their drinks. James takes a long swig of his scotch, swirls it in his mouth and swallows. Brian does not touch his.

"So how have you been doing? Still with Carrie?"

The whiskey leaves a comfortable burn as it slides down James' gullet and he considers telling the truth, but at the last moment it gets stuck in his throat and he says,

"Yeah, we got hitched a few years back, we have a nice place in Boston. You should come by."

"Does she know you're here?"

"Of course." James realizes too late that he doesn't have a wedding ring. He prays that Brian won't notice.

"You're a lucky guy, James."

"It's my greatest skill." James finishes his scotch and calls for another.

"Come on, let me get the next round." Brian has not touched his first.

"No chance."

"Come on, man. You know you can't afford it."

James freezes in place. For a moment he is a cornered animal, a fox that wakes up to find its den surrounded by hounds. He considers his options for a fraction of a second. "Course I can afford it," he says.

"No you can't." Brian's face is contorted into a mask of concern, but one glance into his eyes shows James that there's nothing there. "Not unless you also have three hundred grand for me right now."

The bartender brings James his scotch, but James doesn't touch it. "So you're working for Lewis now?"

Brian shrugs. "Lewis. Friends of Lewis. You owe a lot of people a lot of money."

Without warning James' shock is replaced by raw, angry grief, eating at his lungs and bubbling up his throat, like all the scotch he drank tonight and last night and every night since college had been waiting in his gut to seize control of his body and go fucking apeshit on every aspect of his life. He looks over his old friend and he wants nothing more than to grab him by the neck and choke the life out of him, to beat his head against the hardwood bar until there's nothing on the end of his traitor neck but a slow ooze of brain and viscera.

"Fuck you," he says instead.

"I'm sorry, James. It's nothing personal." For the first time that night, Brian takes a sip of his drink. "I wish I was still singing at Caesar's. But I gotta pay the bills somehow."

The rational part of James' brain has now squeezed in to share the stage with the enraged beast and his eyes are darting around the bar, casing out the exits. The main entrance from the bar to the casino looks open—no, in a corner, staring at him, is a man he recognizes from Montana. The emergency exit is covered by a tall, bony woman that James had a run-in with in Utah.

"I've got guys all through this casino." Brian was following his gaze. "You're not making it out this time."

"I don't owe 300 grand. I owe 200." James' eyes continue to dart around the room, the wheels in his brain working overtime.

Brian sighs, takes another drink. "After the amount of shit you've pulled? I had to talk them down from ordering a hit on you right off."

James says nothing. Now his eyes are fixed on the stage. There's a girl from the college group up there now, absolutely ruining some pop song that he is too old to know the name of.

"Listen, I can maybe spot you 50k if that would help. I don't want this to end in blood, James."

James is no longer listening to Brian. He is listening to the karaoke girl trail off into nothingness, walk off the stage as her friends applaud, the attendant looking at his list, reading it, putting the microphone to his lips and calling—

"Morton Quailey? 'My Way?'"

Never bet against James Morse.

James gives a sparkling grin to Brian, downs his scotch in one go, and walks up to the stage. The vengeful beast that moments ago wanted to turn his friend into a bloodstain now leaps with joy when it hears Brian's incredulous voice behind him say, "No fucking way."

The stage is a proscenium. Garish red curtains hang behind there, presumably to hide a small backstage area with its own exit, leading to the maze of service corridors that keep the casino running. Judging by Brian's reaction, he did not think to put anyone there. James just needs to pull the curtain back, go through the door, and once again run to freedom.

James hops onto the stage, taking the microphone from the karaoke guy. He looks to the audience—big grin, wink at Brian, give a flirty glance to one of the college girls—and then he turns and pulls the curtain back and —

There's nothing there. Concrete brick. No door. Just a curtain and a slab of gray. James' mind goes back into overdrive. Where to go from here? Are there vents? No, that's a ridiculous idea. Maybe he can lose Brian in the bathroom, or maybe he could pay him off, or—

"My Way" begins playing and, almost without thinking, James slides into the first verse, starting out soft and casual just like he did in college. He sings of dying, but the twinkle in his eyes and the humor in his voice tells the audience that this is a joke, a spot of irony, that there is no final curtain, that there never will be a final curtain for James Morse. As he sings he relaxes. He will get out of this. He has a whole song before him during which he can dream up an escape. Brian and his thugs are ants, and right now James Morse is a god. He finishes out the verse in a proud, caramelly drawl, sending the titular lyrics floating down into the bar, through the drunk college kids and drug-addled gamblers and right in front of the stony face of Brian Martino.

The final note of the first verse fades away and James immediately springs into the second, letting the energy fade into almost nothing before bringing it crashing back at full force. *Regrets*, he sings, and then he is thinking of Carrie and his mouth and throat and lungs go on autopilot as his consciousness is shunted away from the stage.

He is thinking of Carrie on the night they met at the Maple Bar. He is remembering her staring at him as he tears up the karaoke stage, catching her eye and thinking that he was young and drunk and that so was she probably, and he is remembering the sex that night, her moaning and him coming on her stomach and then he is remembering six months later when he eavesdropped on her telling a friend that she faked it more often than not, and he walked away and pretended that he had heard nothing.

He is thinking of Carrie when he asked her to be his girlfriend, a month or so after they first hooked up. They are sitting on a picnic blanket at a park looking over the Nashville skyline with a charcuterie board that she made and a bottle of wine that he bought and James has never felt this way before. He's had girlfriends, sure, but Carrie is unlike any woman he has ever met. He does not feel like he has to prove anything to her or do anything to earn her affection. Being with her is easy, stressless, placid.

He is thinking of Carrie when she found out that he had cheated on her, after they had graduated and she was in LA and he was in Vegas. He is at her apartment and she is crying and yelling at him to talk to her but he does not say a word. He does not know how many women she knows about and is afraid he will give away too much information.

He is thinking of Carrie the last time he saw her, at a casino bar with a group of friends in Reno. He stares at her but does not approach, hoping she will catch his eye and take the initiative. She sees him, and, for a moment, he glimpses the same raw sadness that he saw the night they broke up, and then it is gone and she looks at him like a stranger. He has tried to convince himself that it was not her, just someone who looked like her, but he is unsuccessful. He knows it does not matter either way.

James realizes that he has blown right through into the third verse. He is belting now, flooding the room with mournful sound, the very doubt that he eschews in the song poking through and casting its terrible glow upon the audience.

He draws back for the fourth verse, returning to himself and his current predicament. He paces the stage looking around for a clear exit, mind racing from one option to another and each time coming up blank. James is not a violent man, but he's been in a fight or two and now he is thinking that violence might be the only way out. Brian probably has a gun on him; if James gets the drop he can probably wrestle it away and kill him. But then there are Brian's friends, all throughout the hotel if he is to be believed. It's a long shot, but if James plays it slow he could feasibly get them all. He knows the casino better than they do. But even if he pulled that off he'd be at best on the run from the law and at worst shot dead by them. But maybe it didn't have to come to that. Brian would take him to a second location; he wouldn't shoot him on the casino floor. There would be less witnesses there, and James would have a better chance of making his way out.

His thought process is obliterated by the beginning of the final verse, the words exploding out of his mind and into his mouth before he can even read them on the karaoke machine. That would have to be it, then. Resign himself to death and then at the last moment surprise the bad guys and go somewhere far away, north to Canada maybe. Or south to Florida. Maybe he would call Carrie, and maybe he would beg for her to meet with him, and maybe he would prove to her that he had changed, that he could change.

James is sweating through his shirt. His hair is growing unkempt, a strand of it hanging down over his eyes. He is barely singing anymore, it is something deeper and louder and more primal, blasting the lyrics into the bar, each one with the force of an atom bomb. He locks eyes with Brian and for a moment he thinks he sees tears in his friend's eyes.

He holds the final note for longer than he is supposed to, ending only when the instrumentals do. The room is stunned into silence. The college group looks up at him in awe. An old woman has tears in her eyes. James Morse sucks in a breath but it catches in his throat, like the whiskey he drank earlier is fighting the oxygen for space.

The room erupts into applause, blasting back at James all at once the energy he had projected into it. The karaoke man's jaw hangs slack as he slaps his hands together. James smiles, the corners of his lips shaking with nerves. Maybe he can cut a deal, work here as a singer and pay off his debt incrementally. The last twenty years can be wiped clean and he can finally do what he was born for.

He takes another breath and again it seizes up in his throat. He coughs, and red phlegm splatters the stage below him. He suddenly becomes aware of a horrible pain in his chest, working its way through his blood.

James looks across the room at Brian, but his old friend is no longer sitting by the bar. James tries to think but he can't. His brain has become a slow fog, every impulse more complex than raw feeling stuck like a wagon in the snow. He pushes back at it, once, twice, but each time he grows weaker. He surrenders. The grief and regret and pride and scheming ended with the last haunting note of the song and as James Morse falls to his knees he feels nothing but the unyielding applause of the audience and thinks of nothing but the bright blinding white of the abyss and remembers nothing but the stage.

—◆—

George Murray was born and raised in Connecticut before heading off to Ithaca College in Ithaca, New York. After graduating in 2020 he moved to Maine, and then later to Los Angeles where he currently resides. George spends much of his free time reading, playing video games, and going on walks. He has a lifelong passion for writing, in particular short stories about deeply flawed individuals. "The Kneeler" is George's first published work, but you can also find him online as the host of *The Content Button* comedy podcast, where he and his friends lampoon popular television shows.

Chop Chop

A. J. Nelson

The knives need sharpening. The entrails of the first tomato squelch, spread across the cutting board, watery carotene phlegm on golden olivewood. I watch the skin stretch and tear, fantasize about a neat, deep cut.

It's Sarah's job to sharpen the knives. It's Sarah's job to do everything in the kitchen. Most nights I'm only allowed to do the washing up, and even that will be subject to final judgment. There's oil on the Le Creuset. Water spots on her beautiful knives.

But tonight, Sarah can barely manage to open the second bottle of Pinot. "More?"

As if she needs to ask. I shrug, watch the bottle tremble as she fills my glass, biting her violet-stained lips. Her chin quivers, transforms into a walnut. She turns her back, sinks into the sofa.

I attack the tomatoes. Carnage all across her spotless marble countertops. Next comes the zucchini, little half-moons of queasy green flesh. I can barely bring myself to lift the aubergine. Something about its shape, that firm bruised skin. I find myself stroking it, nursing my cold fingers along the swell of it, the way Audrey used to run her hands over the soft swell of her belly. I fucking hated that. The way she'd sit on our sofa next to Sarah and stroke herself with that far-off smile. The way Sarah would hold her hand, watch her expand, like she wanted to eat her up raw. Like she'd starve if she had to wait another four months. In those moments I hated them both.

"We'll try again." Sarah's voice floats over the arm of the couch, knocks against the back of my skull.

Like hell we will, I tell the spaghetti as I break their spines over the boiling water.

Chop

Dull knives are far more dangerous than sharp ones. Ask any medical professional. You're much more likely to take off a finger with a dull knife, with all that pressure behind it. And dull is definitely what we've become. Just try cutting through all that grief with a blunt instrument. It's no good.

And suddenly, neither am I.

I keep having the same nightmare. I'm an improbable child in white knee socks and saddle oxfords. I've swallowed all the seeds of an apple, on a dare. Sarah lurks over me, the resentful babysitter. Tells me I'll be growing an apple tree in my belly. I don't want to believe her. I laugh at her until she cries. But I'm nervous, shaken. Late at night, on my back in bed, I feel the first branches pushing out against my distended skin, like wings unfolding. The dream always ends when I reach down to finger the first sharp green shoot poking through my bellybutton.

Sarah wanted it more than anything. Which meant we both needed the woman it was growing in. I vow never to eat another apple. Fruit of the womb, indeed. The surrogate giveth, and the surrogate taketh away.

Chop

She shouldn't have. That much was clear almost immediately. Uterus for hire.

Audrey had to pay for her university place. Working two jobs was one option. The fetus was another. She would carry it for Dr. Sarah Langham, the maternal Cultural Studies tutor with the unviable eggs. The oldest exchange: flesh for money. Except Sarah kept calling it a baby.

Audrey could taste it. A carefree university life, like her friends whose parents were paying. And she could tell herself it was a good deed. Like the Virgin. Cross my heart, it was a miracle.

Loss of control can be liberating. Sarah told her what to eat, cooked and measured, bought pregnancy pillows and vitamins, drove her to endless appointments, held her hand and stroked her shoulder. But the first time Audrey heard that tiny heartbeat, it felt like drums in the distance. Coming for her.

She asks a lawyer, an old family friend. What would it take? He used to grin, run his eyes up and down her body. Now he looks at her belly as if he's afraid she might explode. He tells her she'd be well within her rights to keep it. Says it through his bifocals while he studies the papers on his desk.

Audrey sees Dr. Langham on campus looking sick thin. But Sarah manages to smile and wave. Relieved, Audrey waves back. Tries to shield her nightshade belly from that hungry gaze.

Chop

The pool lies like a jewel in the basement of the gym around the corner. Sharp chlorine aquamarine. It laps at the edges of my sleep. I wake in the dark, sure I can hear the slap of water, feel the currents I create caressing my limbs. I go early, when it's quiet. Sometimes it's just me and my childhood nightmares of a shark knifing the lanes. My arms slice the crisp water like fins, blood thumps in my ears. Feeling flees from my lungs, bubbles into stillness. Not grief, not even relief. Pushing off the edge, it's anger that rushes down my thinning thighs, along my tight calves, out through my toes. I leave it streaming behind me. A predatory scent.

Five days a week I sweat into the cold clear water, spit chlorine under the tepid shower. Lose ounces and inches. A pound of flesh to the circling sharks of my imagination.

I cook for Sarah, but she won't eat. Pressed up against Audrey's ripening belly, which Instagram documents for us on an hourly basis, Sarah caves in on herself. She perches on a stool at the kitchen island, jeans loose around her hips, her bony crack peeking above the belt loops. I know she's hungry, because I am too. An empty belly I can't fill with food.

We've forgotten how to forget. Social media makes forgiveness impossible. Sarah stores her winter sweaters in our unused oven. She sits in the kitchen, submerged in the underwater glow of her laptop screen. Outside the French doors, the moon washes our tiny overgrown garden in truer, bluer light.

I snap bitter celery, crunch sweet carrots dotted with garlic hummus, pop naked cherry tomatoes. Roll them inside my cheek, crush them between my molars, their juices sluicing my tongue. I gnash a round of eggplant, the purple blades of skin slicing between my teeth. It's all I can feel now. It comforts.

Eggplant is a nightshade. Cooking neutralizes the poison. Sound advice is, never eat it raw. Especially if you're pregnant.

A red rash sprouts between my spreading shoulders, creeps up over my collarbone, vining around my neck. Soon it will reach my chin, my cheeks. Soon.

Chop

I swim. Sarah scrolls. Weeks stand up and stretch into months. I eat my food raw. Sarah drinks. I worry that the baby she can't bear is eating her from the inside.

In the end, it's Facebook that undoes us. Red alerts grab her by the chin and permanently shift her gaze.

"It's happened," she informs me solemnly. I don't ask what.

"He's here." I don't ask who.

Grief has a smell. Nobody tells us that. Some combination of raw cabbage and sliced bird's eye chilis. All crunch and heat and bitterness. Sarah's unwashed body is a daily reminder of my failure to feel it. To feed us.

I slice all the eggplant. I eat the chunks raw. I incubate.

Chop

Late one night, I shiver on the doorstep, my fist around the doorknob. Creeping over our threshold, the smell of butter and rosemary ambushes me. I track it down the hall, around the corner. There's a memory standing before the stove.

Ziggurats of chopped eggplant, blood-red sauce bubbling, raw meat browning in buttery spice. Round red iron pan, an Olympus of shredded cheese. Moussaka.

I force my feet to move, wrap my arm around Sarah's tiny waist.

"You're making dinner?" I try not to sound incredulous.

The bottle of wine next to the stove is nearly empty. When she smiles, her teeth are bruised.

"Would you open another bottle while I finish this?"

I try making small talk at the table. Except I'm the only one eating. Sarah's squirming. I finally ask what.

"We can take it to court." It dawns on me that what I'd taken for a turn was just another loop in the spiral. "It's not about the money," she tells me.

As if I thought it was.

"We'll sue!" she steams.

I inhale, hold in the sigh. "And then what?"

She stabs the table with her butter knife. "We signed a contract!"

"It's unenforceable. You know that. The lawyer told us. No judge is going to make a woman give up her baby because she signed a contract."

"He's not her baby!" Her mouth wide, spitting. Like the Red Queen shouting, "Off with her head!"

Sarah refills her glass, sloshes. She doesn't bother to wipe up. I go in search of a sponge.

Chop

The headaches come first. Nightshade poisoning. I've googled all the symptoms. Nausea comes next. I welcome the waves, stomach clenching, cramps tightening and releasing like a slow-beating heart. This is what it should feel like. Growth. Hatching.

The rash creeps up, lines my chin like stubble.

One frigid morning, I find her in the kitchen, hunched over the sink, shedding tears over a blueberry.

She'd been washing a whole basket when one escaped. Floating in the murky water soaking yesterday's cereal bowls, it looks like Mother Earth suspended in space.

I offer to fish it out, wash it off. No, she sobs. No. She doesn't want to eat the blueberry.

Then what?

"It's just so sad! Like it missed its whole purpose in life."

I don't ask what a blueberry's purpose in life could possibly be. She keeps weeping. I empty the bowl. We watch the berry swirl down the drain, a misty blue jewel in the desolate darkness.

Chop

Once the thought is planted, it grows a taproot.

Deadly nightshade. We'd spotted it in our tangled

garden last summer. At the beginning. When we were happily babyproofing. Sarah wanted to pull it out immediately. I told her we still had time.

The blossoms are so beautifully fragile. The berries mimic blueberries. Its other name: Bittersweet.

I try one berry first. Nothing. Reckless, I up the dosage to five. A little nausea, nothing I can't stomach. I chew my eggplant prophylactic. I think it's time.

Our anniversary. I plan a red carpet meal. Bitter endive stuffed with luscious goat's cheese and golden honey. Wilted spinach salad with sweet-crunch pecans and sour-soft cranberries. Thick spiced pumpkin soup. Duck dripping from the bone, begging to be devoured. This is her chance.

I eat. Sarah drinks.

And then there's the cake. Her favorite. A simple blueberry lemon, sugar snow-dusted, like the frost-spangled garden outside our starved windows.

I plead. Just one piece. I've given up so much time, and she's hardly enjoyed any of it. It's important to me. It'll all be over soon. Please.

She bites. And bites again. The slice disappears. I'd counted as I cut. Eighteen berries. Enough.

The side effects of nightshade poisoning are not so different from drunkenness. Cotton mouth. Poor coordination. Spiked temperature. Dilated pupils. Drowsiness. Blessed numbness. She won't realize until it's too late.

I watch her pale face, her hazelnut mouth. I wait.

She sees me. I see her see me.

I'm not sure I like what she sees.

Chop

I step out into the garden with the rest of the bottle of Barolo. I don't bother with a glass.

The Bittersweet is gone. I took care of that this morning. Even the soil it corrupted is carefully raked. Eventually the grass grows over everything. All that's left is a ripple in the earth. A silver stretch mark.

I take a deep swimmer's breath. The red rash noose around my neck loosens.

I sink into the icy bench. Take another stinging breath. The cold reaches famished fingers into my ears and squeezes.

I'll clean up the kitchen tomorrow.

Chop Chop

=◆=

Alissa Jones Nelson grew up in Southern California and has since lived in Spain, the Czech Republic, Japan, Scotland, and Germany. Her first (unpublished) novel was shortlisted for the Dundee International Book Prize. Her short story "Al-Watan" was highly commended in the 2019 Bridport Prize, and "Elsewhere, OK" was a runner-up for the 2017 Berlin Writing Prize. Her work has appeared in the anthologies *Home Is Elsewhere*, *27 Stories*, and the *Bridport Prize 2019 Anthology*. She lives in Berlin, where she earns her living as an editor and translator.

The Ghosts in West Texas

Andie Ngeleka

Donnie always thought her mother's house was haunted. Not because she ever saw ghosts in the white lace curtains on her window, the small one with the wooden frame that looked out at barren land. One night after finding bliss between the gentle opening of someone else's lips, she came home and dug through drawers for a whittling knife. She found one and engraved the initials of a face that morphed slowly, and bitterly from lover to stranger. But that wasn't the kind of ghost she thought lured in the halls of her childhood home.

When Donnie and Shelly get to the cabin in Terlingua, their sweat is dry on the back of their necks. They get out of the baby blue truck that used to belong to Donnie's mother, carrying a duffle bag each. Donnie takes off her cowboy hat and holds it to her chest as Shelly looks at the crumbling white walls of the house, the vexing sound of the precarious swinging front door echoing over their bodies. A narrow dirt path leads to cracked front steps at the foot of the door. This is supposed to be where they feel safe, in this giant coffin shaped to look like a house. They walk in; Shelly holding on tightly to a leather jacket that had sat heating up in the back of Donnie's truck as they drove up.

Inside the little house there is a small bed with a stool next to it. On the opposite corner of the room there's a disintegrating pile of books. Dust covers the floor, enough dust that it can only barely be called dust as opposed to dirt. The shelves are empty, the doorknobs don't work, the windows have broken glass. Shelly drops her bag at her feet and walks towards the bed. She puts down the jacket and kneels down. She reaches under the bed and pulls out an old wooden box that appears to be in the same condition as the house. Donnie walks towards her and they sit on the raggedy bed, both sinking more than they expected to.

"My daddy ain't always have good to say about my mama," Shelly whispered. "He ain't ever really talk about her nothin', but he told me a story."

Caroline Freeman was named after the state where her parents met. Nevermind that it was the first state to secede over their right to coax agency out of her body with liberty. She never wanted no kids nor no husband. By the time she understood the world enough to understand the function of both, she had been orphaned for five years. She was raised for her first decade by the same woman who raised her mama, the woman who had no patience for ugliness that she said lived in things like the darkness of Caroline's skin. The same woman who had taken care of a host of husbands and children, tended to other people's wounds while neglecting her own. When she died, no one was there but Caroline. Everyone had either been kidnapped or was long dead. Caroline called her grandmother mama, in fact she is sure she never knew her actual name as a child. After her funeral, Caroline decided she didn't have any interest in the business of taking care of others. All she wanted was a house. A house that she owned with white walls and enough room to do anything. She needed only a bed for one and something to put her reading glasses on at night. She knew she wouldn't have the need for things like loneliness and vanity. She went to west Texas because she heard about a ghost town with a population of less than one hundred people. When she got there, she got held up in Plainview because she needed money. She became one of Mama Jackie's girls and used to hang out outside The Rustwater Saloon waiting for anyone to pay her mind. She would sit under the shade of the awning, barefoot, her skin black like vanilla, not at all fighting with the sun. She by that time had realized that certain men had a taste for vanilla. And she enjoyed being desired, but never being held. That's when she met Shelly's father.

"He said that," Shelly continued, Donnie moving closer next to her. "He said, 'I knew the second I saw your mama that she would make me crazy. And she did. But I made her crazy too.'" Donnie's hand holds on to Shelly's right thigh as she speaks. "He said that after she had me there was no stopping her from getting to Terlingua. That she dreamed out loud about getting a house so far away from everybody that even the echo of a gunshot wouldn't wake up nobody. When my daddy brought me up here to see her before we went to San Francisco, she shot at us and said 'I ain't a good shot and I ain't trying to kill y'all, but if I do, ain't no one coming to get you.'"

Shelly opens the box in her lap and inside there's a small pistol with a white pearl handle. Donnie watches Shelly as she stares at the gun in the box—her eyes fixed, her hands tightly pulling at the edges. Donnie stands up. Shelly doesn't move. Donnie puts her hat on and walks out of the house. Shelly, still looking down at the box, now has cold, damp cheeks.

Donnie walks out of the house and sits down on the front steps. She looks out at all the brown and beige in the distance. Smaller, similar houses trail scarcely down the desolate hill. The wind picks things up from between grains of dust on the ground and leaves them at other people's homes. Donnie closes her eyes. She tips her hat down until the wind stops. Shelly walks up from behind her and sits down on the steps next to Donnie.

"Why we here?" Donnie asks. Shelly looks at her for a moment under the shadow of her hat. Her lips are glossy in the light of the sun just above her. Her eyes are invisible. Shelly looks for them, but they've been hiding from her since her half-brother bruised Donnie's arm in that bar the night they decided to stay in Plainview. That was also the night they left. Last night.

Donnie came from a long line of cowboys. Her great-granddaddy Al was a cowboy who moved cattle from Kansas to California. On one of his trips he met a woman named Camille who wrote him poems on the back of torn off posters and married her within a week. They made Donnie's grandmama Sherry that week too.

Al was on his way from Kansas City to San Diego when he got kidnapped and lynched. Camille heard the news when the rest of the cowboys, the ones that managed to escape, got to Texas with the cattle. All they could give her was his horse.

Camille had always considered herself lucky. Her mother had abandoned her with Apaches further out west, while being hunted, so she never knew the sorrow of the plantations which bore her existence. She found a husband, one that she liked and only put his hands on her with a most ardent tenderness, when she was just eighteen. They even got a homestead in Plainview. The only niggers in west Texas that did. But there she was with nothing but a horse and crying toddler. She sold the horse and married one of the other cowboys that wanted to stay in Texas. She raised Sherry up to marry a cowboy too. They had a boy and a girl. The boy died and the girl raised his daughter Donnie, who called her mama. Sherry lived with them while Donnie was a toddler until she got sick. Donnie only remembers her alive because it's easier to repress frightening memories. She spent hours sitting by the kitchen window, her back against the quiet hum of the fridge. Donnie would often curl up in her lap and stare too, but all she saw was a vast emptiness. She would look up at her grandmother's face and not recognize the expression of someone obviously seeing beyond red rocks, dry trees and dusty tin roofs.

"There ain't just dust out there, Donnie," Sherry would say. "If you look close enough you can see faces framed by dark hair and pierced by sunken eyes. There's ghosts walking among us, and we don't even pay them no mind."

Donnie never pretended to understand what Sherry meant. At least as a child. As she stood there in Terlingua watching Shelly cry over a gun, she was sure she knew what kinds of ghosts her mother's house was filled with. Ghosts with gunshot wounds that perforated their torso, cut off heads in mass shallow graves, dismembered arms, defeated souls. All their skin had turned into the brown sand that covered the Texas plains. Their hair can be felt in the softness of a patch of grass under the shade of a giant boulder. Their hands erupt from the ground and hold out branches. But those are the ghosts that haunt the land, they are the guilty imagination of the colonizer. The ghosts people yearn for, the ones they look for in fading pictures and broken necklace clasps, they're harder to find.

"Why we here?" Donnie asks again. She stands up and looks down at where Shelly's sitting, refusing to acknowledge her pleading eyes, she averts her gaze. She puts her boot on the step next to Shelly. She leans forward and then back again. "Why'd we come here?" she says.

"I don't know," Shelly says. She looks back at the swinging door. "Maybe I was hoping I'd see a ghost."

After all the heavy weaponized memories settle down, Shelly and Donnie sit in the bed of the truck. The sun as it comes down takes with it the misery of the day. Shelly's head is in Donnie's lap and she looks up at her face under that hat, a cloudless blue sky standing against her. Shelly squints at the sun in her eyes and Donnie moves closer to her so they can share the shadow of her hat. Shelly burrows herself deeper into Donnie, her arms now around her torso, her head on Donnie's chest. Donnie's hand moves up from the tips of Shelly's fingers, stopping briefly at her wrists, to her neck. She moves her fingers lightly above Shelly's skin, pressing her thumb down gently on her moles.

"The first girl I ever kissed was the only one that ever broke my heart," Donnie said. "She kissed me the same night she kissed a boy in our class, at a school dance. Only I ain't find out until the next Monday. And by that time, I done already carved her initials under my window sill. I never had the heart to sand it even though I was so mad. Anytime I felt lonely I'd sit by the window and trace her initials with my fingers, over and over and over. I ain't sure what I was looking for, I do know I ain't never found it. But I suppose it's the same thing you was looking for in that box."

Later on that day Donnie would leave for an hour to get sustenance, during which Shelly would sit by herself next to the pile of books in the house, realizing that they were quite valuable. Her half brother Darius, who she had only met that week when she got to Plainview, would drive his beat-up Cadillac up to Terlingua just as she found a first edition copy of *Their Eyes Were Watching God* in her mother's dusty collection. He was there at the reading of Caroline's will and he sneered at Shelly as she got the keys to the house. Darius had a white father but that's about all anyone knew about him. He spent his whole adult life trying to become Mama Jackie's right-hand man. That day, the day after he bruised Donnie's arm when he saw her kissing Shelly, he would drive up to the house to find her and get there during the hour Donnie was gone. He was screaming her name before he got to the front door so Shelly hid in the bathroom when she heard him.

As she sat there in the dark, both hands shaking at the weight of the gun, he walked around the cabin knocking things over and screaming about respect. His shouting got increasingly faint as his footsteps got louder. When she saw his shadow creeping in from under the door she closed her eyes and cringed in fear, disgust, anger, as she pulled the trigger. It left her shaking uncontrollably and a hole through the door. She opened her eyes slowly to dusty light piercing through the bullet hole in the door. Then from under the door, again creeping, was Darius' blood. She heard him fall but kept staring at the dust of light coming through the hole in the door until Donnie came back and she moved the body. First away from the door so she could get Shelly out and hold her. Then to her truck. Then to a patch of land that could have been Texas or Mexico.

—=◆=—

Andie Ngeleka is a lesbian writer, comedian and filmmaker based in Los Angeles. Ngeleka was born in the Democratic Republic of Congo, briefly lived in South Africa and then Orlando, Florida before becoming the first person ever to move to Los Angeles to become an artist while attending community college. Her writing has appeared in *Gay Magazine*, *Fifty Fifty*, *Into More*, *Points In Case*, and *HopeIRL*. After being rejected from their journalism school twice, she studied Cinema and Media Studies at USC School of Cinematic Arts. She is a recipient of 10011 NYC's Black Artist Grant.

The Blonde

Bebe King Nicholson

Emma Bates scraped a last mouthful of pea soup from her bowl, then hobbled to the window and yanked the ragged curtain aside. She didn't bother to scrub her bowl or sponge the vinyl tablecloth. That could wait. Right now, it was time for the girl.

Across the street, the girl was already stopping by Mr. Eisenburg's deli. She would emerge in five minutes (she always did) with a paper sack and walk the half block to a square of sooty brick and windows called Horla Apartments.

Five minutes later, the time it took to climb four flights of steps or ride a rickety elevator with stops on every floor, her shutters would fly open. She would be framed like a person in a moving camera by the window she pried open every evening, and she would grow more visible as the hot summer sun flared crimson and waned. When it was pitch dark, she would be perfectly illuminated by the apartment's yellow square of light.

She had moved in sometime during the winter, and Mrs. Bates hoped her presence was a sign the neighborhood was improving.

Each spring and summer Emma Bates lived vicariously, seeing and hearing and sniffing the world that vibrated around 500 Gordon Terrace. When long-delayed warmth sent people streaming to the streets, she opened her window, letting life pour like cacophonous strains of music into her grim apartment.

She had witnessed muggings and break-ins; smelled the odors of frying food drifting from open windows to mingle with the odors of overturned garbage; watched fat, disheveled women water shriveled window plants, scold dirty children, and hang yellowed laundry from lines connecting apartments like arteries.

This summer, the girl was a bright butterfly scattering color along a drab landscape. She wore fashionable clothes and walked spryly, like the women who used to clatter past on stiletto heels before the neighborhood went down the drain. Her hair, fine as corn silk, floated past her shoulders.

In July, after two months of watching the girl move lithely through the dilapidated neighborhood, Mrs. Bates decided to invite her for tea.

"You expecting company, Mrs. Bates?" Mr. Eisenburg asked when Emma stacked almonds and chocolates next to his cash register. He knew she usually bought chicken and coleslaw; maybe some of his pumpernickel bread.

He was a friendly man with a head that reminded Emma of a boiled egg. In conversation, he cocked his head sideways and aimed one oversized but ineffectual ear toward his customers. He was hard of hearing.

"The little blonde girl. The one that moved up the street into Horla, though it's beyond me why she ever moved to that place. The rent in mine's just as low and at least it's clean." Mrs. Bates' thin voice quivered toward Mr. Eisenburg's cupped ear, but it was no use. A person had to stand and shout directly into the ear before coherent sound could filter beyond its flabby lobe.

Mr. Eisenburg tried again, leaning closer. "What's that you say?"

"The blonde girl!"

He nodded, pretending to hear. Whoever it was, it was a good thing they were coming. He hadn't known Mrs. Bates had friends or relatives in the world, but it was what she needed. His hearing might be bad, but his eyesight was sharp as a cat's, and he thought Mrs. Bates looked poorly. Her face was the texture of tree bark, and her eyes were faded like blue jeans dipped in Clorox. But that was the way it was when you got old, he thought regretfully.

Clutching the brown paper sack, Mrs. Bates forced her arthritic joints back through the littered street. For once, she overlooked spilled garbage, paper cups scuttling before the humid breeze and jagged edges of broken glass. With the neighborhood on an upswing, these things would be replaced by window boxes of petunias, ladies in high heels and businesspeople drinking coffee at Hobbs on the corner.

At home, she arranged the nuts and candies in Tupperware bowls and pushed a damp rag across bedposts, dresser, and a Formica countertop marred by Owen's cigarette burns. Then she dug out and dusted her photo album. The girl might want to glimpse her life, so thoroughly revealed in the yellowed pictures of a pretty blonde woman and various, changing friends.

Here was a picture of herself in front of the old Ragamuffin. Dalton Haines, who had liked to dance there as much as she did and had long since become a lawyer, stood smiling and handsome beside her.

Why didn't I marry him? He proposed enough times before he finally got fed up and ran off with Mildred Gupton. Now she lives on Michigan Avenue and I live here. The thought left a taste like green persimmons in her mouth.

And here was one of Arthur Finch, an aggressive man with brains. He died ten years ago, a year before her own husband, leaving his widow rich from the fast-food chain he started. Emma had read about it on the second page of the *Sun Times.* She shoved the picture to the bottom of the pile, out of sight.

There were several pictures of her late husband Owen, a nondescript man; handsome enough until alcohol softened his stomach and failure blurred his features.

Here was her favorite; the picture of herself that she had been looking for. It captured luminous eyes and satiny cheeks ringed by pale hair; a picture preserving beauty in timelessness reserved for photographs.

This is the one that looks like the girl. I could be her grandmother. The idea was startling every time she thought it; every time she saw the girl.

There were no pictures of herself over forty, when Owen pawned their camera. Mrs. Bates couldn't remember getting old. It was almost as if she had woken one morning with someone else's skin draped over her body. Age was a terrible trick. The inner self stayed young while the outer self drooped and sagged and dwindled.

If Emma had it to do over, she wouldn't have ended up here; a woman deteriorating with the neighborhood, condemned to live the remainder of her life viewing the world from her grimy window. She would have taken one of those other roads; the decisions that crop up daily without you realizing that each choice boxes you in a little more.

Emma Bates wanted to say to the girl, *You have life at your feet. Don't squander it. Be wise in your choices. Time is shorter than you think.*

Her plan was to intercept the girl between Mr. Eisenburg's and Horla Apartments the following day, but she woke to a hard, slanting rain beating like kettledrums against the window. Not this morning. It had to be a day when the late afternoon sun danced through the window, brightening the dim apartment.

The rain continued for a week and Mrs. Bates' arthritis flared, sending her to bed. Then, on Monday, sun splintered through the ragged curtain. She got up feeling washed clean, like the world, and decided this was the day.

The hours until six stretched taut as violin strings. Mrs. Bates riffled through old magazines, dozed, filled the pitcher with fresh tea and dozed again. At 5:45 she opened the curtain. The sun's hard glare blinded her, and she cupped her hands over her eyes to stare at the rain-washed street in the direction of Mr. Eisenburg's.

A group of boys lolled in front of the deli, ready for mischief until a policeman rounded the corner and sent them off like a flock of startled pigeons. Some younger children played kick the can, and Mrs. Bates heard the can's hollow clink each time it clattered down the street.

At six, the girl appeared. She was dressed in yellow, the color of her hair, and she looked like a bright canary weaving through a world of drab sparrows.

Mrs. Bates' heart fluttered moth-like against her chest as she pulled away from the window.

The air outside was thick and steamy, hard to breathe. She had to take extra gulps through her mouth. Perspiration beaded like dewdrops on her face and she dabbed it with a handkerchief.

The girl stepped out of Mr. Eisenburg's, and Mrs. Bates struggled through the humid evening to meet her. The sun was slanting into her eyes, making it hard to see.

When she lurched forward, she thought she had tripped. A pain like shards of glass jabbed her chest. The sun was inside her now, filling her with its white-hot glare. She hit the sidewalk with a ponderous thud.

The brassy-haired, thick-waisted girl in yellow was the first one in the circle of people hedging the woman.

"What happened?" somebody shouted.

"Some old woman," said the girl. "She must of dropped dead in the street. I seen her comin' from way over there at Mr. Eisenburg's. Looked like she was makin' a beeline right at me, then she just starts grabbin' her chest and falls."

The boys who had been playing kick the can squirmed through the crowd so they could see up close, this new excitement taking precedence over their game.

The siren's scream announced the ambulance before it flashed into sight. Two men jumped out, felt the woman's pulse, and a minute later were drawing a sheet across her face.

"I could have told you she was dead. I took one look and seen she was gray as fish scales. I said 'ain't no use tryin' to help that one.'" The girl spoke to no one in particular, but to everyone within hearing range.

=◆=

Bebe Nicholson began her writing career as a reporter and newspaper editor after graduating from the University of North Carolina School of Journalism. She has published three books, writes on Vocal Media, News Break and Medium, and her freelance articles have appeared in *Chicken Soup for the Soul*, along with a variety of newspapers and magazines. Her other careers include flight attendant, retail manager, nonprofit director, and mom. She and her partner divide their time between Georgia and South Carolina. When she isn't writing, she is volunteering or spending time with her twelve grandchildren.

Exit Wound

Rachel Pollock

People think a walk in the country is quiet. They're wrong.

Dogs run at you, wild with barking. Deer crash thickets. Cattle stampede. Three hundred pounds easy, even a year-old calf'll spook so bad it takes a hot fence buzzing with 3,000 volts to keep him from running his fool head off. It astounds me how nothing more than a stringy-armed, white-haired Christian woman walking the back fields can set them all in a panic.

Foolish flesh. Fear is built into their DNA. Living in the country, I can't help but think. If our animals had enough brains to realize who ought to be scared, you wouldn't see another one run in your lifetime.

I'm barely home and inside when I hear a car on the gravel drive. And there's my daughter-in-law Deenah, pitching herself up the porch steps to my front door, bloodied and beaten.

She ain't crying, won't call for me, and just drags her broken self one stair to the next. A finch I let roost in the broken gutter above the awning squawks, more surprised than I am.

I grab towels from the drawer, stick them in the sink and turn the spigot on cold and hard. From the window above the sink, I keep an eye out for who might be coming back.

I try to figure whether the .22 Senior used to kill injured stock is in the barn. I think past the barn swallows and vultures roosting there, past the hay turned black with mildew, past Senior's tractor in the field still upturned if no one stole it yet. Couldn't bring myself to use the damn thing if I knew where he kept it, never could stand guns. I might remember Elias tripping on a soft cardboard box half-buried in the coop when he helped me put up the chickens for winter. I might have emptied five shells in my apron pocket and pitched the mushy cardboard in the compost.

I wring out a mass of wet towels, set most of them on the counter. Sink is full with clean water now. It'll be stained before you know it. Deenah makes it up the porch, clops the screen door in its frame as I move to get her.

Clear as daylight the girl can't see through the slits all swelled shut, can barely breathe through the mash where her nose ought to be. My breath catches at the blackness of the blood clotting her pretty orange hair. Hair she can't never seem to pull back, a vanity that drives me crazy every time she and Elias come for Sunday dinner because she's always letting it drag through the gravy. Girl hangs her head so low at mealtimes you don't know how she manages to eat. We don't dare pull it back from her face now. Not without wetting it first. The pulp would catch. Good Lord what a mess these kids got themselves into.

With my whole body I catch her from toppling over and take a quick look around. I can see about two miles worth of empty road through the noonday shimmer and dust.

"Come inside," I mutter. "Elias did this?" And I can't say much more than last time.

It ain't no use asking whether it was my son who did this. Who else? I can't see how it turned out this way when Senior and I raised Elias as gently as we could manage in this hard place.

Mountains and farm dust and iron weed here in the country are a damn sight better than rusted-out trailers and shoddy prefabs falling in on themselves on the outskirts of town. Not much there other than folks long done looking for work now looking for a fix. Growing our boy up, Senior and I made it a point to avoid those outskirts. We kept to our grove and once in a while the church up the road. We know now Elias T. did more than drive through the skirts. Otherwise how could he have grabbed up Deenah to marry.

Elias and Senior at one time were peas in a pod. When Elias was a boy Senior couldn't stand to be apart from his son and the feeling was mutual. At the age he could talk when he needed something, Elias would shut it off if his daddy stayed out late in the field, would stomp around the house when Senior left deer hunting. I never could get him to smile nor eat much if his da wasn't home. How they were was sweet. If they did close me out at times I didn't mind. Of course when Elias married this one here, he became more close-mouthed than before. Then, once Senior passed, I couldn't get the boy to open up again.

Sunday dinners after Senior's accident were silent as his grave.

"Lazzet call?" She speaks. It will take months for that swelling to subside.

Each time she calls Elias "Lazzet," I take a second to know who she means. It's a nickname the kids loose on her outskirt street in Bumville must've started that stuck. Drug-dealers' lingo. I wonder if any of them out there even know his given name. When Deenah's pa Hunter telephoned one day, he didn't know Elias' name, nor what to call me. Called me Missus Lazzet. Course that's Hunter Dice. What a piece of work. In and out of that girl's life, more out than in. The day he called here looking for Deenah, she ran to the phone excited like she won the lottery. She handed the phone right over to Elias, smiling ear to ear. Hunter wants to set up a meeting she said, so he can meet this man of hers, maybe take you kids to a movie or out for a burger, get to know Lazzet some. I had nothing much against it, though I might have thought to myself, here's a case of too little too late. If Hunter stuck around long enough to raise Deenah Dice, maybe she wouldn't have attached herself to my son. What does Elias see in her? I should have hung up the phone. If Senior hadn't taken on that field last March, I bet Elias never would have gotten involved.

"No, he didn't call. Don't mean he's not on his way. What did you all get into this time?"

Deenah turns and faces me. Then, as I'm mopping bits of flesh from her pretty head, she lies. Lies to my face.

"Lazzet's liable to kill me, Mim. He won't stop till I get it."

"Get what?"

"He wants I should get an abortion."

My heart catches to hear news of a grandchild, but something doesn't click. I look down at Deenah's jeans. I can't see pregnant, not even early pregnant.

She says they need money for the procedure. "Money. Five hunnerd."

Something about Deenah is too smooth, too practiced and hopeful—like a dog wagging its tail before you see it's got into the trash. Her forehead needs stitching so I go and get the kit from my sewing drawer.

The last time, Elias fetched Deenah without a word. He come to my door and saw her strung out on the sofa, got down on his knees and lifted that girl onto her feet, her crying the whole time how sorry, sorry, sorry she was. He didn't look mad. Only bothered, like his evening wasn't over but just then getting started. Elias, I said. Elias, how could you do this girl like that? Didn't your da and I teach you nothing? He asked her, Why did you come here? The only thing he said to me was I need to lock my door when it gets after dark and I ought to leave a light on in the hall when I go to bed and where's the dog? We both know Mixer stays outside on account of coyotes.

I guess I ignore all that right now for the fact I feel sorry for Deenah and this phantom grandbaby and I'm mad as hornets that my own son may be up to no good. Beat your wife within an inch of her life for what. For wanting to keep a baby.

"Deenah, you doing drugs?"

I light my big sewing needle to sterilize it. She shakes her head to avoid being scrutinized, but seeing as how her hair is still matted she can't hide behind it now. And I guess I see something. See her flinch. But who wouldn't flinch at a needle. I thread its blackened top, still warm from the flame, and pinch the skin above her temple together with my fingers. Deenah fiddles with the loose ends of her ripped blouse.

She says no, no, she isn't, of course not, Mim. It's Lazzet, Mim. He just can't stand the thought of having a baby right now.

I tell her I can't see how this is true as Elias T. is working steady. Plus, he's never mentioned not wanting children. Neither have you, I said. Don't get an abortion. I'll take care of your baby. I'll love it to pieces and raise it here on the farm in the peace and quiet. You don't have to worry. Elias doesn't have to worry.

To get ready for the stitches she breathes deep and exhales. Look at you, I say. You'll do fine in childbirth I think. You're tough as nails, not scared at all.

She ducks her head, she likes what I said. She's off balance. She don't seem sober.

Lightning quick, I sew her up. Deenah doesn't thank me. She pushes herself into the cushions of my couch until the phone rings. She wets her lips, says (there's Elias through the door) "Don't answer it" he says at the same time.

She's up and running to the bathroom and him full speed after her. I ain't paying for an abortion I let him know the phone still ringing. He knocks over my coffee table, the one his da built by hand, she's made it to the bathroom when I get the phone.

"Who's this?" a man slurs at me.

"Miriam Brenner. Who's this?"

Elias runs from the bathroom where Deenah has barricaded herself, vaults the table to me. I hold the phone up in the air away from him. He's taller some, but not by much. He has to go through me to get the phone. He won't. Except he does.

"Who are you and what do you want?" I throw my voice toward the receiver as Elias T grabs it away.

"Mind your own business, Ma," Elias growls at me, mean.

You mind yours I tell him because it is my house and my phone and you are trespassing and I'm about to call the police so hand that damn phone to me right now.

I grab it so hard he's surprised enough to let go and I hear a voice, Hunter's.

"...never mind about my apartment. Tell her she better have it, because I'm almost there."

"Is this Hunter? Tell who what? Tell Deenah?" but he hangs up as Elias narrows his eyes, turns on his heel and practically rams down my bathroom door.

Deenah is sobbing, sorry. He's my dad.

Elias, he keeps ramming, out of his mind. I guess I am too because I'm not thinking why is Deenah's father on his way, and why is she apologizing to Elias, I'm not calling the police because everyone knows stuck between two counties no one will come for hours and suddenly I remember where Elias Thomas Senior rested the old .22. In the cracked board above the mantle.

I get to the kitchen grab the shells from my apron and drag a chair into the living room.

I barely have the thing loaded when Elias shows up

in the family room dragging Deenah by her hair, her screaming with her face ripped to pieces, arm hanging loose in her sleeve.

I take off the safety and I don't think twice as I shoot my son.

The shot has my ears ringing I lose my balance as I step off the chair and the ground is lower under my left foot than it was when I climbed up and the whole thing tips over then I see deadbeat Hunter Dice in my family room, swaying and jittery and high as a kite and my son, my son sweet pea pod to my Elias Thomas Senior not moving face down on the wood floor. I see Hunter grab his daughter and turn her around and around, his hands everywhere, she's confused but not upset at him touching until I see her realize he's just looking in her pants pocket her blouse pocket for cash, cash he ain't finding and then he comes at me, he spots me and comes toward me hard and fast and his eyes are red-rimmed dark holes and Deenah says in a real little voice, oh no, Mim, and then I see a steel-toed snakeskin boot and not much else.

I don't see how Deenah can stay loyal to a deadbeat Dad who never did nothing right, never showed up for her, never was there for her, but always let her down and who came around only to mess her life when his own couldn't be messed anymore, how can a child love like that, not see poison in her veins as her father sends men to beat money out of her for a habit he won't kick. More than that I don't see how a mother who loves her son can believe such a foul thing about him. Where was my loyalty to either Elias or his Da when I shot our son for something he never did, something I could not believe he ever would do.

Except I did believe it. In the moment I must have, or I wouldn't have pulled the trigger. That sort of thing is hard to forgive. Especially raised as we all are, where no matter what kin is kin.

And then there's Hunter Dice, a bullet who rips through and explodes everything soft in us to bits and then disappears.

I never did call the police. I drove my son to the hospital, him not saying a word to the doctors nor the nurses. Kin is kin. Quite a few raised their eyebrows at us, especially when they saw Deenah and the mess we were all in. Kin is kin they must've said.

I guess we healed some since. Hard to say. When time heals wounds, scars tell the story.

Mid-morning March, a whole year now since my husband's funeral, I walk past the startled cows finally heading to what I come to think of as Senior's field. The neighbor's dog joins me and I don't shoo him away. Truth is, I can use the company because I don't know what's out there waiting for me.

Senior's tractor's been righted by someone. I don't know who. The weeds are pulled. That's nice. I wonder if the tractor still runs, does Elias have a use for it. Some inheritance that would be.

I'll ask. I can do that. I've lived through worse.

I manage to climb up on the thing and sit, dress and all. I must look a sight. The dog does a circle to settle somewhere below my feet. The key's here so I try it. There is black smoke, and something inside turns over then stops. Engine off, I close my eyes and listen. Still seems noisy to me.

I see Senior ride and turn at the end of each row, his heart like lightning, him slow falling as the tractor keeps going with no driver. When our whole world tipped upside-down, did Elias' daddy see a field to be turned, work to be done, an unending ending. Or did he see something beautiful pause like God's shadow or maybe spring.

I stay looking out across his field for a while. I sit there thinking about all the things none of us know. A creek rushes with melted snow. Time to mend the fence or some heifers will sink to their knees.

≡◆≡

R. R. Pollock (Rachel Rebecca Pollock), eclectic writer, teacher and performer is an on-again poet, playwright, and folklife storyteller. Available plays include *Remember How He Told You* and the one-woman show *Journey to Long Nose* that premiered at the Capital Fringe Festival in Washington, D.C. Pollock, assistant professor of Communication, Media and Theater, serves as the director of Forensics, competitive public speaking, performance and debate at Muskingum University in New Concord, Ohio. She is also the artistic director of BiGFiSHFOLKLiFE at bigfishfolklife.org, a non-profit religious organization in New Concord, Ohio to provide worship, performance and retreat opportunities for artists.

Waiting Room

Erin Shea

Sitting in yet another waiting room, I learn that Adam Sandler is the director and producer of *The Price is Right*.

Not *that* Adam Sandler, silly. Not the *Big Daddy*, ultra-rich but casually dressed Adam Sandler we all know and love.

No, this was simply *another* Adam Sandler. One who's probably really good at his job and hates how his name alone will always place him as a runner-up. A less-than.

Now that I think about it, it's a bit odd this man never changed his name just out of sheer convenience. I can already see the Starbucks baristas rolling their eyes. Though he may just have a handful of favorite aliases, providing a different name to each fast food worker: Bill, Steve, Greg, Rod. Maybe he's just the jokester type. The kind of man who says things like "working hard or hardly working?" to retail workers on the verge of shooting themselves.

But wait, what if he gets pulled over? "Adam Sandler" belongs on a hall of fame of worst (but amusing) fake IDs—right next to Fogell's "McLovin."

Screw it, I'm reading too much into this. I'm the connoisseur of overplanning, of expecting the worst.

Anyways, there went the credits. The show ended with a lucky guess, a big prize winner. The waiting room is still nearly vacant and the TV is set to such a low volume, it might as well have been muted.

It's eerily still except for *The Price is Right* on the little mounted television. A show which, when played interminably, could turn into my own personal hell. The kitschy set, those yellow price tags bearing everyone's name, the models. It's almost as bad as spending hours of your life sitting in waiting rooms.

You may be wondering what kind of waiting room I'm even in. Am I waiting to get my teeth cleaned or am I in a hospital awaiting news about a relative splayed out on an operating table? The answer is neither. I'm in a waiting room wondering why the hell I'm here at all—what I'm actually *waiting* for. Chronic illness will do that to you. Doctor's appointments aren't as black and white anymore. I'm not a little kid in animal-themed pediatricians' offices for an annual checkup—getting poked, prodded, vaccinated, and handed a lollipop for my compliance all in fifteen minutes' time. No. Doctors' offices are much more of a devastating arena when you're desperately waiting for an answer that you simultaneously dread. A diagnosis that isn't inherently fixable...

Coping is a vicious word. I've inherited it from white coats.

Inconspicuously, my whole life changed during this mindless hopping between waiting rooms. All of a sudden, I could no longer distinguish sickness from health. There was just pain and respite on a constant loop. I've tried to desensitize myself to it. That's what I'm doing right now. I listen obsessively for the sound of footsteps approaching the door, but all I hear is the receptionist's whispery chatter. Sometimes the phone rings and it startles me. I realize that I'm shaking. There's a timeless, untethered quality to this place, borderline unreal.

The Price is Right switches to daytime soap operas. I can't tell yet if this is worse. At least it signifies that time is indeed passing by. I would estimate I've now been sitting here for about fifteen minutes. Only one other patient has been taken back since I arrived.

Like most waiting rooms I've been in, I find that there is this subtly amusing challenge in the air.

Let me explain.

I scan the room to view my remaining, sparsely scattered sick compatriots, and I feel the need to *prove* my affliction. Like I need to jump up and yell, "I swear I'm sicker than you!" Like I should be wearing a lanyard around my neck with a card listing each and every symptom. Invisible illness will do that to you. If your diagnosis isn't outwardly visible *and* you happen to be quite young, you find that everyone is quietly questioning the reality of your illness. You begin to feel like a fraud no matter how sick you feel.

At long last, the door swings open, and a woman in dark blue scrubs calls my name right as I'm sizing up my competition.

⇒◆⇐

The room smells of antiseptic, underscored by a sweetness that clings to me. I had lathered my arms with floral lotion at home. Some Bath & Body Works concoction that's been sitting on my shelf since before I got my first period. I have an affinity to hold onto things that remind me of my unremarkable youth.

This room is just another manifestation of the waiting room. It's an upgrade in terms of sterility, and it's more doctored (pun intended) to appear as some haven of knowledge. There are always large-framed posters and diagrams in places like this. I've come to learn that they're not entirely for show. I've had doctors whip out diagrams or try and sketch illustrations sedately like some sort of cartoon diversion. I'm the dimwitted guard being distracted so the protagonists can make their narrow, comedic escape.

Luckily, this room doesn't feel cramped, like many doctor's offices I've frequented. The outer wall has one massive window looking out over the urban skyline. It reminds me of how high up I really am. I had to brave ever-winding parking garages and elevator rides to get here. Might as well settle in. Google this other Adam Sandler. Get a visual of him.

The doctor knocks on the door right as I locate a picture. He's on the far left of a group photo. He's bald. His face is indistinguishable. It blends in. I'm annoyed at how ordinary he is. His name should correspond to it. He should change his name to something more befitting, like Adam... Smith. *I always forget if that's the famous economist or the white dude from* Pocahontas. *I tend to mix them up.*

"How are we?" The doctor requires my attention. I look away from Adam Sandler 2.0 and supply his ears with my prepared script. I've developed a knack for listing off my symptoms as one would read a family's scribbled grocery list.

As I talk, he takes notes with a stylus. The letters look loose and free, unintelligible from my angle. I stare at his thinning hair.

When he finally focuses his attention wholly on me, I wonder what he sees. It hurts me even to consider. I can feel my skin thinly scraping across my sternum when I try to sit up straight. My veins bulge out of my pale arms. I'm lightheaded—the warm, artificial air is making it worse.

I wonder if a whiff of pity unfolds before him—if his notes reflect how I grieve over this body still breathing. If he does, he doesn't seem to let on. Instead, he talks about layers, about approaches and confidence, about taking my time. I've heard this spiel before. *These things take time. It's not a race to the finish line. We have to take things layer by layer to try and build you back up. Are you still going to acupuncture? This process is about managing and controlling what we can. How about mental health support?*

Nothing the man with the thinning hair says grips me to reality. For once, I'm not thinking about my body in perpetual chaos. I'm still thinking about the other Adam Sandler.

I don't realize it at first, but he begins to pick up on how I'm just letting him rattle on—that I will not or rather *cannot* grab onto anything anymore. *You're running on empty.*

The man, now more aware of me than I am myself, changes gears before his parting instructions. For the first time, I am able to listen to the *human*, not the doctor before me. It stops me in my tracks.

"I'm proud of you for not giving up on your body," he says.

I can't recall what I replied to that... *if* I replied at all. That was the kind of remark that I'd absorb in a sigh and sit with for years.

He finally leaves, and I feel like crying. But no, that's what dim parking garages are for. I just have to make my descent.

≡◆≡

Back in my car, I sit idle for far too long. A downpour came on, and the parking garage had taken on a muggy and damp but *safe* feeling.

There's a Selena Gomez song playing on the radio. I turn up the volume a smidge. I favor Selena Gomez over other pop stars with a Disney Channel history because she, too, has lupus. When I was seven, I had a poster of her hanging in my room that I'd ripped out of a *Tiger Beat* magazine. Who knew we'd both grow up to lose our grip strength?

I've already forgotten about the other Adam Sandler. Now I'm thinking about my different childhood bedrooms. My borderline-forgotten youth, my fervid adolescence, my plummet into young-adulthood.

I have this habit of fractioning off my memories into categories. Said categories used to be before and after I lost my virginity or before and after I got my driver's license. Now, it's just before and after I got sick. So when the doctor talks about peeling back these metaphorical layers, my mind reverts back to past selves—half-forgotten bliss and youthful ignorance. *A part of me doesn't want it back at all.* I laugh at that, my voice briefly harmonizing with the hum of my car engine. My old therapist would've milked that out of me if I hadn't discontinued our sessions. She preached a lot about throwing off the past and moving forward, shedding our fears and worries.

That said, if the layers *do* peel back, I hope there will be someone left. I hope some core part of me has gone untouched, trapped for years. Someone still holding twinges of childhood security... someone not waiting for the end.

⇒◈⇐

Erin Shea hails from Wolcott, Connecticut, where she resides with her family and beloved cat, Bandit. She is currently a full-time student pursuing a Bachelor of Arts in English. Since childhood, Erin has dreamed of becoming an author. One of her earliest memories is attempting to pen an entire novel by hand. Outside of reading and writing, she enjoys yoga, baking, and curating hyper-specific playlists on Spotify. After being diagnosed with a chronic illness in 2021, she has gained an interest in exploring herbal and holistic medicine to foster healing in her life. "Waiting Room" is her first published work.

Twenty Miles
South of Macon

Melissa Wozniak

One night Mabel kept driving.

Her arms hung heavy on the wheel. Her mind was blank. The fork in the road passed, and with it the turnoff to Harveys Supermarket where she would buy three cans of boiled chicken, a bag of reduced-fat Wheat Thins, a loaf of bread, and a pound of tomato-shaped objects to last her the week. Tillary called them tomato-shaped objects because she used to work at the Macon farmers market and felt the new job was beneath her. A tomato, she said, should taste like something. Trailing vines. Summer rain. These things taste like the tears of the Mexican kid that picked them, and life is not worth living when you've reached the point of eating like this.

Mabel went to Harveys Supermarket on Sundays because that is when normal people shop to prepare for their week, and Mabel liked to pretend she was one of them. It was also when Tillary worked, and the time she spent in the produce department reminded her that she hadn't forgotten how to talk. Squinting flash-blind under fluorescent lights, Mabel mulled Tillary's name tag. It could be a surname. Or the T could be a hastily drawn H. She didn't ask. It took prizefighter strength to pull the parentheses around Mabel's mouth upward into the lead of her cheeks, and when she returned to her car with her tote bag of groceries, she let her face go, returned to silence, and drove home. The brass clock in her kitchen, her grandfather's, tapped its infantry march to next Sunday.

But one night Mabel kept driving. It had been years since she had ventured this far. The four-lane road blossomed into a highway as it approached the city, then shrunk again on the other side. Thirty minutes later, Mabel's courage wore thin and when the beacon of a Super 8 motel rose like a neon sun on the horizon, she took the exit.

Just me, she told the clerk cutting lines of powdered creamer with a business card on the other side of the plexiglass. Her voice was raspy, out of practice, a long-distance call on a tin-can telephone.

She fumbled with the lock of her room and set the chain on the other side. She turned on the TV and turned it off again. For a moment she buried her face in the tissue-thin bedspread, inhaling bleach and cigarette smoke, and then she sat up, stared at her reflection in the window, and for the first time wondered what the hell she was doing.

She wasn't on the run. To be on the run, a person had to have something to run from. Mabel Schwartz had a small house in the suburbs with a rosebush out front, a set of nice serving spoons she never used, and a job annotating legal briefs from her living room that entailed her interaction with no one. She wasn't traveling, because traveling would suggest a destination and someone to call when she got there. Mabel was here, and tomorrow she would be somewhere else. She would be a customer at the diner and then a woman buying chewing gum at the gas station and then a driver who breaks a twenty at the tollbooth. She would pass briefly into people's lives and exit, instantly forgotten.

No one tells you that these things happen. Sometimes your skis get tangled up and you miss the tow from childhood to the real world, and while everyone else rises through the blue bright air with their arms around each other comforted and close, you're at the bottom of the mountain, trying in vain to trudge up alone.

Two more hours before it was late enough to go to bed.

Mabel scrolled through her call log. She listened to her saved voicemails. We're trying to reach you, said a pleasant automated voice, about an opportunity to refinance your mortgage at a low fixed rate. What would you do with an extra three hundred dollars a month? She listened to the message again.

Back in college, Mabel used to entertain a fantasy of being a truck stop escort. She would cross the manicured quad and eye the engineering majors sprawled on picnic blankets in the sun, and in her mind she would be wearing red stilettos and a wife beater with no bra and now, thirty years later, she closed her eyes and tried to remember what it felt like to be young and powerful. Outside, men drowned the evening in three-dollar whiskey. The traffic light that dictates the flow of life in this exit oasis danced its three-toned reflection in puddles to mark the passage of time, green light shimmering on asphalt like psychedelic emeralds. Trucks made their labored rumble from fuel stop to highway. The twenty-four-hour restaurant sold its waffles and black, bitter coffee. This could be anywhere, Mabel thought. It would be at least a month before anyone noticed I'm missing.

There was nothing of her life to wrap up except for a fertilizer order she needed to cancel. Mabel picked up the phone.

You grow things? the woman on the other end of the line asked when they finished the transaction. I can't keep anything alive. Plants, pets, marriages.

I think my rosebush has already moved on, Mabel said.

I make roses, the woman replied. I try to. Out of paper and fabric. I have a book, but it's all in Japanese. I do what I can, follow the pictures. I think sometimes it's better to make your own flowers instead of counting on real ones that die.

Ikebana, Mabel said. It means the art of making flowers come alive. You do grow things.

The woman laughed. By some stretch of the imagination.

Kaizen, Mabel said. A little better every day.

If you lived near Seattle, the woman said, I'd split a bottle of wine with you.

Mabel paused. She pictured the map.

I'll be there on Sunday, she said. She hung up, walked down to the front desk for a toothbrush. The next morning, she bought a tube of mascara and a spare set of clothes.

=◆=

Melissa Wozniak's words and photography come from chapters spent in Africa, Asia, and currently New York. They have appeared in publications including *Playboy*, *Inked*, and *Nashville Scene*. She has created art with refugees in Berlin, collected alms with monks in Myanmar, danced with Rastas in a South African shantytown, and once, in Nepal, had a cross-bearing baba perform a ritual to return lost love that involved holy water and a stick of butter, but she stopped him when it got too weird. She was shortlisted for the Bridport Pize. Visit her online at www.worldwidewoz.com.

A Note on the Editor

Erica Wagner is on the Board of Directors of Creatd, Inc., the parent company of Vocal. She believes that stories can be found everywhere and are told in all kinds of voices—many of those voices can be found on Vocal. Erica is author of *Mary and Mr Eliot: A Sort-of Love Story; Chief Engineer: Washington Roebling, the Man Who Built the Brooklyn Bridge; Ariel's Gift; Seizure* and *Gravity*, and editor of *First Light*, a celebration of the work of Alan Garner. A former literary editor of *The Times*, she is a contributing writer for the *New Statesman* and consulting literary editor for *Harper's Bazaar*.

Special thanks to Jeremy Frommer, Justin Maury, Robby Tal, Rachel David, Jacob Frommer and Joshua Johnson.

The Vocal+ Fiction Awards Shortlist

Ruth A.M., ad, Otis Adams, Gena Adamson, Adrianna, Kimberly Ae, Aggee, Zachary Agman, Catherine Agnes, Ayla Ahmed, Savannah Aichem Alexandria Aji, Katie Alafdal, Bryan Alaspa, Peter J. Albert, Ava Alder, Alex, Bree Alexander, Carrie Ann Alexis, Julia Alfred, alissa , Anne van Alkemade, Greg Allan, Raistlin Allen, Elisha Allman, Christella Almonacy, Caitlin Jill Anders, Sean Anderson, Steve Anderson, J. Andres, Vera Andrew, Alvin Ang, Angela, Glory Anna, Annabella, Kendra Anthony, Marie Antoinette, Miriam Arce, Chelsi Arnold, Sam H. Arnold, Sean Arseo, Rob Asche, Tabby Ashworth, Mehrina Asif, Jordan Aspen, Isabel Atherton-Reimer, Miller Atlas, Alyissa Austin, Sheila Sellinger, Author, Liliam Avila, Stephen Kramer Avitabile, Kayla Holyoak Avondet, Ayban, Marisa Ayers, ayvamitchell, Nancy B, Madison B., Lucia B., Burnt Baguettes, Jessica Baird, Eve Ballard, N. K. Barclay, Alice J. Barker, Kevin Barkman, Blaire Baron, Yasmine Barrett, George Louis Bartlett, Ana Basile, Kishan Baskaran, Basabi Basu, Amadeo Battista, Lissa Bay, Bree Beadman, Ethan J. Bearden, Emily Beck, Becky :), Shayla Beesley, Hayden N. Bell, Myiah L. Bengston, Lauren J. Bennett, Nikki Bennett, Josh Benoit, Kei'Jei Beretta, Danielle Berggren, R. M. Beristáin, Ezra Berkman, Annemarie Berukoff, TC Best, Madison Betcher, Q-ell Betton, Melissa Bezborotko, Victoria Bezzeg, Dane BH, Emile Bienert, Gail Bird,

M. S. Bird, Maggie Blaha, l blickensderfer, Nick Blocha, Noémi Blom, Pryia Blunt, Maryn Boess, Lightning Bolt, Belinda Bonner, Casey Boomhour, Justin von Bosau, EJ Boston, Chris Botto, Bryce Boucher, Jason Bozeman, J. C. Bradbury, Thomas Brand, Will Britton, Kiana Brizendine, Jalia Maléy Brodie, Jalia Maléy Brodie, Marci Brodock, Andrea N. Brown, Glenn Brown, Lance Brown, Sara Brudkiewicz, Yess Bryce, E. L. Buchanan, Fallon Buchholz, Roger Bundridge, Brendan Burns, Carly Bush, Gabriele Del Busso, C. Rommial Butler, Claire Butler, Charlie C, Sammi C, Ellis Cahill, Katrina Cain, Nichelle Calhoun, Josh Call, Katelyn Calvo, Kylie Calwell, Cam, M.R. Cameo, Camille, Joshua Campbell, Philip Canterbury, Courtney Capone, Michael Capriola, Adam Carden, Marieugenia Cardona, Susan Cardosi, Danny Carlon, Jo Carroll, Shelley Carroll, Jalynne Carter, Kathryn Carter, Orion Carter, Kevin Casey, Deanna Cassidy, Lisa Cetinic, Megan Chadsey, Kyra Chambers, Amethyst Champagne, Olivier Champagne, Banu Chandran, Sydney Chapman, Gabrielle R Charles, Chloe Charlton, Alexis Chateau, Tara Chatterton, Jeffrey L. Cheatham II, Simon Chen, Matthew Cheng, Mr Chicken, Alethea Cho, Chris, Bianca Christiansen, Billy Christie, Katelyn Marie Clair, Nathalie Clair, Claire, Robyn Clifford, Adam Clost, Jon Coates, Sandra Coe, Michael Coffey, Kai K Colby, Sandra Tena Cole, Sophie Colette, PK Colleran, J. Arthur Collins, Jessica Conaway, Charlie Conlon, Clayton Cook, Elizabeth Corbitt, Brandon Corrales, Mitchell Coulthard, SJ Covey, Darelle Cowley, Nadia Cowperthwaite, Austin Cox, Emily Coy, Angie Craig, Bri Craig, Jessica Crane, Anton Crane, S. A. Crawford, Laura Cregar, Caitlin Cross, Noel T. Cumberland, Luke M. Curren, Jacqueline Curtsinger, Emese Antal Cuth, Cwrites, Sterling D'Este, Amir Dababneh, Devin Dabney, Cody Daniels, E. K. Daniels, Joshua Daniels, Shamaine Daniels, Meghan Darcy, Ru Dario, Navaris Darson, Prateek Dasgupta, Aleta Davis, Leah Davis, Gabriella Dawson, Alie Day, Phoenixx Fyre Dean, Madison DeCook, Dee,

Joe Deez, Christina DeFeo, J. Delaney-Howe, Joseph DelFranco, C.L. Deslongchamp, Kira DeSomma, Danielle Deutsch, Sadé Díaz, Meagan Dion, Made in DNA, Otto Do, Quinn Docter, Lacey Doddrow, Carlos dominguez, Alice Donenfeld-Vernoux, Thomas James Donoghue, Aisling Door, Catherine Dorian, Devan Douwes, Stephanie Downard, Sleepy Drafts, Michele J Drier, Michael J DuBois, Lese Dunton, Sarah DuPerron, Duskshadows, R. E. Dyer, John Dymale, E, Elbertine Sebastiane Eades, Obsidian Eagle, Cindy Eastman, Danielle Eckhart, Alaina Edgemon, Caleb Edmonds, Kasey Edwards, Susan Eileen, Kainā Padilha Elias, Rebekah Elisabeth, elliot, Peter Ellis, Catherine Elsing, J. C. Embree, jon s emm, Deborah Erickson, Ifeanyi Esimai, Esther, Janet Estrada, Anjula Evans, Ceirra Evans, Merridith Evans, Ardi Everett, J. B. Ezar, Gaia Fahed, Tiffany Fairfield, Cris Farias, Areej Fatima, Ursula Faye, Jim Feeny, Nicole Fenn, EJ Ferguson, Paul Fey, Elle Fielding, Christopher Fin, M. C. Finch, Lottie Finklaire, CL Fisher, jacki fleet, Tia Foisy, Lena Folkert, EJ Fordham, J. N. C. Francisco, S. Frazer, Charleigh Frederick, Sara Frederick, Daniel Freeman, TJ Freeman, Erin Friederichs, Fry, Penny Fuller, Mel E. Furnish, Tay Gallagher, Wonita Gallagher-Kruger, Michaela Gallien, Ash Gallop, Jet Garner, Leigh Garred, Lest Geau, Mark Gee, Rose Loren Geer-Robbins, Sophia Geno, J Gentry, Nancy German, Joan Gershman, Clement Gibson, Gigi Gibson, R P Gibson, Reginald Gibson, Jordan Gilletti, Kelly Girnas, Katherine Glidden, Mark Glover, Sloan Glover, Vicki Glover, Mary Anne Goatherd, Godwin, James Goggin, Alan Gold, James Golden, Naomi Goldrich, Thurman Golemon, Christopher Goodin, D Gordon, Lisa Gott, Marcel Grabowiecki, Anna Grace, Himiona Grace, David Graham, Aimee Gramblin, Aaron M Grant, Ember Gray, Grace Gray, David Grebow, EM Green, Sara Green, Gus Gresham, Concetta Guido, E.N. Gussler, E.N. Gussler, J. Otis Haas, Peter Haas, Hadassah, Anna Hagley, Heather Hagy, Anthony Hall, Isaac Hall, Jordan J Hall,

Sharna Halliwell, Michael Halloran, Logan Halverson-Bergez, Olivia Hamel, Fiona Hamer, Joshua Han, Ben Hanna, Beth (Halo) Hanson, Cassandra Hanson, Meredith Harmon, Lexie Harrell, Corrin Harris, Donn K. Harris, Iris Harris, Leah Harris, Rick Hartford, Jon Hastings, Kiesha Haughton, Alex Hawksworth, Mary Haynes, annie hazel, Nines Hearst, Alexandra Heatwole, Becca Lory Hector, Maegan Heil, Griffen Helm, Kat Helmick, Colt Henderson, Jessilen Henderson, Kristina Henry, Rae Henry, Adrian Herrera, Hester, Sonya Highfield, Alex Higinbotham, Shannon Hilson, Atomic Historian, Mark Hitz, Kate Holderness, Adrian Hollomon, Gerald Holmes, India Howell, Kemari Howell, Brandon Hoy, S. C. Huddleston, Katelyn Hunt, Dawn Hunter, Sabrina Huskins, John Iluno, David Inkwell, Taylor Inman, John Iovine, Kyle Ireland, Frank G. Isadore, Kalina Isoline, isthecoporami, Po Ivey, Tara J, Chloë J., Michele J., Min Ja, Jamie Jackson, Jolie Jackson, Rob Jackson, Sherry jackson, Miranda Jaensch, Frank Jager, Caroline Jane, Maia Jansson, Andrea Jardine, Ruth V Jarvis, JD, Neil Jefferies, Enjonai Jenkins, Kincaid Jenkins, Jess, Robin Jessie-Green, JHR, Tom Jobling, Jahvon John, Bernadette Johnson, Matthew B. Johnson, Nychele Kemper, Rebecca Johnson, Landon Jones, Ivy Jong, Chanelle Joy, Patrick Juhl, K. J. George, k.v.j, Kacie, Tanja Kala, Judey Kalchik, Autumn Kalquist, Samantha Kaszas, Matt Keating, Alisan Keesee, Margie Keith, Edward Kembery, John Kemp, Julie Kennedy, Thomas Kennedy, Catherine Kenwell, Sean Kernan, A. Keson, Marilyn Ketterer, Kgshak, Sana Khan, Killian, Jen Kim, Ryan Kimball, C.R. Kimbrough, Gina King, Merle Kinney, Tara Kjelstrom, Daniel J Klein, A. W. Knowland, Erik Knudtson, Emily Koopman, Konrad Kramp, Carolyne Krans, A F Kraven, Tracy Kreuzburg, Jenn Kruczynski, Anna Kukleva, Susan Kulkowitz, Jeremy Kuzmic, Ashley L, Derrick L., Lori Lamothe, Racheal LaPrade, Shelby Larsen, Elise Lashinsky, Jodi Lasky, James Lassiter, K. Lauren, Monse LaVie, Liv LaVonne, Frank W Law, O. S. Lawrenchuk, LB,

Megan Leach, Kristen Leavitt, Maria Lebada, Lucien Lecarme, Ess Lee, Justin Douglas Lee, Meredith Lee, Rachel Lee, Whitaker Lee, Rose Leffler, Kira Lempereur, Alana Leonard, Call Me Les, David Levins, Mark Levis, Bailey Lewis, Daniella Libero, Ellie Lieberman, Lilia, Andrea Lindsey, Andrea Lindsey, Amy Liou, Liv, Cara Loften, Rebecca Loften, L.C.R. Lohrenz, Morgan Longford, Velton Lorenzo, Francine Louidor, Louis, Chelsey Louise, david love, Kati Love, Scot Loyd, Erin Lucas, la lune, GABRIELA LUPU, Sammy Lycan, S. F. Lydon, Joanna Lynne, Lana V Lynx, Andy M, Yvonne M, Jade M., Laura M., Kimberlain O'Driscoll, MBA, M.Ed, Rachel M.J, Janice Garden Macdonald, David Macias, Ava Mack, Persephone Mackinnon, Alex Maher, E. B. Mahoney, Marti Maley, Miranda Mariana Maloy, Suzsi Mandeville, Mariah Mandwe, Iosefa Manu, Calista Marchand-Nazzaro, Hailey Marchand-Nazzaro, Margaret, Christina Marie, Kelsey Marie, Marie, Rebekah Marie, Theresa Markila, Emma Marks, K. Marley, Natasha Marquis, melissa marsh, Susan Marshall, Julia Marsiglio, Don Paul Martin, Mayra Martinez, Josephine Mason, Mataya, Oleksandr Matvyeyev, Clemence Maurer, Jasmin McCardell, J.L. McCarthy, Liam McCloskey, Graham McCool, Malky McEwan, Luka Mcfarlane, Ashley McGee, Madeline McGrain, Crystal McGraw, Lauren McGraw, Devin McGurk-Nixon, Grayden McIntyre, Rebecca McLeod, Brittany McMillan, Aiden McRae, Michelle Mead, Ayla Meg, PC Melpez, Eli Mendoza, Brad Menpes, Joe Mertens, amy miller, Anna Miller, DeEtta Miller, Eamonn Miller, Daniel Millington, Colleen Millsteed, Majique MiMi, Kayla R. Minguez, Antonella Di Minni, Gleice Miranda, Kaylen Misako, Caitlin Mitchell, Colleen Mitrano, Eli Modiah, Nicole Modugno, Shae Moloney, Joseph Monaghan, Don Money, Ilyssa Monroe, MoodSwingz, Amelia Moore, Marissa Moore, Tiz Moore, Thor Grey (G. Steven Moore), Shannon Moose, Jay Olivier Morel, Zoe Espino Moreno, Dillon R Morgan, Sarah Morgan, Tiffany Morgan, Eugenette Morin, R. A. Moseley,

Ellen Moyer, Melissa MS, Joy Muerset, Sylvia Mulholland, Shauna Mullen, Pohai Müller, Walter S. Munday, Dan Murphy, Kimberly Muta, Mutationist, na'im, Ali Naqvi, Joe Nasta, Natalia, A.W. Naves, Claudia Neaves, Brynne Nelson, Monique Nelson, Linda Neyedly, Valerie Ngai, SJ Nichol, Jenifer Nim, Blanca Nino, Wehttam Kutikim Nnelg, Humira Noorestani, James Nottle, Kat Nove, Josh O'Neill, Paul O'Neill, Nev Ocean, Jennifer Ogden, Emma Ogilvie, Tamika Morrison Okeleke, Daniel Okulov, Valerie Omokhua, Theis Orion, Victoria Osborn, Katie L. Oswald (BookDragon), Marco den Ouden, S.A. Ozbourne, Braden Page, Carla Pahl, Aldo Palaoro, Tristan Palmer, Karina Palukaitis, Joe Palumbo, Samantha Panepinto, Mara Papavassiliou, Sarah Paris, Julladonna Park, Jeffry Parker, Jordan Parkinson, Sophia Partlow, W. Tyler Paterson, Quinn Patrick, Sean Patrick, Hannah Patterson, LD Paul, Rob Payne, S.B. Pedersen, Gillian Pegg, Gwendolyn Pendraig, John Penn, Natasha Penn, Natasha Penn, PeoniePie, Kelly Peppe, Elise Peregrin, Shelby Perez, David Perlmutter, Lilia Peters, Ashanti Pettaway, Adriana M. MD, PhD., Brandon Phifer, Littlewit Philips, R.J. Philips, Byondhelp Photography, Nicholas Pietrowski, Jessica Burns Piraino, Abigail Pollard, Dré Pontbriand, Darcy Pope, Tamara Power-Drutis, Stan Prager, Charlie Pratt, Writer Preet, Laura Presley, Jihaad Pretlow, McKenzie Price, ET Productions, John Pucay, Eye Q, Julian Q., Kit Queen, Arsen Quill, Lila Quinn, Tony Qwade, T. R., Bryan R., Dia Ra, Rabih, ANITA RACHELLE, Joshua Radewan, Lindsay Rae, Margaret Rae, Misty Rae, A. Tonymous Raign, Ella Rainz, Silviya Rankova, Tatiana Raudales, Makayla Ray, Nick Razo, Jack Reay, Rebecca, Hunter Reese, B.D. Reid, L.H. Reid, Robyn Reisch, Natasha Khullar Relph, Rachel Rempel, Rena, Teresa Renton, Blue Planet Resident, Alison Reverie, Rhiannon, Ria, Jem Ricafort, Allison Rice, Steven Rice, Heather Richmond, David Riley, Ashleigh Riley, James U. Rizzi, Jay Robbins, Lexie Robbins, Eloise Robertson, David A Robertson, A.L. Robinson, Frank E. Robinson,

Olivia Robinson, Anna Rocco, Stephen A. Roddewig, Pedro C Rodriguez, V. N. Roesbon, Ethan Rogers, Kevin Rolly, Edith Romero, Stephanie Rosas, Madeline Rose, Ada O. Rose, April Rosele, Michael Donald Ross, Jay Rossignol, Dave Rowlands, Nick Rowley, Wally Roxanne, M.E. Royce, Nina Rueda, Samantha Rusk, Andrew Rutter, Sherry Ryan, Elle S.M., Natan Sahilu, Zachary D. Sajdera, Dawn Salois, MJ Salvati, Élié Sama, Jess Sambuco, Sammy, Koby Sampson, CH Sandler, Dani Sankovich, Kathy Saunders, Marsha Saunders, Skyler Saunders, Liv Savell, Erin A. Sayers, Scarlett, Ariel Schlesinger, Megan Velez Schmid, Kevin Schwandt, Shelby Schwartz, Chris Scoggins, Cameron Scott, Eden Scrafford, Jack Scranton, Melaina Scriven, Lydia Seales-Fuller, Dr Oolong Seemingly, Edoardo Segato-Figueroa, Bianca Serraty, Paula Shablo, Frank Shaw, Jacqueline Shea, Melissa Shekinah, Ben Shelley, CJ Shelton, Raquel Shelton, Joe Shetina, Shlunka, Lucia Carretero Sierra, Reija Sillanpaa, Humberto Da Silva, Savier Silva, Simon, Liz Sinclair, Skaoi_Nott, Steve Sloane, Bonnie Joy Sludikoff, Eleanor Smith, Jon Smith, Kyla Smith, mark william smith, Melanie Smith, Sharon Smith, Jerome Smith-Pula, Emily Arin Snider, Kevin Southgate, Denise Spain, Nessa Sparks, Sarahmarie Specht-Bird, David Spivak, Sara Splendore, Sarah St.Erth, Nicole Stairs, Peggy Stanley, Karlie Steadman, Ellen Stedfeld, Aaron Steele, Dana Stewart, Lisbeth Stewart, Lydia Stewart, Wilkie Stewart, Leslie Strom, Lee Stuart, Kate Sutherland, Bob Sutton, Caitlin Swan, Trudy Swenson, synrie, Louis T, Mira M. T., John T Talbert, A.R. Tanner, Matt Tanner, Leanne Tarrab, Kayleigh Taylor, T. Freya Taylor, Teagan, Fiona Teddy-Jimoh, Brittany Teemant, Phil Tennant, TheSpinstress, R. P. Thirteen, A. R. Thomas, Jennifer Thomas, Noah Thomas, Casey Promise Thompson, Janet Thorley, Tatyana Tieken, Ariane Torelli, ToyaRenee, Destiny Tozier, M. Michael TRARP, Josh Trichilo, Sara Triglia, Maahi Trivedi, C. J. Truman, Kristen Tsetsi, Julie Tuovi, Leigh Ann Tuttle, Jade Utterback, Shelby Valdez,

Ashley Alleyne Van-De-Cruize, Jessica Vann, KM Varilla, Benedetto Varotta, Jennifer Vasallo, A. Vaughn, Karin Venables, S. Venugopal, Mr Rothman W, Caleb Waddell, Jessie Waddell, Scott Wade, Robert Wagner, Judy Walker, Jessica Walker, Adam Wallace, Zak Walters, Bond Wang, sophie may wang, Kavi Warrick, K. H. A. Wassing, Abigail Watson, Aley Way, M. J. Weisen, Travis Wellman, Trevor Wells, Adelheid West, Rosalind West, Wendy Weston, Evan Wettengal, Angel Whelan, Erika Whisnant, David White, Elaine Ruth White, Jeremy White, Tony White, Glenn Whitlock, Mina Wiebe, American Wild, Isla Wilde, SEAN WILDE, Jay Wildfeathers, April Williams, Kerry Williams, Pamela Williams, Rachael Williams, Scott D. Williams, Shannen Williams, Lea Wilson, A. R. D. Wilson, Amanda Wilson, H. Winters, Sam Wit, ben woestenburg, Alex Wolf, H. A. Wolf, Annie Wood, DV Wood, Lesley Woodral, Adam Wright, The Dani Writer, Leslie Writes, Vagabond Writes, Ivy Wynter, Katy Wynter, Anne Xzon, Nika Yasu, Thea Young, Monique Yvonne, Z-Man, Alexandra Zeller, Rue Ziegler (Goblin_Writer), T. D. Zummack